MURDER ON THE ROCKS

MURDER ON THE ROCKS

A HANK REED MYSTERY, BOOK 2

FRED LICHTENBERG

ePublishingWorks!
love what you read.

Book and cover design by eBook Prep
www.ebookprep.com

October, 2019
ISBN: 978-1-64457-089-0

ePublishing Works!
644 Shrewsbury Commons Ave
Ste 249
Shrewsbury PA 17361
United States of America

www.epublishingworks.com
Phone: 866-846-5123

To the memory of:
Kevin Kelly,
Tom Tullio

ONE

Paris topped my bucket list. No other city came close. But try taking in all of the City of Lights in a day and a half, in August, where museum crowds swell. Hell, the way things were going with these never-ending lines, I'd be lucky to catch a glimpse of the Mona Lisa at the Louvre or grab a falafel sandwich at Maoz.

I know, I know. I'm whining. But like I said, I wanted Paris, and here I was. The truth: I didn't spend a dime to get there, thanks to my employer. The Suffolk County Police Department threw in some free time in exchange for my "courageous effort." All I had to do was iden-tify a dead guy lying in a Paris morgue.

That would be easy. I knew the scumbag; I'm the one who put him away. But then he escaped and wound up here. Paris must have been high on his bucket list too—only he tried raping the wrong woman, and *his* lights went out. Love those endings.

That was yesterday. After racing around all day visiting points of interest, my feet begged me to stop. I'd finally obliged them. Now, at five in the afternoon, I entered Café Note, a small, informal eatery near the metro station on Rue Rivoli. The tables were square with toile yellow and cherry tablecloths; black parlor chairs and rustic dark wood floors helped create a comfortable vibe. The place was jammed with tourists and locals, but as fortune would have it, there was one last table in the back. It was for two, but so far, I hadn't been challenged for the extra seat.

I dropped into the chair and waited for my server. Not five seconds later, a woman materialized, smiling. Had she confused me with someone else?

Apparently not. She gestured at the empty seat across from me and rattled off something in French.

I held up a hand. "Sorry, I only speak English. Did you need the chair…?"

"Oh—no. Would it be okay if I shared the table with you? All the others are taken." She looked around and shrugged.

Perfect English with a sexy French lilt. When I hesitated—I mean, she was much too beautiful for me, she said, "I'm sorry, you're waiting for someone—your wife or girlfriend, maybe." She turned and started to walk away.

"No wife or girlfriend," I said.

She paused, turning back, then grinned. "Boyfriend?"

I smiled. "Just me and the two chairs. Please stay." How could I turn away a beautiful woman who needed a place to sit?

"Sure?"

"Yes, of course."

She sat and smiled. "Thank you. By the way, I didn't take you for an American. Sorry."

"Sorry I'm American?" I said with a smile.

"Oh, no, I love Americans. My mother is American." She extended her hand. "Patrice Dubois."

I took it. "Hank Reed."

"You must have thought it…unusual for a strange woman to ask to share a table. I swear this isn't a pick-up."

Too bad.

My eyes stayed with hers. Patrice looked to be in her early thirties, about ten years younger than me, I'd guess. Her brown eyes matched her hair, which was sort of like mine, only hers was straight and long, and looked silky to the touch. Mine was short, styled in a rather harsh military cut. I was—let's be honest—a bit paunchy; she was curvy. I stood at six feet even, while Patrice was around five-three. And her left ring finger didn't sport a ring.

She glanced around. "It's very busy today." She spotted a server and called him over. She turned her attention back to me. "My treat."

I was about to protest, but she held up a hand to stop me before I could start.

"Or," she said, "I can wait for another table." Her smile was infectious. Also, she was very assertive, which I found sexy. I didn't want her to leave, so I relented.

The server, a man in his late forties with a full head of black hair, asked for our order in French.

"Hank, what's your preference this time of day?"

"I've been on my feet all day, so I'm most definitely up for a glass of red wine."

She ordered two. When the server left, she asked, "So, Hank, what brings you to Paris?"

I hesitated, wondering how to answer.

"I didn't think the question was that difficult. It must be very secretive. Let me guess—you're a CIA operative tracking down bad guys."

"Close."

"Seriously?" She rubbed her hands together like a giddy schoolgirl. "Tell me more."

I leaned forward. "I'm a detective from New York. But before we get too far into a Q-and-A, let's wait for our drinks to arrive."

"Are we going to just stare at each other until our server returns?"

I laughed. She was funny, too. I looked out the window for a moment, watched people walk by. I turned back to Patrice. "I've always dreamt of visiting Paris, but never had the chance until now. I'm due back in the States tomorrow. You can't really see very much in just a day."

"Very true. Are you a politician, as well?"

"Sorry?"

"Politicians never give you a straight answer. You were going to tell me what brought you here, not that you yearned to visit Paris." She winked. "Must be a cop thing."

I put up a hand. "Fair enough. Ever been to the Paris morgue?"

Patrice crossed her arms with a look of distaste. "Yes, of course. But I figured you'd be more interested in something like the Musée d'Orsay or the Notre Dame Cathedral." She stopped. "Wait a second. That was the business part, right?"

I winked. "You're good."

"I know. And?"

The server arrived with our drinks. I waited until he left. "An American was found dead in alleyway along the Riverbank. Murdered, actually. The police believe the killer was a prostitute based on the crime scene location." I conjured up images of Snub-Nose Johnson dead on a cardboard box and shrugged. "They haven't found the killer, and between you and me, I don't care. My guess it was self-defense anyway."

"And you were assigned to fly over and identify him since he'd escaped your prison system back home."

"Correct."

She leaned closer. "Sounds like a plum assignment."

"I thought so. Anyway, the guy was a dirtbag with a long history. I had to reassure my people that he was dead, by physically identifying him myself. He was, and I did." I paused. "You only have a slight French accent, by the way. Have you always lived here in Paris?"

"Ah, my turn. The short answer is no. I have a French father and an American mother. They met in New York, got married, and lived in the States a few years before I was born. We stayed there five more years, then off to Paris." She paused. "I have an American boyfriend—or fiancé, actually—who works in New York. We're…working out the logistics." She shot a glance out the window.

My eyes shifted from her left hand to her right. Of course, the European thing. "Congrats."

She showed me her engagement ring, which was modest but classy. "I'm trying to get a transfer to the States. I'm hoping it'll happen soon."

I sensed a momentary lack of focus in her eyes. "Good luck."

She sighed. "Thanks."

"And what do you do besides sharing tables with people?"

She laughed. "I work for Interpol."

"Really?" It dawned on me that this meeting might not have been a coincidence. "Hold on a minute…you know about me, don't you? Were you following me today, Ms. Interpol?"

Patrice threw me a wily smile, then whipped out a business card from her handbag. I figured it was hers, but then she lifted it to the lamplight and read, "'Detective Hank Reed, Suffolk County Homicide Division.'" My jaw dropped. She flipped the card over. "Says here you're working the Johnson case and that you're returning to New York tomorrow on American Airlines flight forty-five. When she looked back at me, her eyes were soft. "Sorry, I didn't mean to deceive you."

I scowled. "You conned me."

She stuck the card back in her bag. "That's a strong term. It was just my assignment du jour. I was told to follow you around, make sure you didn't get into trouble." She paused. "It was quite boring, Hank. Sorry." She paused. "But I really did enjoy chatting with you. I'm afraid I really do have to go, however. Thanks for letting me join you." She stood and dropped a twenty-Euro and her own business card on the table. "I wish we had more time to get to know each other."

"But you're engaged." I shrugged.

Another slight million-miles-away look.

"Give me a call if you get another chance to visit Paris. Though hopefully, I'll be living in the States by then." She turned and began toward the exit.

I was still stunned that I'd been bamboozled.

I shook my head to clear it and called out, "Hey."

She stopped, glanced over her shoulder.

I lifted her business card. "I'll call you."

"Before I get that transfer," she said with a wave, and then continued for the exit.

TWO

My trip to Paris was too short, but I promised to return—and hopefully, not alone. Oscar Wilde was right when he said, "When good Americans die, they go to Paris." Only I didn't want to wait that long, not after feeling the energy, the sensual nature of the environment here. For me, Paris seemed to seduce like no other city in the world. And here I was, alone.

That evening, I took a metro to the Champ de Mars station, where I savored a few hours of people watching. I felt inside my shirt pocket and removed Patrice's business card, flipping it a few times in my hand. My last night in Paris, accompanied by a beautiful woman and sipping a glass of expensive wine at the Eiffel restaurant, would be one helluva way to end the trip. I hesitated, making myself think about the consequences. I was still technically married, and she was about to be. How would it look? I replaced the card.

Instead of a romantic date, I mingled with the crowds. I took in the sparkling lights winking from the tower before heading back to Art Hotel Eiffel, not far from that spot, and tucked myself in.

The next morning, my American Airlines flight to the States was packed with tourists and weary Americans. And a ton of noisy kids. It made sense given it was the height of the summer. My mission didn't include a first-class ticket, so I opted for the next-most-private: a seat near the back row of the plane.

The chatter began to filter out about halfway back. I tossed my carry-on into the overhead compartment, slid into an aisle seat, nodded to my neighbor—an elderly man at the window seat—and closed my eyes. I had a lot to think about. Now that this assignment was over, I needed to sort out my life and next meal ticket. Not that I was being fired—quite the contrary. My decision to leave the department was personal. The Paris gig was the carrot my boss had offered to keep me around, but he knew I needed time to sort my life out. What a guy!

Then there was my buddy, Detective First-Grade JR Greco at NYPD, who'd promised to put in a good word for me there. But working and living in the Big Apple didn't appeal to me. Too many people. So then, what was left for Hank Reed?

A light tug at my shoulder interrupted my thoughts. I blinked several times. Was I just imagining Patrice standing in the aisle beside me?

"Hey," she said, her voice subdued.

I sat up quickly, rubbing my eyes. "Hey, Patrice—what are you doing here?"

She feigned a friendly smile, but I could see the sadness in her eyes.

"You still on my tail?" I asked lightly.

"Afraid not, Hank." She pointed to the middle seat.

Was her finger trembling?

I stood, waited for her to take her seat, then sat and asked, "You okay?"

Patrice placed her purse under the seat in front of her, fidgeted with her skirt a second, then leaned toward me. "Hank, my fiancé is missing."

"Missing?"

"He hasn't returned any of my calls, texts, or emails lately. It's not like him. We talk daily—sometimes several times a day." Patrice took a deep breath and made a concerted effort to speak slowly. "I'm worried. Luke was supposed to be in Newport, Rhode Island, working on an investigation."

"He Interpol, too?"

She shook her head. "He's a freelance reporter, mostly business stuff.

I can't go into all of that right now, but I can tell you he was investigating possible wrongdoing."

"You mean a whistleblower?"

She nodded. "We'll leave it at that. In his last email, he mentioned he was driving up to the Wilson House in Newport."

"From New York?"

Another nod. "That was a few days ago! I know it doesn't sound that long, but like I said, we're usually in touch every day."

"Maybe he lost his phone or—"

She put up her hand. "No. There's always a way to reach out."

She was right. Of course there were.

I checked on the old guy seated at the window. He was fast asleep. Nevertheless, I brought the volume down a notch. "Have you checked with his company? Or the police?"

"I checked with a few newspaper organizations he freelances for. They said they weren't waiting on a story from him." She shrugged. "I haven't called the authorities yet, but I'm afraid he might be onto something big, maybe dangerous." She searched my eyes.

I put a hand on her shoulder in sympathy. It didn't sound good, but I kept that thought to myself. "What about the government? I mean, if he was involved with a whistleblower, he must have gone to someone."

Patrice shook her head. "Apparently, it hadn't gotten that far; it was still preliminary. He was supposed to meet up with his informant once he arrived in Newport." She pulled out a printed copy of an old email and read aloud, "Initial contact at the Nautical Pub, meeting later that evening." She bit her lip. "That was Sunday. Today is Wednesday, and that email was the last I'd heard from him."

I took the paper from her shaking hands and read the quick note.

"You have a plan?" I asked, handing it back to her.

She folded the paper and slipped it back into her vest pocket, then turned to me.

Her tone hardened. "I'm going to find him."

THREE

I t was no coincidence that Patrice had selected a seat next to mine. She obviously needed to discuss her missing fiancé, and what better person with whom to talk through her fears but a fellow law enforcement officer heading back to the United States?

Since I'd been blindsided by Patrice, I had her checked out with the help of JR Greco.

He still had connections with Interpol from his time as a liaison "back in the day." He'd never told me what "back in the day meant," and I'd never asked.

JR's conclusions: Patrice was authentic. That was all he knew, or at least was willing to share.

When the plane reached cruising altitude, I checked in on my neighbor. Patrice was staring absently at the seat in front of her. I guess I would be, too, if my fiancé was missing. I don't have a fiancé, of course, but you get the picture.

She must have sensed my stare, because she turned toward me.

I smiled encouragingly. "Look, I've got a few days off, so how about I drive us up to Newport, and we search for Luke together?"

Patrice settled her eyes on mine. "Are you sure? I mean, I could use some support. But I don't want you to think…"

9

I touched her arm. "My car is at the long-term parking at Kennedy. If we land on time, I can get us to Newport before nightfall."

She squeezed her eyes closed, then opened them. I saw moisture around the edges, threatening to spill over. "Thanks. That means a lot to me. I feel so helpless not knowing where Luke is. I'm really worried about him."

With the help of professional courtesy through a previous phone call, we were able to breeze through customs. My late-model Accord sat waiting for us. Timing was everything, but the snarling traffic on the Van Wyck Expressway—a constant reminder of why I stayed away from Kennedy International whenever possible—made things tricky. Nevertheless, we arrived in just over four hours.

The last burst of the sun lit up the Newport Bridge as we entered from Jamestown. Sunset arrived, but Narragansett Bay and its showcase of small craft anchored about, mostly sailboats, were still visible. Arriving on the Newport side, I said, "Before we start our search, we should check in. I reserved two rooms at The Wilson House."

"That's where Luke—"

"Last stayed, I know. I read his email, remember? Anyway, I called ahead while you were using the restroom at the airport."

"You're resourceful, Hank. Thanks."

The Wilson House was a ten-room Victorian-style inn located on Clarke Street, a few blocks in from Thames Street, the center of everything in Newport. I was told that parking was scarce during the summer months and that any empty spot—outside of a fire hydrant—required a parking permit. Otherwise, you should expect a fine. Double for the fire hydrant.

I pulled up in front of the inn and told Patrice to be on the lookout for a parking enforcement officer.

Besides being a seafaring town, with docks, fishing boats, and beaches, Newport was also the home of mansions—the biggest and most popular of which was The Breakers. It was built by the Vanderbilt family in 1895, and had seventy (yes, seventy) rooms. Could explain the tight parking.

Inside, I was greeted by Brady, the manager. He appeared to have been waiting for us. He had a friendly smile, which lifted his thin, brown mustache a tad at the edges. Dressed in comfortable business attire, his five-eight frame was dwarfed behind an old, dark mahogany desk.

"You must be Hank Reed, my last guest for the day." Brady's eyes searched behind me. "You did say two rooms, right?"

I thumbed toward the door. "The other room is for my passenger. She's on the lookout for the meter maid."

He laughed. "Don't worry, I have a parking permit for you. Didn't mean to scare you, but parking is a luxury around here." He removed a pass from his desk. "Please stick it inside your windshield."

I inwardly rolled my eyes. *Like I would attach it to the windshield wiper!* My grumpiness had to be due to the long-ass flight and the drive, so I gave Brady some slack. "Sure."

"And if you lose it, you'll have to pay two hundred and fifty dollars."
Right.

I nodded and went back outside. After locating a tight spot around the corner on Mary Street, I turned to Patrice. "Let's check in."

When we arrived, Brady was watching the local news. He muted the 13-inch TV, and said, "Damn crime is all over the place. Not here, though, thank God!" He gazed up and smiled at Patrice before turning to me. "You guys aren't together?"

"Just traveling together."

Brady shifted his eyes to Patrice, then back to me, with a too bad for you look on his face. "Sorry, didn't mean to pry."

"Not a problem. When do you get off work?"

"Me?" Brady checked his watch. "I'm off at eight. Something I can help you with?"

"We need to talk when you have more time." I flashed my Suffolk County detective shield. "It has to do with a recent guest."

He scratched his head. "You didn't have to check in to ask a few questions." He stopped. "But you are checking in, though, right?"

"Sure, we might even stay a few days." I stuck the badge back in my pocket and said with a lighthearted shrug, "Depends on the information you provide us."

Brady glanced at Patrice again. "I'll do my best." He reached under the desk and brought up two registration forms. "Definitely do my best."

Exploring the mansions wasn't on my to-do list, but I wanted Brady to feel that I recognized his town was important, so I humored him. After checking in and dropping my carry-on into a cozy Victorian room with lace curtains and a claw-foot tub, I knocked on Patrice's door. We met Brady at his station where he was engaged in a Nelson DeMille novel.

He peered up over bifocal glasses. "This guy's damn good!"

I was a DeMille fan myself, so I knew what he meant. "Luke DuPont."

He marked his page, closed the paperback, and nodded. "Thought so. Nice guy—a little nervous, like he had a lot on his mind. Guess he did, because he skipped out without paying the last night. Not too happy about that."

Brady's voice sounded too even to be concerned about Luke not paying, so I asked, "I thought guests paid when they checked in."

Brady raked his hair with his fingers. "It wasn't quite like that. He did pay for one night, said he *might* need to stay another. I told him it wouldn't be a problem. But then he vanished."

My mind wasn't wrapping around the problem. "So if he left, why does he still owe you for another night?"

Brady slid a guest book onto the desk, flipped to a page, and pointed. "Because his personal belongings were still in his room after the first night's checkout time. I took that to mean he was staying another night."

"So his belongings are still in the room?" Patrice asked her voice racing.

"Were." He closed the logbook. "When he didn't check out after the second night, I entered his room. That's where I found his belongings. The bed was still made up, so I assumed he hadn't slept in it the night before. Then I asked one of my housekeepers. She confirmed that the room was the same as it was the day before." He licked his lips and sat a little straighter. "So, that's when I decided to put his things in storage.

You have to understand, this is our busy season, and if he wasn't returning..."

I scowled. "Did it ever occur to you that there might be foul play involved? I mean, did you even call to find out *if* he was coming back?"

"Look," he said, his hands rising in protest, "I didn't know what to think at the time. And as far as calling, I did, several times. I kept getting his voice mail."

"Call him now," Patrice demanded.

"What?"

"I want to make sure you called the right person."

Brady stared at Patrice for a moment. "Okay." He ran his finger down the guestbook page, then picked up the office phone and dialed out.

"You have a speaker on that phone?" Patrice asked.

Brady glanced at her again through furrowed brows, pressed a button, and waited. After four rings, the voice mail kicked on. A guy with a deep voice answered in typical fashion and asked the caller to leave a message.

I glanced over at Patrice. She gave a small nod.

"Hang up," I said.

Brady complied and searched my face. "It's the same message I got before. Is he really missing?"

That's what we needed to find out. Evidently, Luke thought he needed an extra night. According to Patrice, he was meeting up with his confidential informant that day. There are always delays or no-shows, but then why hadn't Luke returned to his room to pick up his stuff?

I asked Brady, "Did Mr. DuPont come by car? He'd need a sticker, too."

Brady shook his head. "Taxi. I saw it pull up." He kept his gaze on me, apparently waiting for my next question.

"We're going to need to see what Mr. DuPont left behind."

———

Brady dropped Luke DuPont's light-blue denim Billykirk carry-on on the storage room chair. "That's everything."

"Did you take a look inside?" I asked.

He lowered his eyes.

I'd gotten my answer. "What did you find?"

He fidgeted.

"Come on, Brady, I can have my team process for fingerprints within an hour," I said, knowing I don't have a team, at least, not in Newport.

He squirmed. "Okay, I did peek inside. But I didn't take anything, I swear. I was just…curious."

Right. Curious.

"What were you hoping to find, DuPont's dirty underwear?"

"It wasn't like that. The whole up-and-leaving thing seemed weird. I thought maybe I'd find something to help me get in touch with him."

Patrice unzipped the bag. She must have caught a whiff of Luke's cologne, because she whispered, *"Amour."* She reached inside and removed a blue checked poplin sport shirt, holding it tenderly in her hands. She then removed the remaining contents. Luke traveled light. Then again, he hadn't been planning on an extended trip.

She pulled out a Lenovo ThinkPad X1 Carbon laptop. That alone would have paid for several nights—and the fact that it was still in the bag vouched for Brady's honesty. That, or his concern that Luke would return and confront him if it were missing. Patrice removed a flash drive and some printouts from the bag.

I asked Brady, "Anything else you were 'curious' about?"

A quick twitch in his eyes told me he was holding back.

"Come on, Brady, you keep giving us piecemeal information. I want all of it now or we're going to have a problem."

Brady dug his hands in his pockets. "Okay. The same day, I got a call from a guy asking for Luke DuPont. I told him he wasn't here, which was true. He asked for his room number, which I found strange considering I had just told the guy DuPont was no longer a guest." He stopped. "I probably shouldn't have even told him that, but the whole thing sounded crazy at that point." Brady paused. "Anyway, that afternoon a guy walks in with an FBI badge and tells me he wants to see Luke DuPont's room. Not Luke, just his room. Now I'm really wondering what's going on. Plus, there was something off about the guy.

I mean, he didn't look like an FBI agent to me. He was wearing street clothes and sneakers, not a suit like I would've expected."

Brady's eyes drifted to Patrice's. He continued, "My father was a cop. He'd tell me stories about how people tried to impersonate law enforcement. To me, this guy smelled like a phony."

Brady hesitated a moment. "I told him it wouldn't be a problem, considering I already had DuPont's things safely locked up. He started looking through the drawers, the closet, the bathroom—then he demanded to know what had happened to DuPont's suitcase. I mean, come on, this guy must have thought I was an idiot. I told him Mr. DuPont took it with him." Brady stopped, rubbed his mustache between a thumb and forefinger. "He didn't like that answer. He mumbled something and left. That's the God's honest truth."

"And it didn't dawn on you to call the FBI, maybe?" Patrice blurted. "What the hell?"

"I swear I was just giving it another day."

I said, "Well, under the circumstances, you did the right thing—though you should have come forward sooner."

Brady bowed his head. "Look, we run a legitimate business here. The last thing I need is bad publicity."

Patrice opened Luke's computer and fired it up. She entered a password, but was rejected. "Damn."

"You know his password?"

"I was guessing."

"Leave it for now," I advised. My eyes swept the room then settled on the carry-on. Evidently, Luke's secret meeting wasn't that secret. Some interested party had found out where he was staying. Fortunately, Brady had been smart enough to sniff out the imposter. It was obvious the phony FBI guy wasn't looking to snatch Luke's poplin shirt. The laptop and flash drive were the only worthwhile items in his carry-on.

I turned back to Brady. "How do you know we're not playing the same game as the phony FBI guy?"

Brady grinned. "Easy, you paid for the rooms in advance."

Back in Brady's office, I inserted Luke's flash drive into Brady's PC and waited for instructions. Patrice stood next to me, fidgety; Brady had gone off to make us some coffee.

The computer recognized Luke's flash drive. I clicked on the option to open the folder, and found more than a dozen documents to choose from. I scanned the file names, searching for one that might provide a hint as to Luke's whereabouts, but nothing jumped out at me.

I turned to Patrice. "Anything grab you?"

Her index finger moved along the monitor, but didn't stop until she reached the bottom of the screen. She shook her head. "Nothing."

Brady returned with a tray laden with mugs of coffee and a few biscotti. "Thought you might be hungry," he said, finding an empty spot on the desk. "I did have a box of chocolate cookies around somewhere, but I think the staff snatched them. They have a tendency to do that, even when I write my name on it."

I gazed up from the monitor. "Look for chocolate stains on their lips."

He cracked a smile. Brady must have glimpsed the screen, because he said, "Looks like Mr. DuPont was interested in some local sightseeing spots." He pointed at a file named "Cliffs."

"What's that?" I asked with sudden interest.

"You never heard of the Cliff Walk?"

"I'm from Long Island. We don't have a lot of cliffs out there."

"Well, you're in for a treat. It's one of Newport's top attractions. It runs about three and a half miles, most of which is paved. The best part: a free view of the mansions!"

My friend here was definitely pushing the mansions.

"Luke loves to walk. Maybe he decided to check it out," she said her tone hopeful.

I peered over at Patrice and raised an eyebrow. "Before or after his secret meeting?" Then I thought: Unless the Cliff Walk was the meeting place. I clicked on the document, which turned out to be an event calendar. Luke apparently had a full schedule the day he disappeared. A quick run along The Cliffs was on his calendar, then lunch at The Nautical Pub, and then simply meet at eight in the evening.

Meet whom?

"Hank, Luke mentioned that pub in his email, and as far as The Cliffs, he is a runner." She pursed her lips.

Brady said, "The cliffs are more for walking. It's pretty rocky in parts and not great for joggers. Plus, it's about seventy feet above the bay, so if you fall…"

Could be Luke wanted to do a dry run—or walk—in case he needed to make a quick exit later that night. I asked where The Nautical Pub was located.

"A few blocks north," Brady said, pointing with his nose. "It's on Washington Square. They have an extensive beer menu. I'm a regular."

"Luke's last email mentioned something about The Nautical Pub, so it coincides with his calendar. The message was brief. He didn't say who he was meeting with. Top secret, I guess. That, along with the meeting that evening." Patrice screwed up her nose. "What's that all about?"

I grabbed a biscotti and bit into it. "Let's find out."

Brady had already heard too much, so I wasn't about to whet his appetite with more gossip. I instructed him not to call the local authorities unless I told him to. It didn't take much convincing—especially when I promised a great review on TripAdvisor. He seemed to like that deal and agreed.

Though Luke was missing, I didn't want every law enforcement agency crawling along the Cliff Walk until Patrice and I had a chance to investigate. After all, there might have been a legitimate reason Luke hadn't been picking up his phone. He could have lost it, for one, and didn't have a quarter for a pay phone (okay, I'm reaching). I didn't really believe it, but stranger things have occurred in my line of work.

Another theory: Luke might have been in the middle of some top-secret meeting and didn't want to be disturbed. Even by his fiancée. However, more likely, Luke was already in trouble. I wanted to test that possibility first.

By all appearances, Patrice seemed to have left her friendly and upbeat personality in Paris. I felt she was becoming paralyzed, or at the least, withdrawn. I was hoping we would find some evidence that indicated Luke was alive.

Around nine-thirty in the evening, we entered The Nautical Pub. Its cozy interior and dim lighting made for a romantic atmosphere; somehow, I don't think that's what Luke had in mind. The hostess greeted us with a captivating smile and asked our preference: a booth or a seat at the bar. I scanned the restaurant, with its black-and-white tiled floors. It had a charming, homey feel, similar to Salty's Bar and Grill back home —a favorite after-work hangout of mine. I considered Luke's purpose for the meeting and asked for a booth. I pointed to the back, away from the bar crowd.

After settling in, I surveyed the restaurant a little more. For a weekday, the place was fairly busy—mostly with tourists, judging by their casual dress and out of town accents. Patrice and I ordered a couple of Killian's Red Ales. Our thirtysomething server, who had short blond hair with a streak of pink in the front, returned with our beers, and I asked her if she'd worked the day shift over the past few days.

"Sweetie, I have two small kids at home. Unless my boss is willing to let them run wild in the kitchen, the answer is no. Why do you ask?"

That was my opening. "A friend of ours recommended a few places in town, including this one." I leaned forward. "So I was wondering if maybe you saw him eat here." I paused. "He reviews restaurants for a newspaper."

Her eyes lit up. "Really?"

I nodded.

"You have a picture of him?"

I turned to Patrice, who had already taken her cell out. She handed the phone to the server. Her gaze hovered on Luke's face for several seconds before she shook her head. "Sorry." She moved to hand it back, but stopped. "Let me check with Maureen. She's here most afternoons."

Before she left to find Maureen, we ordered our grub—both choosing the Nautical Pub burger (an Angus patty in pocket bread with melted Swiss cheese, fresh spinach, sautéed mushrooms, and crisp bacon —I was already salivating). It came with fries or salad; I chose the fries. Patrice claimed she was watching her diet and ordered the salad instead.

I guess that's why I had a slight paunch, and Patrice (I couldn't help but notice) had one killer body.

An attractive, middle-aged woman approached our table soon after, her bright-red hair styled in a punk hairdo. She held the cell phone in her hand and introduced herself as Maureen. She squeezed in next to me, handing the phone across the table to Patrice. "Your restaurant reviewer friend was here, all right. In fact, he sat in this seat. What a coincidence."

Patrice perked up. "When, what time? Was he alone?"

I tapped Patrice's knee, attempting to send the message to settle down.

Maureen said, "I think it was Monday afternoon. Wait, no, that can't be right. I wasn't here Monday. It must've been Sunday around noon. Yeah, right, we had a busy church crowd at the same time."

That sounded right. If Luke had followed his calendar's timeline, he would have gone to the Cliffs that morning, then here for a bite. His calendar didn't mention any activity between lunch and his evening meeting.

"Alone?" Patrice repeated, a little too loudly.

Before Maureen could answer, I jumped in. "Did he have a laptop or pad and pen with him to write his review?" I wanted to make it sound official.

Maureen lifted her head to the ceiling and closed her eyes for a moment. "As a matter of fact, yeah, he did have a laptop sitting on the table. I guess that was to write the review, right?"

Patrice's eyes shot across the table at me, and I could tell Maureen's response had registered: Luke must have left his laptop in the room after being here, and before the meeting that evening.

Our server arrived with our food, but neither of us wanted to dig in yet. This was valuable information.

Maureen said, "And then she came along, and he closed his laptop."

"She?" Patrice blurted out. "What did she look like? Was she young? Pretty?"

I tapped Patrice's knee a little harder. Easy, cowgirl.

Maureen nodded. "Oh, yeah, gorgeous. I guess she was his girlfriend. They got real chummy, if you know what I mean. Probably why he asked for a quiet booth in the back."

The pain that registered on Patrice's face made me feel like telling Maureen to leave. "This woman, what exactly did she look like?" Patrice asked again, not giving up.

Maureen shook her head, gave a little eye-roll. "Blond, great body— very top-heavy. Her outfit was to die for." She shot a glance at me, as if I cared about the woman's clothes. "I got a chance to check out her shoes before she left: red, opened-sided pumps, three-inch heels, rhinestones on the toe buckle. Shew—couldn't forget those babies."

"So they didn't leave together?" Patrice asked.

I'd run out of knees, so I touched Patrice's arm. She got the hint and sat back with a deep breath. She feigned a smile.

Maureen thought a moment. "As I recall, she left without ordering. I mean, she had a glass of wine, but no food. Guess she wasn't part of the review team?"

"What did he order?" I asked.

Maureen glanced at my plate. "Come to think of it, a Nautical Pub burger, same as you. Think he'll give us a good review?"

Patrice obviously hadn't been expecting to hear about another woman. She kept blabbering about Luke and the blond and the chumminess and the cool spikes. I put a hand on her shoulder.

"I know you're upset, but Maureen might have just been exaggerating. You need to hold off until we know for sure what's real. Maybe he was playing this woman to get information." That was unrealistic thinking, but I wanted to calm her down.

Patrice glared. "Easy for you to say. It's not your fiancé or wife or loved one that's missing. God, and the whole shoe business."

At least she didn't bring up chumminess.

"Look," I replied. "All I'm saying is you can't appear to be desperate. Besides, Maureen might just have been blowing things out of proportion. She doesn't know Luke is your fiancé."

"That makes it even worse, Hank! If she did know, she probably would've been less forthcoming." Patrice emptied her beer then called over our server for another bottle of Killian's. I declined.

We left the pub around ten-thirty and backtracked to the Wilson House. The night was dark and quiet—kind of like Patrice, who was definitely in a sour mood. She hadn't even touched her burger or salad.

She picked up her speed along the bricked sidewalk, and it was all I could do to keep up. "Stop for a minute," I said, a little out of breath. "It still doesn't mean anything. Once we find Luke and confront him..."

She stopped and turned to me, her face blanched. "Right, like he'd be honest with me." She looked away. "Who the hell is she anyway? His informant? Forgive me for being suspicious." She huffed then turned back to me, searching my eyes for answers.

When I said nothing, she said, "I was faithful to Luke from the start..."

"You're assuming again," I replied. "That's dangerous. Look, I was in a similar situation...forget it. We need to stay focused and find Luke. Maybe this blond woman knows where he is. We need to find her."

"They're probably together."

There was no winning with Patrice's frame of mind. I said, "We won't be able to think clearly until we get some sleep." I checked my watch. "Jet lag has to be wearing us out. How about we meet for breakfast and discuss a game plan?"

Patrice shook her head in defeat. "I'm sorry I got you into this...this cat and mouse chase, Hank."

I smiled. "That's okay, I love animals."

The inn was locked up for the night, but my key let us in the front door. I bid Patrice goodnight, knowing she'd be up for quite a while, if not the whole night.

We had adjoining rooms. I opened my door and turned to her. "Hey, knock if you need me."

A weary nod.

She slipped into her room, flipped on the light, and closed the door.

Being a member of law enforcement has its disadvantages. We tend to obsess over our investigations, and though I wasn't technically on duty, this one counted. Especially since another fellow law enforcement officer's loved one's life was on the line. And so half the night, my eyes gazed at the dark ceiling. I assumed Patrice's were doing the same.

Around eight the next morning, Brady greeted me in the upstairs study. He pointed to the coffee pot and Danish on the table, then told me that a full breakfast was available next door in the dining area.

"Danish and coffee works for me," I said, looking around. "Have you seen Patrice this morning?"

"Yeah, she was up pretty early. Said she was going for a walk."

I lifted an eyebrow. "Did she say where she was going?"

"Nope. I'm guessing the Cliffs, because she asked for directions. I gave her the short route toward the beach."

I grabbed two pastries, filled a Styrofoam cup to the rim with coffee, and asked Brady for directions by car, which happened to be the same route. Apparently, Patrice hadn't been interested in a full breakfast. I munched on the first cheese-filled Danish and washed it down with a couple gulps of joe.

I didn't expect to find Patrice before arriving at the Cliffs, and I was right. I parked the car at Easton's beach (having purchased a nonresident sticker from Brady), wolfed down the second Danish—prune, which probably wasn't a good idea—grabbed my half-finished coffee, and bounded for the Walk.

The narrow trail sat about seventy feet above the shoreline, overlooking Easton Bay. Magnificent mansions from the gilded era, reminiscent of the Vanderbilt, stood on the south side of the Walk. Unfortunately, I didn't have time to stop and admire these excesses of the past; my mission was to find Patrice, Luke, and maybe the blond, in that order.

From the north side, the Walk started at the western end of Easton's Beach and continued south, with major exits at Narragansett Avenue, Webster Street, and some others. It ended at Bellevue Avenue at the east side of Bailey's Beach, locally referred to—I kid you not—as Reject's Beach.

I reached Narragansett Avenue and the Forty Steps, a dramatic stone staircase that dropped about two-thirds of the way down the side of the cliff to a balcony over the bay. I tossed my Styrofoam cup in a receptacle, then asked a few people milling around if they'd noticed a woman walking alone. I described Patrice.

All negative responses. I picked up my pace until I reached the Breakers Mansion, the grandest of Newport's cottages. Right, I thought. Cottages. Maybe for Commodore Cornelius Vanderbilt II. For the rest of us, the seventy-room 'cottage' would accommodate more than a few families comfortably.

I followed the path, passing the Chinese Tea House that was part of the Marble House property on my right, walking through a narrow stone tunnel and exiting the other side—but still no sign of Patrice.

It wasn't until I reached Sheep Point that I glimpsed her ahead. Obviously, she hadn't found anything, or anyone, because she was steadily making her way toward the second tunnel at Gull Rock.

Beyond the tunnel, the conditions were rough, with chain-link fences and thick, unpruned hedges insuring that walkers wouldn't stray onto private property. I called out, but Patrice, too busy moving to hear me, disappeared inside the tunnel. I picked up my pace, wishing now that I'd given up Boston cream donuts. I entered the tunnel and spotted her exiting the other end. She was picking her way over the stones.

When I reached the end of the tunnel, I noticed that the trail broke up alongside chain link fences with padlocks on the gates that guarded the remaining private mansions. 'Private Property – No Trespassing' and 'No Thru Way' signs glared from the edges of the properties, large enough for the most visually-challenged to see without trouble.

At this point, the only way out would be to turn around or finish the Walk, since there were no emergency exits on this last stretch of the path.

"Patrice," I called out, competing with the waves crashing below.

I finally got her attention. She turned back and waved.

I caught up with her, stepping over loose rocks, nearly falling. "Why didn't you wake me this morning?"

"I couldn't sleep, Hank, so I started out early." She glanced behind me. "No sign of Luke?"

I gazed past her at the rocky beach, or more specifically, at an object near a large boulder a few feet from the water. Whatever it was, it sparkled in the morning sun. I kept my eye on it as I negotiated the rocks and stepped onto the sand. The closer I got, the stronger the glint from the object became.

A shoe? As I inched closer, I realized it wasn't just any shoe. It was a red, open-sided pump, with a three-inch heel and a rhinestone buckle.

My head darted about, eyes hunting for the owner. How many women wore expensive heels along a rocky trail or the beach? Who would walk along this beach at all without a lifeguard present? I had a sinking suspicion the shoe belonged to the blond with whom Luke DuPont had shared a table at The Nautical Pub. My flimsy hope was that she'd only lost it.

Patrice stared at the shoe, expressionless, then knelt down to peer at it more closely. She removed a hanky from her belly bag and handed it up to me. With the hanky, I lifted the pump to the sun, squinted at it, but didn't find any blood. Aside from the heel angling off to one side, the shoe was intact. Spying a large boulder near the water, I jogged over to it, but Ms. Size Seven was nowhere to be found.

I wrapped the heel in the hanky and handed it to Patrice, who glared at it. I suspected she was thinking about the owner—or rather, her fiancé and the owner.

Scanning the shoreline without binoculars, I could only see sand, and nothing floating along the coast.

"Let's have a look around."

For the next hour we trudged across boulders, pushed through high, unpruned hedges, and wound up at Bailey's Beach at the east end of the walk. I looked down and understood why the locals called it Reject's Beach. No one in his right mind would attempt the descent to the glacial boulders, riprap, and Armour stone to the water.

We retraced our steps to where we'd found the shoe. Patrice said, "Hank, it looks like foul play, but I swear Luke wouldn't be a part of something like that."

Her comments seemed way premature, as though she felt the need to protect Luke. I wasn't about to accuse anyone at this point. Besides, one shoe in the sand might be nothing more than a wild night on the beach. But I'd keep that thought to myself. I did hope the blond was still alive and willing to help us find Luke.

"Let's not speculate," is all I said. As a detective from another state potentially holding evidence to a crime, I had to make an executive decision. "We might have to visit the locals soon. I mean, the shoe could mean nothing, but given Luke's disappearance…"

Patrice said nothing, gave a reluctant nod.

I drew my cell phone from my pants pocket and asked Patrice for Luke's phone number. I let it ring until his voicemail greeting came on, and then hung up. As we retraced out steps back, I kept dialing, praying his phone hadn't run out of juice. As we approached Gull Rock Tunnel, I stopped and dialed once again. This time, the ring from his phone sang out ever so softly.

"You hear that?"

Patrice looked around. "No."

One more call. "Now?"

"Nothing."

My eyes searched the crevices between the rocks. "There!" I took off, pressing the call button again.

"I hear it!" Patrice ran past me, jumping over a few smaller, flat rocks. "Call again."

I did. She stopped. "I see something shiny." She stuck her hand between two rocks and scooped up the phone. Emotionally charged, she was neglecting protocol. Her damn fingerprints were all over the thing now! She didn't stop there. Next to the phone was another object, silver, and round in shape. A medal?

She held up the phone in one hand and the medal in the other. I called one more time.

"It's his—Luke's—and this is his St. Christopher medal."

With her fingerprints on both.

FOUR

G iven the exchange between them at the pub, it wasn't surprising that we found Luke's phone close to the mystery woman's shoe. Still, what I found strange was that Luke hadn't answered or returned Patrice's earlier calls. According to Maureen, Luke was there, chatting it up with the blond—meaning he was alive at the time.

There had to be a reason Luke held back on contacting Patrice. And it seemed improbable that he'd lost his phone at the beach before he disappeared. I mean, come on, who can live without a phone nowadays? Not to mention burners are available everywhere. Maybe Luke simply hadn't been in a talking mood, at least with Patrice. So what did that say about their relationship?

We sat opposite each other on a few flat rocks, Patrice staring out at the bay, apparently in deep thought. I was eager to view Luke's cell phone log, but held off. "How was your relationship with Luke?" I asked pointedly.

"Great."

She'd answered too quickly. Clutching his phone as though it too would disappear, she added, "I know what you're thinking, Hank. We were going to get married."

"That's not what I asked. I know you *planned* on getting married. Had there been any bumps lately?"

She wasn't as quick to respond this time, so I guessed Patrice needed a moment to think about it. She loosened her grip on the phone and rested her forehead in her other hand. "All relationships go through bumps at one time or another. Ours was no different." She turned to me, her eyes begging for reinforcement.

I nodded. I understood, of course, since I was going through a similar situation with my wife, Susan.

Patrice thought a moment. "It's possible Luke and this…woman had a platonic relationship and her husband or boyfriend found out and misinterpreted it. Or, more likely, she was part of the investigation and things went badly."

Mistaken relationship or transaction gone badly. Patrice was reaching.

"Are you certain the bumps were smoothed out?"

Patrice squirmed, said nothing.

"Let's take a look at Luke's phone." I hoped he didn't have a security access code. Patrice must have known what I was searching for, and began swiping. She peered up. "There are at least a dozen calls made to or from one phone number with a six-four-six area code."

"That's New York City. Dial it."

She hesitated then dialed. I could hear the voicemail kicked in, and I watched her listen to the message. She turned off the screen and handed the phone over to me.

"The bastard!"

I flipped through Luke's phone log myself and found that all but two calls had been placed to the same New York City number: my guess, the blond. The first turned out to be a local number without a voice messaging system. The second was to The Nautical Pub.

I stood out of range of Patrice and called JR again. When he picked up, he announced, "Sex academy, number one in his class speaking."

I indulged him with a chuckle. "Number two calling."

"Hank, my friend, I knew it was you. And by the way, you'll only become number one when I slow down, and that's not happening for another thirty years."

"I'm glad you knew it was me, or NYPD might admonish you for handing out false information."

We both laughed. Pleasantries aside, I asked JR for another favor.

"Not a problem, but what happened to your data bank system in Suffolk?"

"Oh, I'm sure it's working, but I'm not home. It's a long story, but thanks for reminding me. I'm in Newport, Rhode Island."

"Nice place to vacation."

"Would be normally, but I'm not exactly on R and R. I'm working pro bono. It has to do with that woman I met in Paris, Patrice DuBois."

"You devil."

"It's not what you think." I gave JR the abbreviated version, starting with the background he had provided me on Patrice and Luke when I was in Paris.

"So after the boondoggle in the City of Light, you meet this sexy woman who just happens to need your help tracking down her boyfriend. Sounds like fun."

"Fiancé," I corrected.

"And now there's a mystery woman with a missing shoe. Hank, it sounds like her fiancé has his own sex academy. There's probably a guy out there real pissed off."

"Except her fiancé is part of a whistleblowing investigation. Could have something to do with that."

"Yep. Could be both. Okay, give me the number and keep your phone handy."

"Thanks. Oh, there's another number here in Newport that doesn't have an answering machine. Check that one out, too." I passed the numbers to JR. "Before I go to the locals, I'd like to search a little longer." I turned toward Patrice, who was watching waves crash against the rocks. I lowered my voice. "Who knows? I might find a body."

"Or two," he added.

"I hope not."

"While you're waiting to hear back, check out the Cliff Walk. I hear it's pretty cool."

Right. Cool.

While I waited for JR to get back to me, Patrice and I drifted in silence along the Walk, the cliffs and bay aligned to our right. I thought about this unsanctioned investigation and how far I was willing to take it. I could get busted if this thing turned out to be long and messy.

I'd previously told my boss I needed some time to reflect on my life, and like a caring guy, he'd squeezed in a few extra days—with pay, a gift for my superlative job in Paris. Of course, he'd been laughing at the time. What a guy!

As we approached the jutting Forty Steps, my cell phone sang out.

It was JR. He confirmed what we already knew, that the phone number belonged to a New York City resident. Then he passed the particulars: an Elena Sullivan, thirty-five, single, lived on West 85th Street on the Upper West Side of Manhattan. And—JR's words—she was very sexy. He told me to check my text messages for a present. It was true. I had to agree with JR: Elena Sullivan was indeed very sexy.

I responded to the pic, "No commentary needed."

"Here's what I found out about Ms. Sullivan," JR continued on the call. "She's an administrative assistant—what used to be called a secretary—to the CEO of the Fox Reynolds Corporation. Get a load of this. The guy's name is Preston Hartford, III. Some blue-blooded guy, I bet."

"Sounds like it. What's Fox Reynolds into?"

"Medical devices. It's privately held, but I hear they're looking to go public."

I moved out of earshot of Patrice.

"What's the connection between Sullivan and Luke DuPont other than a bunch of phone calls?" I asked.

"It may be nothing, but I was told Ms. Sullivan left for Newport on vacation, to meet her boyfriend." He paused. "And you're looking for Luke in Newport. Coincidence?"

"Boyfriend?" I turned back to Patrice, who had settled for a wooden bench near the steps. "Not good. Especially in light of our server's description of the two of them in the pub. According to her, they were quite chummy."

"Well, if Luke is the boyfriend, someone's gonna get hurt. Probably the woman you're helping out locating him."

"I hate to jump to conclusions, JR. Could be she's the whistleblower. It might be innocent."

"Hank, I think you're being naïve. Sounds like you're trying to protect Patrice from the truth."

"Maybe I am. Does this boyfriend have a name?"

"I'm sure he does, but I wasn't able to get it. I think we have to assume Sullivan was meeting up with DuPont. Maybe the boyfriend thing was just a ploy to hide her real reason for being in Newport." He paused. "Except, maybe after they met…"

There goes the wedding.

JR added, "You said you found Elena's shoe and Luke's cell phone on the rocks. Could just be they were frolicking hard."

"Yeah, or it could be something menacing," I added. "That's what I need to find out before I head home. If these two are just messing around, that's one thing. And sad for Patrice. It's another if there's foul play. And whistleblowers could easily find themselves in danger if the target finds out. The question is who's the target?"

"Could be Preston Hartford, III. Sullivan seems to have an important position at his company."

"Makes sense. By the way, were you able to get the name of the other person Luke called in Newport? The number without an answering machine?"

"Oh, right. It belongs to a Warren McKenzie, no pretentious number after his name. He lives in Jamestown, Rhode Island. I think it's just across the Newport Bridge from you. I'll text you the address."

"Thanks. Any connection between the players?"

"Nothing so far, but that can change. Where are you staying, just in case I get a day off?"

"The Wilson House on Clarke Street."

There was a long pause, and it sounded like JR was shuffling papers. "You there?"

"You said Wilson House?"

"Right."

"What a coincidence. That's where Elena Sullivan was supposed to meet up with her boyfriend."

———

"Let's go back to the pub."

"Hungry?" Patrice asked.

"Only for answers. We'll stop off at the inn first. I want to show Brady a photo of Luke's contact person." After I said it, I grimaced, realizing I should have chosen my words more carefully.

Brady shook his head as he scrutinized the photo. Then, to me, "Never saw her." He handed back the phone, his lips curling up ever so slightly. "Believe me, Hank, I'd remember that one. As far as I know, Mr. DuPont was always alone."

Right. Alone.

Patrice let out a small sigh of relief, but this whole rendezvous thing didn't add up. Nothing made sense.

I thanked Brady, and we stepped back outside, taking in the clean New England air. At least, I did. I doubted Patrice had breathed deeply in a while. I was keenly aware of the pain she was experiencing in doubting a loved one. It was unlikely Brady would have seen Elena Sullivan if DuPont had checked in alone. And if Elena had had an ulterior motive, she wouldn't have wanted to be seen anywhere near the inn with Luke. Yet, according to JR, she was meeting her boyfriend at the inn.

My eyes fell on a young woman walking across the street toward us with a handful of towels.

"Excuse me," I said, approaching. "I'm staying at the Wilson House." I nodded over my shoulder. "I was supposed to meet a friend here." I showed Elena's photo. She studied it a few moments then glanced away.

"Something wrong?" I asked.

The woman squeezed the towels a little harder before meeting my eyes. In a slight East European accent, she said, "She was here a few days ago, but left."

"She left by herself?" I pressed.

The twentysomething woman, whose name tag read Maja, gave the towels another squeeze and then nodded.

I smiled. "She's not my girlfriend. Just a friend."

"Oh." She returned a relieved smile. "I saw her leave a room late, maybe ten at night."

"Whose room?" blurted Patrice.

"Don't know his name. The man in 203."

Patrice described Luke to Maja.

She turned her gaze to me, and then back to Patrice. "Think so."

Patrice was visibly crestfallen.

"You were working late that night?" I asked.

She shook her head. "No. Only daytime. I work here in summer, so Mr. Brady gives me a room with another girl. It is next to the man's room. We were walking back from the movie. It finished before ten." She pointed to the corner. "That theater there."

I looked. It couldn't be more than a five-minute walk.

"She left the room with her bag. She…was in a hurry. Didn't say hello."

"A handbag, you mean?"

Maja thought a moment. "Bigger than a handbag, like a small suit-case. They call them overnight, I think. It was expensive looking."

"How about her shoes? Did they look expensive too?" I asked.

Maja smiled. "Oh yes, very." She described the shoe we found, and I side-glanced Patrice.

"Can you take us to Room 203?" I asked, knowing what her response would be.

"He's gone."

My expression feigned confusion. "Oh."

She squeezed the towels one more time. "He left soon after her and never returned."

"You mean he checked out in the middle of the night?"

"Um, maybe you should ask Mr. Brady."

Maja was clearly uncomfortable, and since I already knew the answer, I held back. "Okay, I only have one more question. Did you notice if the woman got into a car?"

Another frozen moment.

"It could help."

"My friend and I followed her to the door and looked out. She walked down the street then turned toward the beach." She pointed left. "I don't know if she had a car." Maja paused. "Soon after, I heard his door close. I saw him leave, too. He didn't have a suitcase, so I thought he would be back."

I nodded. Elena could have driven to the inn, but with restricted parking, she would have needed a decal, or she'd face a parking fine. And she certainly didn't get one from Brady.

I thanked Maja, then pulled out my phone and called JR. I asked him if he could find out how Elena Sullivan traveled to Newport, and, assuming she drove, to get me a make, model, and plate number.

"Sorry, Hank, I'm up to my ass in traffic."

"Perfect. Next time you stop make a call or two."

"Asshole! Not you, the idiot who just cut me off. Okay."

I hung up and returned to the inn. Brady was apparently looking to help us, but I told him three was a crowd. Then I thought about Warren McKenzie, the other name Luke had called on his cell phone, and asked Brady if he was familiar with the guy.

"Yeah, he's got some kind of medical business here—McKenzie and Company. You think he's involved?"

"No, and don't spread rumors. I need to get my prescription for Lipitor filled while I'm here. He was recommended."

Brady's mouth twitched, suppressing a grin.

"What?"

"Not that kind of business. Medical devices. I heard they also have something to do with drug testing, stuff like that. You need to pee in a cup, Hank?"

"Funny."

"Anyway, he lives on the other side of the Newport Bridge in Jamestown. Off of North Main Street. Quite a place, I hear."

I'm sure.

Especially if Warren McKenzie's pee-in-a-cup business was ripping off the government.

FIVE

B ack at The Nautical Pub, I showed Maureen the photo of Elena, minus the shoe.

"Yep, that's her. She hasn't been back since then. She part of the review team, too?"

Even though Maureen wasn't part of the investigation, I told her no. "I'll let you know if she comes back. You have a card?"

Patrice quickly pulled one out and asked Maureen to call if either Elena or Luke showed up.

She took the card without looking at it, and then grinned at me with a flutter of her lashes. "How about you, sweetie?"

How could I say no? I handed her a card.

Patrice made a show of rolling her eyes.

Maureen eyed my card and scrunched up her face. "Detective Hank Reed? You're a cop? So this whole restaurant review thing was a ruse?" She turned to Patrice. "I had a feeling something was up by your questioning about the blond. And the guy's yours, I'm guessing."

"Long story," I said. "But since you've been so helpful, once we find Luke, we'll make sure he writes a glowing review for you personally."

I was eager to pay Warren McKenzie a visit, and I reminded Patrice we had an appointment. We wished Maureen a good day.

We drove in silence on Thames Street, the historic cobbled road in Newport that runs parallel to the waterfront. As we approached the Jamestown side of the Newport Bridge, I said, "Patrice, you're going to have to tell me more about Luke's whistleblower investigation. I need to know everything you know. Did he ever mention specifics? You have to trust me." I glanced over at her.

Patrice shook her head. "Don't you think I would have told you what I knew? Why would I hold back?" She held back tears, but she was clearly out of sorts.

"Sorry, but we have very little to go on."

She crossed her arms. "Luke was very secretive about the whole thing. In the past, he'd mention his assignment, what he was working on, but said this was different." She paused. "I know Luke trusted me, but this was big, and he needed to keep it totally secret. He did say that if all went well, his investigation would implicate some wealthy people. Heads would fall, with prison time. He joked that it might produce a Pulitzer." She hesitated again, then said, "He's either deep in cover, or…"

In deep shit!

I gave her time to recover, thought about McKenzie. If he was the target of the investigation, why would Luke contact him in the first place? How would that conversation go? *Hi, Mr. McKenzie, I'm Luke DuPont, and I'm investigating your company—or rather, you.* And for all we knew, Luke might have dialed the wrong number when he'd called McKenzie. One thing that bothered me: Both McKenzie and Hartford were in similar businesses, and one was likely a crook.

Something else: What the heck were we going to ask McKenzie? *We're looking for Luke DuPont and think you had something to do with his disappearance, so where the hell is he?* Not likely.

My thoughts were interrupted by my cell. I didn't put it on speaker.

"She flew into Providence," JR said, "but didn't rent a car, so I'm guessing someone was waiting for her. That or she took a taxi. I'd say it was the former."

Patrice and I arrived in Jamestown, a town situated almost entirely on Conanicut Island and one that was ranked pretty high on the wealthiest places in the United States—this according to Brady. We drove on

North Main until arriving at a private road that displayed a threatening sign: NO TRESSPASSING – VIOLATORS WILL BE SHOT, SURVIVORS WILL BE SHOT AGAIN.

I snorted. "Think we should have called first." A nervous chuckle.

I followed the gravel road a few hundred feet and stopped in front of a circular driveway with a McMansion on one side and a four-car garage on the other. I studied the contemporary Victorian estate and wraparound porch. Brady had understated McKenzie's digs. The place was breathtaking to say the least. His company must be doling out lots of pee-in-cup products.

"Luke told you his investigation would implicate some wealthy people. Look around, this place drips money. " I pointed at the house. "Good place to start."

Before I got out of the car, I sized up my surroundings. There weren't any snipers on the roof (always a good thing), and there were only a few lawn cutters attending the grounds. A white truck stood twenty yards from the house, its rear door opened, apparently used for storing the riding mowers and other grounds equipment. Black lettering on the side of the truck read The Perfect Cut. The groundskeepers looked over at us with indifference then went back to work.

"I don't think weapons are required for this one."

Patrice was lost, mesmerized by the enormous estate.

"Earth to Patrice."

"Sorry, pretty impressive." Her eyes met mine. "What's the game plan?"

Good question.

I thought a moment. We couldn't just drop in without a plan. "Let's hope McKenzie hasn't read his trespassing sign lately."

An attractive Latina dressed in a white domestic worker's uniform opened the door with a look of slight apprehension. When I showed my shield and identified myself, she stiffened. But when I explained I wasn't from Immigration and that our interest was solely in finding two missing people, she relaxed and showed us in.

It was apparent that McKenzie, who wasn't home, had a flair for the nautical. The family room was large, with minimalist decor. On a light-colored wood coffee table sat a round, silver tray accompanied with fresh flowers, driftwood, and coral. The neutral sectional sofa rested on ivory marble floors. But what caught my attention the most were the sheer window draperies framing a sweeping, spectacular view of the bay.

The woman appeared to be in her mid-thirties. Now that she was more at ease, she revealed a captivating smile, and she had striking dark-green eyes and black hair tied up in a bun. Quite honestly, she could have passed for a telenovela actress.

"How can I help, señor?" she asked, her accent heavily flavored with Spanish.

"We were told Mr. McKenzie might help us in finding a few missing people." Patrice showed her a photo of Luke and waited for a reaction. She shook her head. "No."

Patrice had refused to even view a photo of her nemesis, so I showed McKenzie's domestic a photo of Elena, the one JR had provided.

She nodded. "Sí."

It turned out that my fellow investigator's Spanish was impeccable, and she began expanding her questioning. I, on the other hand, gazed around the room, which equaled two of my former living room on Long Island. I noticed a hallway that probably led to one of the bedrooms. My head shot back to them when my rusty Spanish ear heard the words *"¿Ella estuvo aquí?"*

"You mean she was here?" Patrice asked impatiently. "In this house?"

The domestic nodded for the second time.

"¿Cuándo?" Patrice inquired.

I understood that, too, but then the woman's words began to rattle on and lost me. When she finished speaking, Patrice turned to me. "Ana Lucía—that's her name—told me Elena was here about two weeks ago. And then last Friday, McKenzie told Ana to tidy up the guest bedroom, that he was expecting a friend Sunday afternoon. She claims it was Elena. At least, she thinks so."

Patrice paused. "That sounds right, considering she and Luke were seen earlier at The Nautical Pub. Luke was supposed to meet his CI later that evening at the Cliff Walk. Someone other than Elena?"

Ana Lucía—nice name.

"Was the woman in the photo Señor McKenzie's girlfriend?" I asked with a smile.

"Friend, maybe." I took that to mean Elena and McKenzie were involved in business or the bedroom. Or both.

"Is he married?"

"Señor McKenzie is divorced."

"I see. Does anyone live here with him? A friend?" I pressed.

She looked down and away, evidently uncomfortable with the question, maybe concerned for her job, but she said, "Sometimes he has girl-friends."

I nodded, looked around then returned my gaze to Ana. "Where is Mr. McKenzie now?"

She hesitated, possibly not wanting to provide personal information on her boss. "He has a business in Boston."

"So he's not here during the week?" Patrice said pointedly.

Ana turned to her and shook her head. "Only weekends."

I considered that it must be lonely here during the week for Ana Lucía. "May I use the bathroom?" I asked.

"*Sí, por supuesto.*" She pointed to the hallway I'd noticed upon arriv-ing. I gave Patrice a barely perceptible wink and excused myself. My bladder really was full, but I also needed time to explore, so I passed the bathroom and continued until I found a closed door. I tapped lightly then entered. It was a bedroom. True to the living room design, this room was also nautically inspired. There was a circular, blue-and-white wooden piece of wall décor with an anchor in the middle, with the message, "Welcome Aboard."

I went directly to the walk-in closet. Unless McKenzie was a drag queen, the designer dresses and expensive shoes belonged to one of his girlfriends. Judging by the fact that there was only one dress size, I assumed McKenzie had a favorite.

At the moment, though, I was more interested in the shoes. I found a rack with at least a dozen, in many seductive styles. Like the dresses, the shoes had one commonality: the size, seven. Elena's size. I took out my cell phone and snapped a few pictures, then knelt down and noticed a shoe toe extending ever so slightly from the rack. I pulled a handkerchief from my back pocket and carefully lifted a red, opened-sided stiletto sandal with three-inch heels that showed signs of abuse. The damaged shoe was missing a rhinestone. In its place, there was a small, dark-gray object. I took a pen from my pocket, removed the cap, and picked at the object with it until it came loose and fell on the floor. I picked it up and lifted it to the light. It was a beach pebble. I snapped a picture.

Cinderella's other shoe.

Not wanting to get Ana in trouble with her boss, or put McKenzie on to us, we told her it would be wise to forget we were here.

She had no problem with that.

Back in the car, Patrice wanted to know what I'd been doing in the bathroom so long. "You're too young to have a prostate problem, so tell me, what you were looking for?"

Very discerning woman.

I carefully removed my folded-up handkerchief. I opened it, displaying the pebble I'd found inside Elena's rhinestone pump. "Guess."

Patrice was about to touch, but my hand got in her way. "Could be evidence." I brought the handkerchief up to her face.

"It looks like a pebble to me. And you found it…?"

"Lodged in a shoe inside a bedroom closet. I left the shoe for obvious reasons, but it's identical to the one we found out at the Cliffs. I'm guessing it belongs to Elena. The closet was full of expensive dresses and shoes probably purchased at Macy's or something."

Patrice glanced up at the ceiling and smiled.

"What?"

"You obviously aren't a woman. If what you're saying about the clothes is true, those shoes are more Manolo Blahnik and Jovani."

A blank stare, then I got it. "Oh, the rock star."

"What? No—not Bon Jovi. Jovani. Think Saks Fifth Avenue. Anyway, I'm betting she and McKenzie are an item," she said, her tone hopeful.

"Quite possible," I replied, hoping to reduce her anxiety. "Only I don't know where Elena fits in. If Luke was meeting an informant, I doubt it would be her. She doesn't work for McKenzie, and if she and McKenzie are lovers, and she knew what he was up to—assuming he was up to anything—what would she gain by turning him in? Judging from the closet full of expensive goodies, I'm sure McKenzie and Jovani are taking good care of her." I smiled.

Patrice gazed up at the house. "Let's get out of here. Ana Lucía is watching us."

Midway over the Newport Bridge, I noticed Patrice becoming fidgety. "What's up?"

"I'm just trying to link Luke with Elena, that's all. We've been thinking McKenzie might be dirty and the target of Luke's investigation, because Luke had his phone number. What if he isn't? What if Elena is cheating on him with Luke and McKenzie found out about it? I hate that theory, obviously, but let's just say."

McKenzie would still be dirty if he was involved in their disappearance.

"Possible, considering Maureen found Luke and Elena...friendly."

She sighed. "That would be bad for us," she said almost to herself. Then turning to me, she asked, "How did they meet?"

A woman had a right to know.

"Well, for one thing, Luke and Elena both work in New York..."

"New York is a big place, Hank!"

I'd definitely hit a nerve. "True, and once we find him...them, you'll have plenty of time for questions."

Another sigh. "God, I just want to know. This entire missing business is making me crazy." She paused. "But you're right. When I find Luke, I will question him to death."

Spoken like a true professional.

When we reached the Wilson House, I turned off the engine and tapped the steering wheel before turning to Patrice. "If we don't find Luke or Elena soon, we might consider sniffing around Boston. That's where McKenzie's business is located, remember? And according to Ana, he sleeps there during the week, so he has to have a place locally. Could be someone saw Luke and Elena in the area. I'll ask JR to get me an address."

She nodded absently.

"Something's bothering you."

She gazed over. "Just trying to piece together their timeline. She left the pub first, and at some point, they met up. I hate saying it, but I have to believe that's what happened. Ana claimed Elena returned to McKenzie's place that afternoon. I'm assuming she still had both shoes at the time. I'm also guessing she hung out with him for a while since he's there on weekends." She stopped, gave it some thought then continued. "Then she tells McKenzie she's going out for a while."

"Okay, and?"

"More than likely, she meets up with Luke until the eight o'clock meeting." She closed her eyes hard.

My own eyes stayed glued to Patrice's pained expression. "But what if Elena was the informant?" she continued. "Then who was Luke going to meet at eight? From what we found, we know they visited the Walk at some point…"

"Right, the shoe and phone," I added.

"And the St. Christopher medal."

Let's not forget ol' Chris.

"Unless both of them were meeting the informant. If you're thinking foul play, why weren't there any signs of a struggle? For all we know, the whole thing was staged."

Her expression rejected that thought. "Why the hell for? Certainly not for me. Luke didn't even know I was flying over." She stopped and offered me a grave look. "Not staged, Hank. Maybe McKenzie tailed them. One thing led to another…"

I had a problem with her theory. "Then how come I found Elena's other shoe in his house? The police would eventually find out about him and Elena and search his place."

She shook her head. "You really think Luke and Elena staged this and then took off in hiding? That's crazy. I can't deal with this."

She stepped out of the car and stormed into the inn.

I watched her disappear inside. She was much too close to the investigation, which made my job difficult. Patrice needed to keep an open mind, but until we found Luke, that wasn't about to happen.

I filled my lungs and let it out, then remained in the car a bit longer. Foul play wasn't a stretch if McKenzie and Elena were a couple—especially if he'd discovered she was becoming sweet on someone else. But where was the struggle? And where were the bodies?

I looked up at the inn. The thing that bothered me was finding Elena's other shoe in the closet. Maybe McKenzie was just some sick guy holding onto his lover's worn shoe for posterity.

I found Brady inside, crumbs and chocolate smears on his lips betraying a gobbled cookie. It made him appear like a clown, or a four-year-old kid. When he saw me, he downed a glass of milk, wiped his mouth and mustache quickly with a tissue, and smiled. "I found the cookie culprit. She admitted taking them, claimed she was having a hypoglycemic attack. She brought fresh replacements this morning. Want one?" Brady brought up a box.

"Homemade, nice." I shoved one in my mouth, chewed with delight, and took another.

"I know. I got a pretty sweet upgrade to my usual store-bought."

I scanned the area for Patrice. Brady pointed to her room. "From her expression, I'm going to guess you didn't have any luck."

I shook my head and popped the second cookie in my mouth.

"'Fraid not."

"Well, I might have a bit of news. I asked my staff this morning if anyone had seen something or someone unusual around the inn Sunday or Monday. I mentioned there was a tip in it for good information." Brady removed another cookie from the box. "We have a security guy who patrols the area at night for several of the inns in the neighborhood. Kind of like a community watchdog. Chuck's his name. He tells me he remembers a guy walking his dog a few minutes after nine Sunday night. He stopped by our place, walked up to our door, and tried opening it. It was locked, of course, so Chuck says the guy put his face up to the glass to look inside. When Chuck asked him what he was up to, the guy gave him some bullshit story and left." He stopped, gave me time to digest it. "Chuck followed him until the guy got into a white Camry and drove off. He described the guy, and between you and me, it sounded like the same phony FBI guy. I guess he's trying more stunts to get inside—this time with a dog."

"Chuck say what kind?"

"Nah, he's not a dog lover, so all he said was that it was small. Possibly a poodle."

"Strange. Did Chuck get the license plate?"

"Not really. Like I said, it was dark. He spotted a few numbers," Brady looked down and picked up a yellow Post-It stuck to his desk. "One-six-nine, that's it. He said it did have the lighthouse insignia on the left side, so definitely Massachusetts. He never followed up, since nothing else unusual happened over the next few days."

Brady bit into a cookie, then handed me the Post-It. "You might want to check it out." He smiled then made the cookie disappear in his mouth.

Massachusetts license plate—as in Boston. As in McKenzie's company's headquarters. Coincidence? I mean, who takes a dog out for a walk at night only to drive away with it? I thanked Brady for his good detective work and told him we'd be staying at least one more night.

I debated knocking on Patrice's door, but within a few minutes she showed up more refreshed.

"Sorry about before."

I guided her outside and asked if she wanted to file a missing person's report. It was her fiancé, and thus, her call.

She took a deep breath. "Hank, I'm scared and angry, but my gut

43

tells me that by now, whether we did or not, it wouldn't make a difference." Her pained eyes searched my face for an answer.

She was probably right, and although the authorities might have better luck tracking down Luke—dead or alive, I decided to hold off. I said, "How about we try McKenzie's place in Boston first?"

Boston was a little more than seventy miles from Newport. After taking the infamous I-95, we switched to I-93 until we hit North Street in the downtown area. JR, who was frustrated with his own murder investigation, returned with McKenzie's Boston address. I owed him big time and told him so.

It turned out McKenzie's company owned an upscale condo on Broad Street close to the Boston harbor. After circling the block twice, I pulled into an underground parking garage next to McKenzie's condominium. I grabbed a ticket from the machine, then parked two levels below. As we approached the street, I noticed an old guy with a wrinkled face and short, wiry gray hair in the booth. He was checking us out—or, rather, Patrice. He smiled at her and gave a little wave.

Picking up on his friendliness, she turned to me. "Let's ask him." As she approached, his eyes lit up. At the window, she produced her credentials, along with a photo of Luke. "Hey, I could use your help."

"Really? Sure."

She pointed at the photo, and the old man's eyes dropped to the grinning image of Luke. "Have you seen this man?"

"He in some kind of trouble?" His eyes met Patrice's with a look of genuine concern.

"Please answer the question." She glanced at the name tag on his shirt. "Mickey."

He nodded. "Okay, yeah, I think I seen him. He was here with a woman earlier in the week."

"This woman?" I asked, showing him Elena's photo.

Another nod. "That's the one."

"You said you saw them together?" Patrice's voice became rushed.

"Right, together. I see customers walking in and out all the time." He pointed to a mirror in his booth. "These two seemed like a regular couple."

"Regular how?" I asked. "And when?"

Mickey closed his eyes. "It was…Monday afternoon." He opened them. "They were dressed businesslike and walking fast like everyone else around here. Nobody has time for talking to nobody anymore these days. Just in a damn rush all the time."

"Monday? You're sure? That was a few days ago," Patrice said quickly.

The old guy chuckled. "Yeah, I remember. I paid attention to her. She was a hottie, like the kids say. The man, he was good-looking, too, but she—"

Patrice broke in. "Were you here when they left?"

"Yeah, I was here, only he was alone. Too bad." He smiled wolfishly at Patrice and winked. "Believe me, I woulda remembered if she'd been here."

I didn't even try to conceal my eye-roll. Today was Thursday, and I wondered if Elena was still in McKenzie's condo. I spotted a closed-circuit television system at the front of the garage and whipped out a hundred-dollar bill in front of Mickey's face. "How about letting us view the feed on the CCTV for that period?" I pointed to the camera.

The guy's head darted about. "Oh, I'm not sure I can do that. This job supplements my social security check." He eyed Benjamin Franklin. "Can you be quick?"

"How quick can you get the feed?"

It took about ten minutes, but we managed to glimpse Elena and Luke walking out of the garage then turning towards McKenzie's place. No hand holding, not even that fast, just a normal pace, side by side. Good sign. Also, Elena was dressed more casually, in black pants and a white silk top. No heels this time.

I stopped the video, and for the first time came into contact with Luke once removed. He stood at about six feet, with short-cropped brown hair. I could see Patrice's attraction in him, looks, anyway.

I turned to Patrice, who was studying the stopped footage. She

45

sighed. "At least he was still alive on Monday. She didn't mention Elena for obvious reasons."

Mickey, who was standing at the doorway between the office and his booth, started breathing heavily. I prayed he wasn't having a heart attack. He began hopping from foot to foot.

"Mickey, since you had eyes for the blond, what would you say her disposition was like? She seem friendly? Anxious?"

"Normal, I guess. You almost done?"

"She didn't smile at you as she passed by?" This from Patrice.

"They were both looking straight ahead. All business, like I said, in their own lives. Things on their minds, no time to stop and smile. She was still hot, though."

Christ, the old guy needed to get a life.

"Please, I need to get back to work."

"Go ahead. I'll let you know when we're done."

We spent another twenty minutes viewing, and then Patrice pointed. "There's Luke again."

I stopped the video. "Like Mickey said, he was alone." I checked the time on the feeder. "Monday evening, seven ten p.m." And still alive. I continued the feed and watched as a dour Luke disappeared into the subterranean garage. A few minutes later, he appeared again, driving a fancy black something-or-other, and disappeared after making a right onto Broad Street.

"Rewind," said Patrice.

I followed orders.

"Luke lives in New York City and doesn't own a car. It must be a rental."

I rewound again and stopped when the back of the car appeared on the screen. I zoomed in. It had a Rhode Island license plate. It read: MORE4ME.

Definitely not a rental.

We continued watching the video feed, waiting to see if Luke returned, or if by some chance Elena had entered the garage. Negative on both accounts.

"Let's pay Elena a visit," I said.

We thanked Mickey, who was happy to see us leave, and I slipped him the hundred. We walked to McKenzie's condo building. Luxury was the appropriate word to describe the glass, stone, and brick exterior. I counted the number of stories, stopping at twelve, and wondered if McKenzie's digs were the penthouse.

"Did you see that? A car just pulled out of McKenzie's condo building. He has private parking." Patrice pointed.

I glanced over. "So what was MORE4ME doing in public parking?"

"Maybe the condo only provides one spot. And since MORE4ME doesn't appear to be a rental, it could be McKenzie's second car. That can only mean his private parking spot is taken." Patrice stopped. "She may still be here."

I eyed the front entrance. "Let's find out." The interior construction also spared no expense: there was marble and glass all over the place. The security officer was sitting at his desk, watching us as we walked in.

"Hi," he said. "Can I help you?"

Friendly enough.

The guy was mid-fifties, white, lots of gray hair, and a smile, at least, so far. His name tag said "Carey."

I showed him my shield. "We believe there's a fugitive on the run and he might be in the area." I nodded to Patrice. "Show him his photo."

She brought up her cell phone. "Have you seen this man?"

He eyed the photo then asked to see my shield again. "New York?"

He can read.

"Right, Suffolk County, Long Island. You want to call them, see if I'm on the level?"

He searched my face then looked to Patrice. "You Suffolk County, too?"

She grinned, showed her Interpol badge. "One better."

Carey studied it a moment. Evidently he was not familiar with Interpol—that, or he just liked her photo. "Yeah, he was here." He removed his sign-in book from underneath the desk then stopped. "I just realized, he was here with the owner, so he wouldn't need to sign in. We're very careful about unwanted visitors."

"Understandable," I said. "You said he was with the owner?"

"Right, Ms. Sullivan. But he left a day or two ago, and she left this morning."

Two cars for sure.

"You're sure the unit doesn't belong to someone else? Maybe Ms. Sullivan rents the place?"

He shook his head. "Not possible, renting is prohibited in this building."

I side-glanced Patrice, then showed Carey Elena's photo. "Is this Ms. Sullivan?"

"That's her. She in some kind of trouble? I hope not. She's nice, only comes here occasionally, mostly to get away from the stress. That's what she tells me, anyway."

The guy seemed to know her pretty well, so I asked, "And this man, he come here occasionally?"

Carey shook his head. "First time, as far as I know. Could be a new boyfriend."

A soft guttural groan rose from Patrice. "So she's had other boyfriends in the past?"

The guy glared at us. "Are you interested in her or him?"

I figured he must be a retired cop. I moved in on him. "What would happen if another boyfriend turned out to be like this guy? A real piece of work. Huh?"

The guy stepped back. "Look, she's been living here about a year. When she arrives—when I'm here, anyway—she's alone. And no one has come in and asked for her, okay? If she parks her car in the garage, I can see it with our monitor camera." He pointed to his desk. "She left from the garage this morning. Believe me, Ms. Sullivan is safe in this complex."

I smiled. "You'd make a great cop."

He relaxed. "I was on the force for twenty-five years. District A-one, here in Boston."

"No hard feelings. We're just trying to do our jobs."

"I gotcha. Me too."

I handed Carey my business card. "In case you see the guy again. And discretion is everything. Please don't alert the locals."

"I might not have a choice. You have to understand, like I said, I was a cop."

I nodded. "Give me first dibs, if you don't mind."

He took my card. "Professional courtesy, I get it."

"Thanks. Oh, one other question: does Warren McKenzie also own a unit here?"

He shrugged. "Who's that?"

SIX

"What was that all about?" Patrice asked outside the building. "I thought JR told you the place belonged to McKenzie."

"He actually said McKenzie's company owned it. Maybe this guy doesn't know that. He's probably assuming it's hers."

I glanced inside the building and saw Carey on his cell phone, talking a mile a minute. He noticed me peeking inside and turned his back. Maybe he'd get a big Christmas tip for keeping his mouth shut. But what was the big deal who owned the condo?

"It's possible that McKenzie's company transferred the unit to Elena. Only, I'm sure JR would have picked up on any change in ownership." I shrugged, keeping my eyes on the security guy. He hung up then turned to me and smiled. I nodded and waved.

Patrice said suddenly, "Let's get the ownership answer later. We need to find Luke."

She was right. When we returned to our car, I speed-dialed JR. He didn't pick up, which didn't surprise me. He was probably caught up in his own muck. I texted him: Need owner and address of RI plate MORE4ME. Pure vanity.

After picking up the car, I handed Mickey my parking stub, paid the

50

rate, and thanked him again. Then I slipped him my business card. "In case either party pops up again."

I felt as though I was chasing two ghosts in two cars, in two states. At this point, I hadn't a clue what to think about the situation.

And then Brady called.

"Where are you now?" Brady asked.

Christ, another mother?

"Boston. We're heading back to Newport. Why do you ask?" I said, backing out of my spot.

"I guess you didn't hear. They found something below the Cliff Walk, near the Forty Steps."

"Something or someone?" I asked my voice racing.

"According to the local news, it's too early to tell. The police got a call this morning about clothes strewn about. Probably a male, if it's a person. Could be just kids messing around. It is a cool place to hang out at night."

Right, cool.

"Did they at least identify the type of clothes? Youthful, business?"

"Nope, didn't say. I'm keeping an eye on the news, though. I'll get back to you when I know more."

"Appreciate the heads up, Brady. You did good."

After I hung up, I turned to Patrice, whose blanched face was all panic. She must've held on to every word of the conversation. I passed on Brady's information and told her we shouldn't jump to conclusions.

"Hurry," she pleaded.

I exited the garage. "It could be anyone, if in fact it wasn't a prank," I said, trying to reassure her.

Patrice stared straight ahead, said nothing. She fidgeted in her seat, took out her Android, and made a call. The conversation began in rapid French; I didn't speak the language, but by the sound of her intense and rushing voice, I concluded she was trying to get help. When she ended the conversation, she turned. "We'll find out soon."

"Interpol, I'm guessing."

She nodded. "I have a source that can pull things out of a hat. Anywhere. They know why I'm here and will do anything to get me back to Paris." A smile barely made it through tightly pressed lips. She played with her phone a little then stared out the window.

The traffic to Newport was lighter than usual, and we arrived at the inn in less than an hour and a half. Inside, Brady's face was glued to the local news. His head shot up as we entered. "Nothing more. Still thinking it could be a hoax."

Hopefully.

"The Cliffs must be swarmed with local enforcement, so how do we get near the Forty Steps to find out what's going on?" I stood next to him, my eyes on the screen.

"Parking's a bitch," Brady said. He glanced over at Patrice. "Sorry for my language. Anyway, you might want to just walk." He gazed out at the late-afternoon gray, threatening sky. "Or maybe not. Park as close as you can to Narraganset Avenue. It's probably ground zero."

Brady wasn't kidding; police cars swarmed the immediate area. I drove a few blocks before pulling into the McKillop Library parking lot on Ochre Point Avenue. The sign read: "For Patrons Only."

"What's the worst that can happen? I get a parking ticket?"

Patrice glanced around. "It's on me if we do," she said, but her voice was strained. As we approached Narraganset Avenue, Patrice's cell beckoned her, and she answered on the first ring. As we continued walking, she nodded several times and thanked the caller.

"We have to find Detective Jackson."

"You gonna tell me a little bit more, partner?"

"Like I said, my department has worldwide connections. I didn't want to use up my brownie points before, so I held off. I told them about Luke, but he wasn't on anyone's radar when I left, and since they hadn't contacted me, I assumed they still didn't know where he was. But now, with a possible murder, this was the time to tap my sources."

"And this Detective Jackson?"

"Apparently, he's in charge." Patrice picked up her pace as we entered the Walk, and like a puppy, I followed her toward the steps. When we saw a uniform, she removed her credentials and asked for Jackson. "He's expecting us."

At the top of the Forty Steps, Detective Jackson was surrounded by a half-dozen men and women in blue. He peered over their heads and waved for us to approach.

"Interpol?"

Patrice nodded. "Thanks for letting us in." She introduced us.

"You're a long way from home, Detective Reed. Must be important."

I let Patrice fill Jackson in, starting with Paris.

"Quite a coincidence, you being in Paris, and then helping her out here."

"Law enforcement folks look out for each other everywhere," I said.

"Touché."

Jackson was a ten-year homicide detective veteran originally from Hartford, Connecticut. He'd joined Newport's force about three years ago. Dressed in street clothes, he was a slight, wiry guy in his late thirties, with a military buzz cut, clean-shaven. He was the lead homicide detective, and the fact that he was here meant something more than simply finding some clothes had developed.

Two guys approached from the Steps carrying a body bag, dripping with seawater. From what I could tell—or couldn't—our investigation might sadly be over. But then Jackson said the victim was a white male in his mid-fifties with gray hair, and broken bones throughout his body.

Patrice let out a breath she'd been holding for who-knows-how-long.

"He could have been dead a number of days for all we know right now." Jackson pointed to the waves crashing into the rocky coast below. "The water was cold enough to keep him from rotting out. We'll have a better idea once we get him to the coroner."

Patrice might have been relieved, but I wanted to know more, and asked Jackson how the victim had died. Luke and Elena might be safe for now, but I wanted to know if the guy had been murdered.

"Hard to say. Based on a preliminary visual, the vic suffered severe head trauma. Of course, he could have accidentally fallen off the Walk. That would certainly do some damage. We'll get a better sense once we obtain a toxicology report." He tilted his head. "Then again, he might have been pushed. One thing's for sure," Jackson said, "The guy isn't saying."

Later that evening, we caught up with Jackson at the stationhouse. He wanted to fill us in on what he'd learned in person. He offered us a seat.

"The victim's name is Warren McKenzie," he said, meeting my eyes. "Ring a bell? He owned a place in Jamestown across the bridge."

My stomach took a hit. *Our Warren McKenzie?* I didn't wait for Patrice to answer.

"Yes."

"Yes? Okay, please expand on that, Detective."

I nodded. "We discovered that Luke DuPont made several phone calls during the course of last week. One of them was to McKenzie."

Jackson lifted a brow.

"We don't know for sure if Luke ever spoke to him, at least by phone, because when I tried the number there was no voice message feature, and the call was dropped within seconds. That's all we know."

Jackson turned to Patrice. "And your fiancé never mentioned McKenzie?"

"He was very secretive about the investigation. It was his first whistleblower case. So no, never." She then said, "Detective, if McKenzie was the target of the investigation, why would anyone be interested in killing him?"

I tried getting a read on Jackson, who appeared to be mulling over Patrice's question.

"Fair point. What I'm hearing is that Luke had no reason to kill McKenzie. Just the opposite. If he knew Luke was on to him, McKenzie might have had his own plan to quash the investigation, correct?"

She nodded in agreement.

"And Luke is still missing. Maybe they met, got into an argument, and your fiancé won. Maybe he's hiding out, figuring his next move. Is he violent?"

She shook her head briskly. "Only on paper. He's a dogged reporter, but not a physically violent person. But, if he were attacked, I'm sure he would fight back."

"I'm sure," Jackson said his tone suspicious. "The reason I asked you down here was to inform you that we believe McKenzie was pushed over the Cliff Walk. We discovered a shred of clothing, probably from his shirt, in an area on the Walk. Looks like he fought with someone before being tossed over." He stopped and gave Patrice a grim look. "Until we piece more together, we can't rule out either self-defense or murder. Meaning your fiancé is a person of interest."

Patrice closed her eyes.

"Help me find your fiancé, Ms. Dubois."

She nodded, a tear forming in the outer corner of her right eye. "Believe me, we've been trying for days. I want answers more than you do. Especially now."

"Okay, then, thanks for coming by. I understand you folks are staying at the Wilson House. Say hello to Brady for me. Nice guy."

We left Jackson and sat in the car in silence, trying to take in McKenzie's murder. Could Luke and Elena be next if McKenzie wasn't the target? They were either missing or hiding out somewhere. We had to find them, and fast—which meant I couldn't leave just yet.

I had already called my boss and told him I'd probably need more time. He must've known I was up to something, and word had gotten out that I was contemplating leaving the force. He politely told me to get my shit together, meaning if I wanted to stay on payroll, I'd better return soon.

I turned to Patrice. "What if McKenzie wasn't the whistleblower's target? What if Elena and Luke were working *with* him? What if McKenzie was feeding them information? Elena works for Preston Hartford's company, which is McKenzie's competitor. Maybe she discovered her boss was crooked?"

"I thought of that. Luke might really be in trouble, and not for the reason Jackson thinks." She turned to me, her eyes pleading.

I cranked up the engine. "I think we oughta pay McKenzie's domestic another visit first thing in the morning, before Jackson decides to investigate."

Patrice said nothing, so I continued. "Once Jackson searches his place and finds a closet full of clothes, he's going to start asking questions, and she might wind up telling him we had already been there. It's not good for us if he thinks we've been holding back—which we have."

I flipped open my cell and called JR. "Any luck on the plate number?"

"Oh, right, sorry. You can't even imagine my life right now. Or maybe you can. Hold on a second."

I heard clamor in the background, probably radio dispatchers. *I could imagine.*

"Two cars are registered in McKenzie name: a Mini Cooper sport, and the car you asked me about. Both registered in Rhode Island."

"Makes sense. He lives there."

"I also found a company car registered in Massachusetts, a crystal black pearl Acura RLX. Sexy color."

"They belonged to McKenzie," I said. "He turned up dead this morning. Likely pushed over the Cliff Walk. We're working with a local detective on the case."

"And the fiancé?" he asked. "He turn up yet?"

I glanced at Patrice who sat patiently.

"Not yet."

At eight the next morning, we arrived at McKenzie's Jamestown home and found the place quiet. Must have been an off-day for the landscapers. Fortunately for us, Detective Jackson and the investigators hadn't shown up yet.

I knocked on the door, and when no one answered, I peered through a window. No activity. I eased over to the garage and found a late-model, beige Hyundai Accent parked outside. I peeked inside the car. There was a Spanish-language newspaper on the passenger seat with today's date.

"Someone's here," I told Patrice as I approached her. "Follow me." I hustled around the back. "Wasn't there a yacht tied up here last time?"

"I think so. Maybe." She stopped. "Think that's how McKenzie got to the bay?"

I shook my head. "Unlikely. He was pushed from the Walk. Besides, Jackson would have mentioned finding an abandoned boat offshore near the crime scene if it was there. Someone took it."

As I turned back toward the house, I was certain the sheer curtain moved.

"Cover the front!" I shouted as I ran to the back door. A shadow inside skimmed quickly by. I banged on the door, calling out Ana's name, telling her the cops were on their way.

The door opened slowly, and there stood a woman with her hands raised, her eyes wide.

"You're not Ana Lucía."

She was the same height and shape and could have passed for an older Ana, but her hands were rough-looking like a real domestic, not like Ana's, whose French nails had been perfect, now that I thought about it.

"Who?" she asked.

I showed my shield. "Ana Lucía, Mr. McKenzie's domestic."

Her face angled in confusion. "I am his housekeeper, señor," she replied with a heavy Spanish accent.

"You are? What's your name?"

"Isabella."

"Is that your car parked near the garage, Isabella?"

"Sí, Señor McKenzie allows me park there. Something is wrong?"

There definitely was something wrong.

I described Ana to her, but Isabella shook her head. "I have been Señor McKenzie's housekeeper for five years. There is no one by that name who works here."

I scratched my head. "Do you live here in the house?"

She shook her head. "No, señor, I live with my family in New Bedford."

There was a knock on the front window, and I could see Patrice waving. "Would you please let my partner in?"

Patrice entered and gave Isabella a confused smile, then turned to me and raised her eyebrows. "What gives?"

"I'll fill you in later. Isabella works for McKenzie here at the house."

"Then who is Ana Lucía?"

"Not the domestic." On our last visit, I'd noticed a security camera attached to the front of the house. "Isabella, I need to see Mr. McKenzie's video feed for his security camera."

"¿Cómo?"

Patrice initiated her perfect Spanish, pointing to the front door then faced me. "I asked Isabella where Mr. McKenzie keeps the DVR recorder for the system."

"Ah, sí!" Isabella pointed to a small cabinet on the far side of the room. "Is locked."

"Do you have the key?" Patrice asked.

Isabella nodded, then retrieved a set of keys from the kitchen wall and proceeded to open the cabinet door.

"Dios mío, is gone!" She shot me a look. "Was here a few days ago, señor, I swear it. Someone must have…"

Not good. I glanced through my eyebrows at Patrice. "I need to look around."

I began with the guest bedroom—no sense in wasting time. I wasn't surprised to find the closet empty. I searched the other rooms and closets, and didn't find anything belonging to a female.

Who are you, Ana?

Returning to the family room, I shrugged. "Nothing."

"According to Isabella, McKenzie stays in Boston during the week, which is the same thing Ana told us. But he didn't want his house empty, so Isabella works Monday to Friday."

"Then how come you weren't here yesterday?" I asked with authority in my voice.

She hesitated. "Señor McKenzie's office call me, say I did not have to come until today, but I would still get paid."

I shot Patrice a look. "I see."

"She say Señor McKenzie had guests for the weekend who would still be here yesterday. They wanted privacy."

I'm sure.

"And when you returned this morning, did you find anything unusual? Stuff from messy guests or garbage bags filled to the brim?" Patrice had to translate that one.

Isabella took a quick look around the room. "Very neat guests." She smiled.

I met Patrice's gaze and nodded. "Isabella, there's been a terrible accident. Mr. McKenzie has been killed."

She placed a hand to her mouth and made a quick sign of the cross, then began to cry. Patrice found her a tissue in the bathroom and helped the poor woman to a seat on the sofa.

I called Detective Jackson and told him we'd located McKenzie's home in Jamestown and interviewed the domestic there. If I was going to get a quid pro quo from Jackson, I needed to keep him in the loop. He thanked me and said he was on his way.

I sat down across from Isabella on the loveseat and asked her if she knew what had happened to Mr. McKenzie's yacht.

She wiped her eyes and gave me a bewildered look. She stood quickly and went to the curtains. "*Dios mío!* They have taken the boat!"

"Who?"

"I guess the people who stayed here."

"The police are on their way," I said. "We'll let them know." I offered her my best encouraging smile.

"Do you know the name of the boat?" This came from Patrice.

"The boat has a name, señorita?"

I held off rolling my eyes. "Yes. It would have been written on the back."

"Oh! Sí, I remember. It was *Pretty Diagnostic*," she said, having some trouble with diagnostic.

Christ, another write-off.

Patrice showed Isabella a photo of Luke, and like before, I produced one of Elena. Patrice had finally seen her nemesis from the CCTV tapes in Boston but refused to keep the one I had of Elena in her cell photo file.

Isabella shook her head. "Never seen them."

I took Patrice aside. "Look, I know you don't want to keep a picture of Elena in your phone, so just text me a photo of Luke. We shouldn't have to produce two cell phones all the time. It's unprofessional."

She huffed and looked away, and then nodded.

Jackson and a few uniforms arrived twenty minutes later. "Can you believe that warning sign outside?" he said when he saw me.

"You're safe today," I said. "But I guess McKenzie wanted to keep out the Jamestown riffraff, whoever they are." I introduced him to Isabella, who appeared put-off having a bunch of people tracking through McKenzie's clean house.

I took Jackson aside and updated him on the domestic interview, including the part about the missing boat.

He immediately put a call into the Coast Guard. "Unless the yacht sunk, or our escapees made it to their destination, we might get lucky."

I told him McKenzie had a condo in Boston, but held off informing him about our visit. There wasn't much information to offer from that escapade, anyway. And then I remembered the landscapers. I knew the name of the company, but didn't want Jackson to know that, for obvious reasons.

"Isabella, who are Mr. McKenzie's landscapers?"

She went inside for a moment and returned with a business card.

"The Perfect Cut—sounds like a hair salon."

Jackson gave me an impatient look.

I shrugged. "Everybody hires landscapers these days. Maybe they saw something."

"Good point."

"You never know unless you ask. I'll be glad to check it out if you want."

Jackson thought a moment. "I'll have one of my guys accompany you."

"Of course." I then mentioned the stolen security DVR, but left out Elena's wardrobe from our previous visit. I did tell him about the call Isabella received from her boss's secretary about guests.

Jackson surveyed the room then looked back to me. "It looks like it's getting a little more involved, wouldn't you say, Hank?"

"Looks that way, I'm afraid."

I hated investigating with a shadow, but there was no way Jackson would allow me to interview anyone without one of his men present. My appendage's name was Matt Sterling, a uniformed patrolman from the

Newport PD. He was a local kid in his late twenties, with brown eyes and short, curly brown hair. By the size of him—about six-one, and broad shoulders, he might have played fullback in high school.

I parked the car in front of The Perfect Cut's command post, a small warehouse that was part of an industrial park off East Shore Road. The sign above the window featured a guy on a lawn tractor cutting through two feet of grass.

Patrice turned up her nose. "Not a very classy sign for a business."

Inside, we found a white male in his fifties, sporting a worn-out Boston Red Sox ball cap. He was swearing and shaking his head at a John Deere riding lawn mower, its hood up.

"Tough day?" I asked, walking over to him.

The guy peered over the hood at me, threw one more profanity at the tractor, and said, "Fuckin' engine won't start." He glanced at Patrice and apologized.

"Oh, I've heard worse," she said with a tired grin. "We'd like to ask you about one of your clients. Well, a former client, as of today. Warren McKenzie?" She arched a brow as she scrutinized his beer belly.

His expression changed from friendliness to confusion. "Who are you guys?"

Patrice and I displayed our shields. "Not sure if you've heard, but the police found Mr. McKenzie's body below the Cliff Walk."

"Dead?"

"Quite." A half-dozen tractors were scattered around the warehouse. They looked like oversized toddler toys. Bags of fertilizer shared the space with hedge trimmers, edgers, and leaf blowers. Outside a large window leading to the back stood young crab apple, crepe myrtle, and other New England trees waiting to be planted, as well as an assortment of perennial plants. "Are you the owner here?" I asked.

He crossed his arms "I am. And you're not local."

The guy was smart.

I wanted to tell Mr. Red Sox his team sucked, but I needed information from him. So with as friendly a smile as I could muster, I mentioned that we were working with the local police. I threw my thumb in my shadow's direction; Matt shifted uncomfortably.

The man appraised Matt's blue uniform and nodded.

"We're not here to ask if you have an alibi," I said with a grin. "Just following some leads."

"So you are the owner, then?" Patrice asked again.

"Yep. Been a family business for over thirty years. We have a clean record, don't hire illegals—knowingly, anyway—and have never had a problem with the law. I'm Nick Parisi, check me out."

"We're not from Immigration, Mr. Parisi, so you're offering way too much information. We're only interested in asking employees who worked on McKenzie's property a few questions, and not about his demise. We're trying to track down two people who might've been seen at his house while your landscapers were working there."

His body relaxed. "Sure, okay. I have a list of clients and workers at my desk." We trailed him over to a metal industrial desk, where Parisi removed a composition notebook. He turned a few pages. "Too bad," he said, and sighed. "Warren McKenzie was a good customer. Always paid on time." He stopped, gazed up. "He does owe for this month, though. I still hope to get paid."

Very sympathetic.

"I'm sure the estate will take care of the bill."

He nodded. "I hope it was an accident. You don't see murders around here, really. Anyway, it's not good for business."

I almost felt sorry for this guy. "So," I said, "now that your almost-up-to-date client is dead, we'll need as much information as you can tell us about him."

He glared at my sarcasm. Then, with a shrug, said, "Not much to say. He owns—owned—a large estate in Jamestown—you already knew that, I'm sure. As I recall, he owned over an acre of land, so I generally use three guys." He tore a blank sheet of paper from his notebook and jotted down the names of his workers, along with their cell numbers. Parisi turned a few pages and looked up. "They're in Newport today." He added the address. "I'll call and tell them to expect you. Please be mindful of the client's privacy."

"Of course," I assured him. "And just in case anyone gets nervous, tell them we're not from Immigration."

I smiled. He didn't.

Parisi's employees were working a three-acre residence on Hammersmith Road, near Fort Adams State Park, located at the mouth of Newport Harbor. My tires crunched on the long graveled driveway, until we reached a white, contemporary farmhouse. Unlike at McKenzie's place, we weren't greeted by any threatening signs.

Patrice gestured toward two of the three landscapers driving their green-and-yellow John Deere tractors in uniformity about fifty yards away. As one arched toward us, he motioned to his partner.

They negotiated between a few fruit trees before arriving, then killed their engines and approached us.

I scanned the area. One tractor stood idle near the truck. "Your boss said there were three of you working the yard."

"Chewy had an emergency," the taller one said. He appeared to be in his late twenties and was mahogany-skinned from the sun. An outdoor-job perk. His partner was about the same age but shorter, also sporting a rich tan. Both wore Red Sox caps. Must have been a job requirement.

The taller one looked beyond me and said, "Hey, Matt."

Matt donned a cool smile. "Andrew." Then to his partner, "Josh. You guys behaving yourselves?"

I turned to Matt. "Friends, or priors?"

Matt laughed. "High school buddies. They took a different career path, but as far as I know, they've never been in trouble with the law. Right, guys?"

"Never," Andrew defended.

"Should I assume you also know the missing guy, this Chewy?" I asked Matt.

He shook his head. "He's not local, is he, Josh?"

"Chewy's from New York. He's working through the summer before he heads back home for college. At least that's what he told us."

That raised my antennae. "And this emergency, when did it occur?"

"Right after Nick called to tell us you guys were coming to ask some questions," Josh said. "Chewy got nervous all of a sudden, said he just got a text that his mom—his mom, right, Andrew?" Andrew nodded in confirmation. "Yeah, his mom was in an accident. So he took off."

"On foot?" Patrice quickly asked.

"Yeah. He just scrammed out of here."

"For New York?" Patrice pressed.

"I guess." Josh glanced at Matt. "Is he in trouble?"

"Hard to say," Matt answered his friend. "I mean, he took off in a hurry. Maybe the timing of the emergency was a coincidence, maybe not."

"We do have a couple questions for you two," Patrice said, crossing her arms. "Like what's Chewy's real name?"

The two looked at each other, apparently hoping the other one knew. "I don't know," Josh said. "He went by Chewy."

We were getting nowhere fast, but I had to ask, "What's with the nickname, anyway? Star Wars superfan or something?"

Josh replied, "He told us he got the name in high school for chewing gum all the time."

"Seriously, we don't know much about him," Andrew added, then removed his cap and wiped his forehead. "He pretty much kept to himself. We'd go out for beers once in a while, but after a couple, he'd leave. Said he had to get back to his room and get ready for his fall classes."

"He say what college he was attending?" Patrice asked, keeping eye contact.

Josh looked at his partner. "I think NYU? He said he was going for law."

"So he might live in New York, then?" Patrice pushed.

Josh shrugged. "He mentioned a place, but it didn't sound familiar."

"Upper something or other," Josh said.

"Upper West Side?" I helped.

"Sounds right."

"Guys, you gotta help me here," I pleaded. "He was rushing somewhere to see his mother. He wasn't walking. He must have a car somewhere. Where does he live locally? You guys must have gone to his place at least once, had a few beers, right?"

Both shook their heads. "Just the bar," Josh said. "He always arrived by bike. Don't know if he has a car."

I scratched my head. It sounded like Chewy cherished his privacy, or maybe wasn't interested in making friends with Red Sox fans. "Did you guys hear about Warren McKenzie? The police found him dead below the Forty Steps."

They gazed past us looking nervous. "You don't think Chewy had something to do with it?" Josh asked, turning to Matt. "He's a good guy."

"I'm sure he is, but you gotta admit, his sudden disappearance, and then McKenzie's death, know what I mean?"

"What about you guys? Did you know McKenzie?" Patrice asked, stepping closer.

Josh took a step back. "Us? You're kidding, right? He's just some rich guy."

"He was a good tipper, especially at the end of the season," added Andrew.

With Matt behind us, I hesitated asking whether they'd noticed unusual activity at McKenzie's place lately: people stopping by, the maid, *us*. I took a chance anyway. Both shook their head.

I shot Patrice a look of satisfaction as I produced photos of Luke and then Elena—I made an executive decision to have both photos in my possession. Patrice was fine with that. "We're looking for these people. Think you might have seen them around town, the bars?"

Both shook their heads. "Sorry."

I surveyed the immaculate grounds and asked, "What happens when you guys have to pee?"

They snickered. Josh threw a glance back toward the house, and then whispered, "See those trees? 'Course, we make sure nobody's watching."

"Except," Andrew started. "Chewy didn't like to use trees, said it was disrespectful to client's property. He generally asked if he could use the indoor plumbing." He shrugged. "He was serious."

That struck me. "How about the last time you cut McKenzie's grounds? Did he use the indoor plumbing?"

Andrew and Josh checked each other. "Think so."

They kept looking over their shoulders. "We really need to get back to work," said Josh.

I asked Matt if he had any questions—important to make him feel part of the team, I guess.

"These are good local boys, Hank. I'm sure they told you everything they know." To them he added, "Right?"

Quick nods.

"One more question," I asked. "By any chance, did Chewy ever mention McKenzie's boat?"

"Boat? Oh, yeah. He said his father owned one like it, only not as big," Josh said. "Please, we have other jobs to do."

"Okay, guys, the lawn is all yours. Oh, and don't call Chewy."

"Okay."

"But if he calls you, don't mention what we talked about, or I'll have Matt charge you with aiding and abetting."

I watched them return to their tractors. I got the sense Chewy wasn't just some middle-class kid looking for summer work. But until we found him, nothing was certain. One thing I now knew, according to the landscapers: Chewy had used McKenzie's bathroom the day we'd been there. The same day the faux domestic, Ana Lucía, had opened the door and greeted us.

SEVEN

Sitting in the car, I tried Chewy's cell, knowing he wouldn't answer, and left a brief, non-threatening message. "It's important, please call back." I then called Nick Parisi, who picked up on the first ring. I guess he was anxious to hear what his employees had had to say.

"One of your guys is missing in action: kid named Chewy. Your call set him off."

"What do you mean, MIA? He's the one I spoke to."

"I'm guessing he forgot to mention he had an emergency. According to the other guys, Chewy claimed his mother had been in a car accident and bolted."

Hesitation. "Well, it's possible, I guess. Look, Chewy's a good employee. He must've just forgotten to tell me."

Right, or he forgot to say get me out of here now!

"He hasn't picked up his phone, either. What can you tell me about him?"

Parisi thought a moment. "Chewy, that's what he goes by. It was a high school thing about him chewing gum a lot. He told me he got into trouble with his teachers over it sometimes." Parisi paused. "Anyway, he showed up late springtime and asked if I was hiring. He told me he was a student at NYU but needed time off. A college student, good-looking, and strong. Hell, I needed someone strong and reliable, so I hired him on the spot."

"No paperwork?" I asked, watching Josh on the riding mower as he circled a crabapple tree a little too quickly.

Easy, Josh!

"Well, sure, he filled out an application. I have it on file."

"Can you get it? I'll hold. I'm hoping the application has his given name and local address. And a social security number."

"Right, if it has anything necessary for taxes. Be right back."

I held my hand over the speaker. "Might be nothing," I told Patrice and Matt. "But given that he scooted out of here in a hurry, you never know." Matt began taking notes. To Patrice, "And he used the McKenzie's bathroom."

"Could be the reason…"

I put up a hand and mouthed, Parisi.

"Hold on," I said into the receiver when Parisi returned. To Matt, I said, "Can you rip out a piece of paper? And I need your pen."

I jotted down the information. Chewy didn't use a local address. I asked Parisi if he had a photo of Chewy. "Otherwise, I'll have to ask your boys to describe him and his mannerisms, and that might take them away from their work."

"Christ." He thought a moment and said, "I'm not sure I have one. It's not like we socialized and took selfies or had office parties. Wait, I think I might have something…" the phone clattered on the desk.

I surveyed the property while I waited. Josh had negotiated a tree without ramming it. Andrew had begun edging near the house. Then I glanced at Patrice. She smiled at me, a genuine, eyes-that-sparkle smile, and I smiled back. God, she was beautiful. Luke was an idiot.

When Parisi returned, his voice was rushed. "Okay, I found something! A license photo. It's not very clear, but you can make out his face and information. I snapped a photo and texted it over to you."

Great things, these smartphones.

After a second, I got the notification of the MMS. "Got it, thanks. Listen, if Chewy gets in touch with you, which I doubt he will, call me."

Parisi was right. The photo on the right side of Chewy's New York license wasn't clear. The facial details were dark. I deciphered a round face with short hair. His smile, though, was clear, showing a chipped upper front tooth. The name of the motorist belonging to the photo was Timothy Jerkens, male. His DOB made him twenty-three. He had green eyes and was five-eleven. His address was listed Upper West Side, New York City. At least Josh got that part right.

I showed Patrice and Matt the photo.

At that moment, my cell trilled.

"What the heck is going on in Newport?" JR laughed. "I love murders. Wish I could join you."

I reminded him he was already knee-deep in his own murder investigation, but agreed it would have been interesting to work together.

JR and I never worked a case as partners, since we were from two different police authorities—though he had helped me solve a murder case I was working on once. Good detective. "Hey, can I ask you to run another name and social for me? Since you miss me so much." I passed on Timothy Jerkens's license information. "Kid goes by Chewy."

"I'm tempted to ask. But I won't. Okay, it shouldn't take long."

"See if you can find any priors, family members, the good stuff. He told his boss he was a student at NYU."

"Gotcha."

"Oh, and see if there is a yacht in his family."

"I should have never called."

"Admit it, JR, you love sticking your nose into my investigation."

"Yeah, like I said, I wish I were there in the flesh. Give me an hour."

We returned to the stationhouse, where I updated Jackson on the missing landscaper and mentioned how invaluable Matt's assistance had been, especially his note-taking. Jackson laughed and thanked me. He then suggested that McKenzie had been murdered, because the ME had found no trace of drugs or alcohol in his system. And he would've seriously had to trip over a high fence.

"What a way to go," he said.

"Suicide is always a possibility," I suggested. "But now would be a good time to find Chewy. No one seems to know where he's living locally, and by the time we find out, he'll probably be halfway to New York."

"Not good."

"I have an NYPD contact in the city. I'll feed him the information on Chewy's license and have him snoop around until I get there. I have to make a trip anyway," I lied.

"Sure, Hank. But make sure you keep me in the loop."

We had at least an hour to kill before JR would get back with news on Chewy. I wasn't about to hop on the highway to New York and waste three hours only to find out his mother really was in an accident, so I asked Patrice if she was hungry.

"Starved, actually."

"Good, me too."

Brady recommended the popular Red Parrot Restaurant on Thames Street. The building itself was listed on the National Register of Historical Places in Newport—it had been built in 1898. We were led to a table in the front and handed a menu by a twentysomething pixie-cut blond woman with an infectious smile.

I studied the demographically mixed, clearly relaxed crowd, and then gazed over at Patrice, who I found staring at me. "What?"

Her right hand covered mine on the table. "Hank, I know I've told you before, but I can't thank you enough for helping me find Luke. I mean, I know we haven't found him yet…oh, you know what I mean. It's been crazy."

My eyes rested on her hand on top of mind. I blinked. There was something missing: her engagement ring. My gaze found hers. Evoking a tender but wistful smile, she said, "I made a decision: I'm going back to Paris. There's too much negative energy here. I mean, even if we find Luke, our relationship is dead."

My stomach tightened. I felt blindsided. I'd never expected that Patrice would drop her search before finding Luke—dead or alive. And yes, I'd been hoping she'd stick around a while. Maybe my feelings for her were more than I wanted to believe they were. I'd been hoping to get to know her better, and if her relationship with Luke was dead, maybe I would have a chance. My shock was accompanied by a pang of anger, as well: Why should I keep searching for her fiancé if she was abandoning the investigation?

I shared none of this, of course. Instead, I nodded. "I understand."

Her hand squeezed mine gently, lovingly. Or was I just imagining things? She withdrew her hand, opened the menu, and told me lunch was on her. "It's the least I can do."

I was about to protest, but she raised a hand.

"Okay." I opened the menu and selected a basic burger, while my partner settled on a sliced avocado and baby spinach salad with bacon, bleu cheese crumbles, walnuts, dried cranberries, grape tomatoes, and red onions with strawberry balsamic vinaigrette. That was quite a mouthful of healthy.

When our lunch arrived, she began playing with her food, tossing her salad back and forth with her fork. She lifted her eyes to mine. "I'm sorry. I guess I'm feeling sorry for myself." A quick smile—but not with the eyes this time, I noticed.

I wanted to tell her I'd been in that situation, with all the doubts, and that it gets better. But does it?

I was two bites into the juicy burger, with warm grease dripping onto my plate, when JR called. I quickly wiped at my mouth with my napkin.

"You're in for a surprise, Hank. Timothy Jerkens, a.k.a. Chewy, is dead. You're chasing his ghost. Jerkens died two years ago when he leaped in front of an oncoming subway car near the NYU downtown city campus."

"Jesus Christ." I almost choked on my burger.

"Wait, there's more. The real Chewy was adopted at birth. I tracked down his adoptive mother. She was more than a little upset that someone would steal his identity, especially under the circumstances."

Maybe that was the point.

"So this phony Chewy needed identification for some reason—open a credit card account maybe."

"Or something more sinister," added JR. "Let's face it, all he had to do was snatch one close in age by trolling through obituaries."

I'd seen similar identity fraud schemes in the past, and it was always heartbreaking for the loved ones. That was certainly the case here. And now, two years after killing himself, Chewy's mother had to revisit his death.

"Maybe the kid just wanted to disappear from his past, acquire a new name and live out the rest of his years in peace. And he might have, if we weren't looking into McKenzie's murder. The two might just be a coincidence," I said, glancing over at Patrice, whose eyes were riveted to the one-way conversation. I put up a finger.

"Maybe, but until we find this guy, we won't know for sure."

We. JR definitely wanted to be part of the team. I grinned to myself, sparking a look of confusion on the face of Patrice. I shook my head, waved it off.

"I think it's too much of a coincidence that McKenzie, Chewy's boss's client, winds up dead, and then he immediately disappears when you start asking questions."

I had to admit, unless McKenzie died from his own doing, Chewy the Second was a person of interest. Along with Luke. For all I knew, there could be a connection between the two of them. And then there was Ana Lucía. According to the lawn guys, Chewy had used McKenzie's bathroom the same day Ana, the supposed domestic, happened to be in the house.

JR's assessment appeared solid. "Here's something else: McKenzie was found dead on Thursday. According to Detective Jackson, he could have been dead a day or two before that, which would make the time of death Tuesday at the earliest. If his business was in Boston, where he worked weekdays, what was he doing in Newport then?"

"You'll figure it out, Hank."

"Thanks. It's a lot to digest," I said, then glanced at my half-eaten burger. I snorted at the unintended joke and glanced at Patrice, who playfully rolled her eyes. "I'll have Jackson put out an APB on our friend." I thanked my buddy and told him I'd be in touch.

The call over, I gave my attention fully to Patrice, whose eyes were filled with questions. "Seems the real Chewy killed himself two years ago, and this...imposter fellow has been cutting McKenzie's lawn. I don't know what to make of it yet."

"Coincidence?"

I grabbed my burger, and before taking another bite, said, "Unless you're catching the next flight to Paris, we're going on a road trip."

Patrice decided to hold off on flying home. I think she became intrigued by the new development. Not to mention returning to Elena's Boston apartment might provide insight as to who her competition was. Assuming, of course, we could get into her condo.

I probably should have informed Jackson of our trip, but I wasn't in the mood for another shadow, even if it was likeable Matt. It's just that sometimes I do things a little unorthodox.

I contacted Brady on the way and gave him the good news: we were staying a while longer. He was thrilled. It was clear he was getting a kick out of his insider view of the investigation.

We arrived an hour and a half later and pulled into the same public garage near McKenzie's condominium building. I chatted with Mickey a few minutes at the parking booth, but he had nothing new to offer on the missing duo.

Then we met with Carey, the security guy at the front desk. I broke the news to him about McKenzie.

"Yeah, I read it in the paper, but like I told you before, I don't know anyone by that name. Hell, I wouldn't recognize the guy if I bumped into him."

A little too late for that.

"Far as I know, he's never been here."

Got it.

I informed Carey that Elena Sullivan was still missing, and that checking her condo could prove invaluable to our investigation. As a professional courtesy, maybe he could make an exception, let us snoop around. One cop to another, I told him.

His tired gaze swept the lobby. Seeing it was just us, he sighed and said, "I really don't want any trouble. How long will you be?"

"An hour tops. In the meantime, I can call for a warrant if you like."

He waved me off, then opened a closet near the desk and pulled out a set of keys. "How come no one else is looking for her?"

I grabbed the keys from his hand. "We're smarter than they are."

He looked at me dully and said, "Be quick."

We entered the unit on the eleventh floor. The room had a magnificent flagstone fireplace, and a large, square mirror on the mantel with small, white-framed contemporary paintings perched on it. The Brazilian walnut flooring created a pleasant natural contrast. But we weren't here to appraise the unit: we needed answers, and in an hour or less.

I could tell by Patrice's silence that she, too, was impressed with the place. She'd mentioned her small Paris apartment to me, with its cracking plaster and unnavigable flow. She was probably comparing this condo to it, maybe wondering if she was in the wrong profession. A hint of forlornness in her eyes confirmed my suspicion.

We snapped on latex gloves and separated, me taking one bedroom, she the other. I focused on the closet, which was filled with expensive suits, shirts, sweaters, and outerwear, the names mostly Italian. Had to belong to McKenzie. I checked the rest of the room, under the bed. Nothing unusual.

I called out to Patrice, but when she didn't answer, I walked over and found her engaged in a newspaper article. "Time to read?" I said with a smile.

She looked up. "Sorry, I got engrossed." She handed me the two-year-old article and a blank manila folder.

"What's this?"

"You'll see."

A Boston Globe article, taken from page six—the regional section—was short and to the point. "NYU STUDENT LEAPS TO DEATH IN FRONT OF ONCOMING TRAIN."

I glanced up.

"Keep reading."

The article mentioned that a young man named Timothy Jerkens was the victim of a suicide. I glanced over at Patrice. "What the hell is going on here?" I snapped a copy of the article with my phone and handed the file back to her. "Where did you find this?"

"In the drawer, underneath some sexy panties." She pointed. "What about you, find anything interesting?"

"Nothing as interesting as that. Just some expensive men's clothes."

"So what do you make of it, the fact that this is here in McKenzie's condo?"

"Or Elena's?" I added.

She nodded. "Right, might have something to do with her."

My eyes surveyed the room as I thought. "Let's check out the closet."

Patrice hesitated, and then reluctantly fingered a few articles of women's clothing in the walk-in closet. I noticed the clothes were equally expensive as the ones in the closet I'd checked. It appeared that Patrice was now counting shoes. I'd stopped at twenty. She lifted a pair of electric-blue, suede pointy-toe pumps and held them out to me between thumbs and forefingers, grimacing.

"Size seven. Same as hers."

Still hard getting Elena's name out.

"Makes sense, given she lives here at least part of the time."

Patrice gave me a hopeful expression.

"What?"

She shrugged. "Maybe nothing, but it seems we have a 'his and hers' bedroom. I mean, there's plenty of room for his clothes in there."

She was reaching, or just being hopeful.

"Could be," I said in an attempt to be encouraging.

The first part of the trip back to Newport was spent in silence, me ruminating on what we'd gleaned from McKenzie's place. Patrice? You'd have to ask her. What was McKenzie, and/or Elena, doing with an article on Chewy's suicide? More importantly, what was the common thread between them?

The newspaper article had produced a cryptic clue into McKenzie's murder—or was I reading too much into it? I hoped "Phony Chewy" had the answers. All we needed to do was find him.

"McKenzie, Timothy, and…Chewy," Patrice said, breaking her silence. She was slouched in the passenger's seat, arms folded across her chest. "Chewy was employed by a company that did landscaping work for McKenzie. He also hijacked Timothy Jerkens's name, the guy who took his own life. And now, we have an article addressing the suicide found hidden in *her* bedroom drawer." She turned her head toward me. "What do you make of that?"

"You wanna know if there's a connection between Luke and Elena and this murder business, I'm guessing."

"Don't you?"

I nodded, keeping my eyes on the road. We were approaching the Newport Bridge. "Right now, I don't see a connection." I side-glanced her. "I believe we have two separate situations."

Patrice sat back and stared straight ahead, obviously unconvinced.

I felt I had bothered JR too much for one day, and asked Patrice if she mind doing some research at the local Newport library.

"That's what I do at Interpol, Hank."

I laid out my thoughts. Patrice listened intently; she was quick and smart, so even though she didn't take notes, I knew she wouldn't forget. We arranged to meet at the local library in a few hours.

"So, what? You don't like research?" A playful smile.

"Me? I'm a hands-on guy, more intuitive."

I dropped her off, watched her trudge up the concrete steps to the library doors, and then drove to the inn, where I found Brady standing in his usual spot behind the desk, watching some news channel. "Anything new happening in the world?"

"Only that they're saying now McKenzie was murdered, probably pushed. They have a person of interest." He crossed his arms and looked at me, perhaps waiting for me to elaborate.

Chewy. News travels fast. "They say who?" I asked, already knowing Jackson wouldn't let the word out this soon.

"They're only releasing the guy's description to the public." He met my eyes. "I hope it wasn't random. That would scare away the tourists for the rest of the season, maybe even longer." He sighed.

"You won't lose everyone. We'll be sticking around for a while." I will, anyway. "I kinda like Newport."

"You're welcome to stay as long as you like, Hank."

I started for my room then stopped. "Say, Brady, how did Luke DuPont make his reservation? Phone, internet?"

"Probably like most people these days, through our website. I'll tell ya, it makes my life easier. I don't have to pick up the phone as often."

"Except in my case. I called ahead."

"Right. Hold on." He hopped on the computer and scrolled down the page. He clicked a few times and stopped.

"Actually, he didn't." He looked up. "Someone else made the reservation, but used his credit card. It came from a woman's email address, at least according to the name she used." He turned the monitor around to face me. "See?"

I stared at the reservation. Sure enough, Elena Sullivan had made the reservation for Luke DuPont. "Print out a copy of that for me, will you?"

Inside my room, I removed Luke's computer from the closet and fired it up. I knew his password, thanks to Patrice, and began opening each personal file, searching for anything I might have missed the last time. Nothing new stuck out. Patrice and I had followed his calendar of events. I opened it again and this time jumped ahead a month, and then another. Both months were blank. There was nothing about meeting up with Patrice—or anyone, for that matter.

Most people made at least some notations on their calendars during the year: a birthday or anniversary, for instance, but so far, nothing from Luke. I recalled Patrice mentioning that her birthday fell on October twenty-fifth. I went to that date, but it, too, was blank. Strange, but not too strange. A lot of guys tended to be forgetful when it came to special occasions.

I jumped ahead, and when I reached December, I found a notation on the tenth of the month. He'd typed in two dollar signs, and below them, "free at last."

December was months away. Patrice had told me they were waiting for her to get a transfer or job in the States, so they could get married. Yet Luke's notation appeared to mean something different.

Free from Patrice after coming into money?

I was curious as to why Elena had reserved a room at the Wilson House for one adult—Luke—and had used *his* credit card. Where was she staying, this woman with whom Luke apparently had more interest

77

than he did some whistleblower contact. Unless, maybe at the time, the two weren't romantically involved.

I called Patrice at the library and asked if December tenth meant anything to her.

She whispered back. "No, why do you ask?"

"Curious." Then, "How about your birthday, you and Luke have anything planned?"

She sighed into the phone. "Well, if you want to know, it's a special day for both of us. It's when he proposed to me. Kind of romantic, right?"

Not according to his calendar.

With the library closing in an hour, we agreed to meet at The Nautical Pub at eight fifteen. I settled back in a chair in my room, its padded paisley print cushion torn at the edges, and made a mental note to suggest that Brady replace it before his next guest arrived.

I wasn't finished playing with Luke's computer just yet. Somewhere inside his hard drive was the key to his game plan. Staring at his laptop background photo, I was intrigued by the peaceful, tropical beach scene, with its fine white sand and gem-colored water. I'd noticed it previously, but that was before my discovery of Luke's penchant for freedom. The scene on the laptop was devoid of vacationers, as though the photographer had wanted a natural backdrop—at least until the happy couple showed up. For sure, it wouldn't include Patrice.

I drummed my fingers on the laptop and wondered what sites would entertain Luke in his spare time. His search engine history might hold a clue. I opened Chrome and hit Ctrl-H, then scrolled down a few pages.

His surfing ran the gamut from finance to porn, the latter, I thought for a moment, would have been to help him through not seeing Patrice. But then, scratch that, he had Elena. I started getting into interesting territory: politics, music, expensive cars, and homes in Belize. I stopped. Was he just bored, or thinking ahead?

I stood, stretched my legs, and walked over to the window. Dusk had set in. I was now convinced Patrice had gotten her fiancé all wrong. But why would Luke go through the trouble of getting engaged if his plans didn't include her? Unless they had until Elena came along.

My cell beckoned me from the nightstand.

"Sounds like revenge," Patrice suggested when I answered, her voice rushed. "There's more to this suicide story. Guess who taught classes as an adjunct professor at NYU? McKenzie," she said, not waiting for a reply. "And Chewy—the real one—was one of his students. Go ahead, ask a question."

I had several regarding Patrice, but held off on those. "You're saying McKenzie was Chewy's professor?"

"Chemistry professor. I found an article that quoted a close friend of Chewy's. The kid suggested Chewy was despondent over a failing grade for an important class—one that would make or break his entrance into medical school. He said Chewy became withdrawn. We know he eventually took his life by jumping in front of an oncoming train at the Eighth Street Station near NYU. The article wasn't accusatory, but it's interesting to note that McKenzie never returned to teach again. One could easily read between the lines…"

"Teacher and pupil." I stared at the floor, rubbing my forehead with my hand.

"If you ask me, it's too much of a coincidence. Chewy must have told his friend, who knows, maybe the guy who ended up stealing his identity, that McKenzie was making his life hell. That he might as well say goodbye to med school."

I thought a moment. "What was McKenzie doing teaching a course? I mean, the guy had a business to run. In Boston, no less."

"Apparently, he was scouting around for potential employees. It's better than using a head hunter."

"I guess Chewy wasn't a candidate."

"Quite the opposite. According to another article, McKenzie thought Chewy was brilliant and wanted him to get his undergraduate degree and then work for him. Chewy rejected his offer because he wanted to continue his studies. That's when McKenzie played hardball and made the kid's life miserable. That was the takeaway from the article, anyway. Whether he thought he was pushing Chewy over the edge isn't clear."

"Nice phrase."

"Right, over the edge, it's appropriate. It sure sounds like revenge to me, especially if the friend was convinced McKenzie was responsible for Chewy's suicide." She paused. "I just don't see how Luke fits in."

Back to innocent Luke.

"You really have a lot of faith in him, don't you?"

After few awkward moments, Patrice said, "Hank, I've been holding back from you, but I can't anymore. We need to meet."

EIGHT

What the hell did that mean?

I arrived first, and Maureen offered me a quiet booth in the back. My mind kept latching on to Patrice's words, "I've been holding back from you." A few minutes later, she walked over to the table, her expression pained and her smile forced. I noticed a few wrinkles around her eyes. Were they there before?

"Hey," I greeted her.

She settled opposite me without saying a word, but her body language told me she was about to broach a serious admission. When she began with an apology, I sensed I'd been wasting my time searching for Luke.

"Luke and I aren't getting married. He broke it off."

I guess I wasn't that shocked, given what I found on Luke's calendar. I let my eyes settled on her and waited for her to continue.

She twisted a bit of hair around her finger and averted her eyes. "The last time we spoke, before he was scheduled to meet with his whistleblower informant, he told me he needed time, and that it had nothing to do with me. That's a standard line, but I was still blindsided. I tried rationalizing that it was the investigation and that he was overwhelmed."

She looked back at me. "I believed him, at first, that it wasn't me. I mean, why would it be?" She paused, wiped an eye. "He'd never lied to me in the past, as far as I knew. But then my female intuition got the better of me and I sensed there was another woman. At that point, I made a decision to find out for myself.

"I needed to see him, to talk about it, but he flat-out refused, and told me he would contact me when the investigation was over." She paused, smiled thinly. "When I told him I was flying over, he got upset, forbade me from doing so. And went as far as to tell me my presence would be disruptive."

She narrowed her eyes. "That was an understatement. Especially now that I know about...them." She puffed up her cheeks, blew out air. "And then you came along. Or rather...remember how I told you I'd been assigned to watch over you in Paris? That wasn't exactly accurate. When I learned you'd be there, I saw an opportunity and decided to leave with you and fly to the States."

I leaned back in my seat. "You set me up."

"Hank, it wasn't like that. I thought you'd be able to cut through the red tape with your law enforcement connections and find him quickly. Okay, I was naïve. But I never figured we'd be involved in a murder case. You have to believe that."

I hate being played.

"Why should I believe you now?" I asked with an air of sarcasm.

She reached for my hand, but I pulled back.

She looked away. "Why do you think I didn't want any pictures of *her* on my phone? What would you have done, Hank?"

She had a point, but I remained silent.

"Bad judgement on my part, I agree."

I leaned in. "There's more you're not telling me. Why come forward now?"

"No reason."

"Bullshit! There's always a reason. You said Luke wasn't dangerous, but suddenly one person is dead and another on the run. And Luke is still missing and not because he's lost. We've been chasing a guy who doesn't want to be found. What do you suspect?"

She wrung her hands. "Okay, Luke can be unpredictable at times. Not dangerous, but he does have a temper. I've always kept him in line."

Until now.

Patrice's expression had morphed from anxious anguish to fear. She feigned a smile, but she was unmistakably uneasy; her breathing was quicker, her eyes wider. Christ, if Luke could be unpredictable, why be involved with him in the first place? I didn't get it.

I took a calming breath and said, "I think your decision to fly home is a good one. You're only going to get hurt if you continue looking for him. You know he's cheating on you, so there's no reason to confront him anymore. Anyway, I think that's what I would do."

Patrice got up to leave, but I reached out.

"Let's have a drink, talk a bit, friend to friend."

She nodded, sat back down. I called over our Maureen and ordered a few Harpoons. We remained silent until the beers arrived. I took a sip.

"What did you find at the library?"

"You sure you want to know? After all this?"

I smiled. "Yeah. I don't like loose ends. Besides, it's a different subject."

She took a long gulp of her beer. "McKenzie was never accused of instigating Timothy Jerkens's suicide. Turns out the guy had been depressed for a while, and if McKenzie had harassed him to the point of suicide, it was a fine line. McKenzie claimed he hadn't known about Chewy's depression and the meds he was taking, and that even if he had, his teaching technique—though perhaps unorthodox—had led no one else in the class to commit suicide. Though that might not have been the most justifiable defense. Nevertheless, McKenzie was asked to leave after the final grades were released.

I took a slug of beer, let Patrice's story sink in. I remembered a case involving an IRS agent whose supervisor had constantly badgered the guy until the poor agent snapped and jumped in front of a subway car. (What is it with subway cars?) No action had been taken against the supervisor, and he retired five years later. Everyone knew the bastard's management techniques had been over the top, but there had been no direct link outside of the guy's being a hard ass.

Patrice placed her hand on mine. "Hank, I'm sorry I lied to you."

Her soft hand felt warm on mine, like it had at the Red Parrot. But this was not a time to get cozy. Still, her touch stirred feelings inside me. I smiled wistfully. "You'll be fine. I promise."

She rubbed my hand gently, and I slowly removed it from under hers. I took a final sip from my mug and called over Maureen.

"Still waiting for that review, Hank. Did your friend get cold feet?" She smiled.

"Hopefully not." I took out my phone and opened my photo log. "Does this guy look familiar to you? Maybe a customer."

Maureen grabbed the phone and narrowed a look on faux Chewy. "Nice-looking guy, but no. He a restaurant reviewer, too?" she said with a snarky grin.

"Landscaper. You sure?"

"I study people, sweetie, especially in my line of work. I would have remembered. You should see some of the characters who come in and start hitting on me. When I tell them I'm in a relationship, they leave a crappy tip." She snorted. "Maybe I should let them tip me before I reject 'em."

Right: Tip first, reject later.

I glanced beyond Maureen, my eyes settling on a patron sitting at the bar. I'd noticed that he'd been sneaking glances our way for a while. There was something about him that interested me. I asked Maureen to casually turn around and check out the guy with thick salt and pepper hair.

Like a pro, she *accidentally* dropped her pen and then slowly bent to retrieve it, looking over toward the bar. The guy turned away. "He's not a regular, but I've seen him in here a few times. Gives me the creeps, actually—always staring at people. You know him?"

Not yet.

"Do you recall if he was here around the same time our couple of friends were?"

Maureen thought a moment. "Mm, can't say."

"Point me to the men's room, please."

"You mean you don't know where it is yet?"

I gave her a look, and she understood. "Oh, right." She reached over and pointed to the back of the restaurant, behind the bar.

"Thanks." I told Patrice to guard the bathroom door in the event the guy decided to join me. Then I excused myself, walked past Mr. Nosy, and pushed into the bathroom, stopping at the first urinal. A few moments later, like I'd figured he would, he stepped into the men's room and stood at the urinal next to mine. I shot him a look. "I understand you're looking for a friend of mine, Luke DuPont."

The guy froze for a second then recovered. "Excuse me?"

Since I hadn't yet unzipped, I moved aggressively and pressed his head against the wall. "You heard me, shithead. Why are you looking for him?"

He tried to yank away, but I held his arm behind his back tighter.

"I don't know what you're talking about," he blurted. "I don't know any Luke whatever-his-name-is."

"Wrong answer." I jerked his arm up and he groaned. "If you're going to pretend to be an FBI agent, act like one. I slipped my hand in his pocket and whipped out an ID. "Everett Sexton, Private Investigator. Well, well. So who are you interested in, Mr. PI?" I gave him enough slack to turn around and face me.

He remained silent a moment then said, "Elena Sullivan."

"Is that right?"

"Swear. Her boss hired me to follow her around." His squinting, watery eyes met mine.

"Go on."

He shrugged.

"That's not an answer." I pulled harder.

"Goddammit, I don't know who you are or what you want, but I'm not saying anything else."

I offered him a humorless smile, took out my shield, and shoved it in his face. "If you know her whereabouts, holding back information might present a problem for you, PI Sexton. Elena Sullivan is a person of interest in a murder investigation. So if you know where she is—"

"The fuck you talking about? I don't know anything about her being a person of interest in any murder."

I finally released him. He stood in place, rubbing his arm.

"Look, her boss—boyfriend—is jealous. He thinks she's fooling around on him, that's all." Sexton shoved my shield out of his face and attempted to push past me, but I tripped him, sending him to the floor.

"You okay in there, Hank?" Patrice said, knocking on the door.

"Out in a minute."

I tried picking Sexton off the floor, but his arms flailed hopelessly. "The fuck, get off me."

I held off and watched him get up on his own.

He glared. "I haven't seen her in a few days. She was with someone, okay?"

"Where do you think Ms. Sullivan vanished to? And who was the someone?"

"I don't know." Sexton growled.

"I'll show you mine if you show me yours."

"The fuck you talking about?"

I whipped out my cell and showed Sexton a photo of Luke. "This the guy?"

He nodded. "Yeah, that's him. What's your interest, since you have a picture of him?" he demanded.

"Show me a photo of Elena Sullivan first."

He hesitated, then removed his cell and brought a photo up to my face. Elena was gorgeous, even in jeans.

"Hand me your phone."

He protested, but I swiped it out of his hand and texted my number from his. When I heard the ping, I handed it back. "Now you have my number."

"What do I get out of this?"

"We're friends now. If you answer a few questions, I'll notify you when I find her."

He studied my face. "Fair enough," he said warily.

"Tell me a little about your gig, PI Sexton"

He hesitated, probably wondering if he'd violate some client privilege if he talked. When he'd apparently decided it was all right, Everett Sexton told me he worked out of New York City and maintained a lucrative practice following people around.

"Like Elena Sullivan?"

He nodded. "Her boss hired me, said he thought she was cheating on him."

"You said that before. Only you said boss and lover."

He cracked a smile. "Right, both. She told him she needed a few days off on account of her stressful job. The guy must've had a hunch she was cheating, because the job wasn't that stressful, at least according to him. There were other suspicious things, too, which aren't relevant here. So he hired me to follow her, which I did, and landed here." Sexton shrugged. "That's pretty much it."

"So it has nothing to do with work?" I asked, wondering if he knew about her meeting Luke regarding the whistleblowing.

He shook his head. "Straightforward jealousy is how I understand it."

I didn't know if Sexton was holding back, but he wasn't about to broach the subject if he did know.

"Hence the FBI ruse," I said. "Okay, show me what you discovered by following her around."

Sexton narrowed his eyes at me, but then nodded. "Only if you promise not to leak it out, at least until I present it to my client."

I inwardly crossed my fingers. "You have my word."

Sexton lifted his phone in my direction. A diabolical little grin appeared on his face as I viewed the first photo. His smile grew as I flipped to the second and third, and continued, each photo more compromising than the one before. Elena's boss was right: she was clearly cheating on him.

"Text me a few of the most incriminating."

"Come on…"

I grabbed his wrist. I can take your phone and you'll have nothing, or you can be a good citizen and help out my investigation."

"Fuck. Okay, but only a few." He sent four—a little stingy, but I really didn't need more than that.

"And this guy was the only man you saw her with?"

"You mean she might be screwing around with other guys?" He sounded discouraged, as though he might have missed something important.

"Just curious."

"As far as I know, only him."

"Okay, then. I guess with your goodies, you'll be heading back to New York."

Sexton grinned. "I could use a mini-vacation, and I'm rather fond of Newport. Ever been to the Cliff Walk?"

Right.

I drew Sexton in to me, aimed my phone, and took a selfie. "Let's stay in touch."

Sexton brushed past Patrice and scurried out of the pub. I was tempted to follow him, but he'd probably assume that's what I'd do. I took Patrice by the elbow. "Let's finish our beers and head out."

She watched me down my Harpoon. "Are you going to tell me what that was all about?"

I wiped my mouth with the back of my hand.

"That guy, he's a private eye. Actually, I recalled Brady's description of the phony FBI agent, so I took a chance. His name is Everett Sexton, and he's from New York City. Apparently, Elena's boss hired him, to see if she was hooking up with someone." I regretted I said it, but let it register. "Anyway, Sexton swears he knows nothing about McKenzie's murder." I opened my cell photo gallery page and showed her the selfie. "Sexton and I are friends now."

Patrice said nothing, so I let her stew for a moment and waved Maureen over for the check.

"Your friend ran out without paying."

"He was in a hurry. Something about work," I said with a wink. "Add his bill to mine."

"Sounds like your bathroom meeting went well. You find out something important?"

I smiled thinly. "I think so."

I now wondered whether Luke was involved in a whistleblowing effort at all. Was there even an investigation? Or was he just screwing around?

I asked Patrice, "How come I never came across one file on Luke's laptop that alluded to him working on an investigation? Not one."

"Is that what the PI told you? That Luke and Elena were just having a romantic encounter?" She glared. "You think I lied about the whistle-blowing investigation, too?"

I put my palms up. "Hey, I'm only suggesting. Maybe that's what Luke wanted you to believe. Makes sense, doesn't it?"

"I hope the bastard is dead!" She spat then caught herself. "Sorry."

I shook my head and covertly scanned the pub. At ten at night, only a few patrons remained, all at the bar, and they seemed to either be engaged in chitchat or drunk. I made an executive decision, perhaps to solidify any remaining doubt I had about Luke's and Patrice's relationship.

"I wasn't going to show you, but there's no reason to hold back now. You have the right to know the truth. Sexton took these." I selected the text message I sent from the PI's phone to mine and showed Patrice the happy couple.

She managed to remain calm as her eyes flipped from one scene to the next, stopping after the last photo.

When she finished, she handed back the phone. "I'm leaving tomorrow. For sure." She then stood up and dashed for the door.

I paid the bill and caught up with her a few blocks away.

"I thought you should know," I said again, but her silence felt calculating.

When we reached the inn, Patrice headed straight for her room without saying a word. I entered mine, plopped on my bed, and searched the ceiling for God knows what. I, too, was ready to leave Newport.

I closed my eyes, searching for answers. One name kept surfacing: Ana Lucía.

It felt like I'd been laying there for hours when I heard a knock on my door. I sat up and glanced over at the clock on the night table. It had been less than an hour.

I opened the door and Patrice rushed in my arms.

"Hold me."

NINE

She was gone before I woke. I hadn't slept that soundly in a long while and hadn't heard her leave. Maybe it was just as well. After making love, I'd had a sudden pang of guilt. What was I thinking showing her those compromising photos? Was sleeping with me nothing more than throwing Luke a big *fuck you*?

I took a quick shower and was about to go ask Brady if he'd noticed the time she left, but a note perching conspicuously on the nightstand stopped me.

It was written on the Wilson House stationery. Her note was a painful admission in believing in her relationship with Luke. She was heading home and asked that I not try to stop her. "As for last night, Hank, it wasn't a rebound. Our lovemaking was real. You're very special. I could easily fall for you, Detective Reed. Love, P."

I read the note a few times and let out a sigh. It *had* been special. I decided to call her, but it went straight to voicemail. I left a message. "I feel the same way," I said, then hung up.

I felt empty, lost, and rudderless. I wanted to tell Luke how much of a jerk he was for mistreating Patrice, only I'd have to find him first.

Brady was at the front desk, and when he saw me, he waved me

90

over. "Patrice left in a hurry this morning. Said she had an emergency at work. I hope it's not serious."

Right, an emergency.

"Nothing life threatening," I assured him. I hoped it was true.

He gazed at me. "Are you okay, Hank? You look like you lost a close friend."

I feigned a smile. "It's been a long couple of days, but I'm fine."

"Are you checking out, too?"

Was I?

The real question was: should I?

Brady waited for my reply.

"Not just yet."

The Wilson House had a small but comfortable living room for guests. After pouring a cup of coffee from a silver carafe, I sat on the beige sofa across from a glass cocktail table. I sipped and thought.

Where to, Reed?

I'd been sitting a while, thinking quietly, when my phoned purred. I didn't recognize the caller, but the area code belonged to Boston.

"Detective Reed?"

"This is he."

"This is Mickey from the parking garage in Boston. You told me to call if I saw someone."

I sat up. "Go on, Mickey."

"That guy you showed me a picture of, he just pulled in. Same cool license plate as before."

Luke. "Was he alone?"

"Yes, and he looked like he was in more of a rush than before."

"I'm on my way. Call me if he returns to the garage."

"Okay, I will."

"And thanks, Mickey. I owe you."

An hour later, I found Mickey engaged in the *Boston Globe* sports section. He looked up and waved.

"Guy hasn't returned yet."

I was about to dash next door, but took my phone out and showed Mickey a photo of Chewy.

He nodded. "Oh, yeah, I remember that guy. He had a nervous look to him. He paid cash and left within an hour without saying a word."

My heart quickened. "When was this?"

Mickey put his hand to his chin. "I think it mighta been the same day you were here, only in the evening. Right, I got paid overtime."

"Do you remember the car he was driving?"

"Some old clunker, a Chevy or something. You wanna check the video?"

I did, but I needed to find Luke and had no idea how long he'd be sticking around.

"Later."

Carey was sitting behind the lobby desk, looking bored, and when he saw me, he threw a nod my way and smiled. A good sign.

I showed him a picture of Luke, but he shook his head. "Not today."

"I know he's here! His car is parked in the garage next door. I have to see Ms. Sullivan's unit."

He gave me a grave look. "You need backup?"

I waved him off. "I'll let you know. Right now, I just want to talk to the guy."

Carey took the keyring from the cabinet and handed it to me. "Okay, but like I said, he never came in this way. I would know."

As I entered the elevator, my hand brushed against my handgun. Luke could be *unpredictable*, Patrice had admitted to me.

Getting off the elevator, I checked the hallway, then walked over to Elena's door and placed my ear against it before knocking.

I entered, but the unit was quiet. I checked every room and every closet. I even opened the refrigerator, which was nearly empty.

Where are you, Luke?

Deflated, I sat on the bed and played with Elena's house keyring. Three keys, different sizes and teeth shapes. I called down and asked Carey about the other keys.

"One's for the main entrance, one's for the unit, and the third is for the storeroom. Every owner has one in the parking garage area. Hers would be near her spot. Hold on." When he returned, he said, "It should be in front of number two sixty-seven. You find the guy?"

"He's a ghost. I'm heading down to her storage room now."

I flipped on the light to Elena's storage room. The six-by-six dungeon had enough space to store most anything, within reason: a bike, skis, or boxes of stuff you don't want to clutter your apartment with. I stepped inside and kept the door ajar. Apparently, Elena wasn't into sports, but she sure liked cartons—seven to be exact—though none were labeled. I painstakingly placed each on the metal table in the center of the space, and started to make my way through them.

The first six revealed that Elena liked books, picture frames (sans photos), and scrapbooks from her childhood—certainly nothing important to the investigation. The seventh carton started off the same, but as I removed a few designer magazines about midway down, I noticed folders, all containing cryptic titles that meant nothing to me. I opened one and began reading what appeared to be accusations, only none directed at McKenzie. In fact, his name never appeared.

I rummaged through a few documents, more folders, and then, on the bottom of the carton, I removed a five-by-seven, ordinary wooden frame, with a photo inside. My cell went off at that moment. I glanced at it, but I didn't recognize the number, so I blew it off, silencing the ring. I was too intent on wondering if the photo had anything to do with the documents. I suddenly had the feeling I wasn't alone, but before I had a chance to turn around, my world went dark.

My body ached like it'd been poked and prodded, and I opened my eyes to find Carey attempting to revive me.

"Ah, there you are. I tried to alert you, but you didn't answer your phone."

My fuzzy brain didn't register the meaning of his words. I touched my skull and winced. "What happened?"

"I saw her car enter the garage, and called you."

"Elena Sullivan?"

"I assume so, but I didn't actually recognize the driver. She—or he —had a ball cap riding low on the forehead. I guess you were too busy to pick up your phone." He glanced around. "Boxes."

My eyes shot over to where box seven had sat. It was no longer there.

"You might want to have that tended to. It looks nasty. I have a family doctor—"

"I'm good, thanks anyway. Can I use a bathroom?"

"Upstairs. Come on, I have a first-aid kit."

I gazed around, my eyes weighing the spot where box seven had been filled with incriminating evidence. At least, the documents looked incriminating. I held my throbbing head and thought of the framed photo. I now had my doubts about McKenzie being the target—at least, as far as the whistleblower investigation went.

"I'm guessing he or she took off already."

"I assume so. Her parking space is empty."

I nodded. My head felt fifty pounds heavier than it had before the love tap. "Take me upstairs."

Walking tentatively toward the elevator, I realized this investigation had taken another turn. McKenzie's murder was only a side trip. The photo I'd found presented a very different picture. McKenzie, Elena and Ana appeared to be a very happy threesome.

After allowing myself to be treated by Carey, I searched the condo garage's most recent CCTV video. Sure enough, either Elena's or McKenzie's car left soon after the person got what they were after, including my consciousness.

"Whoever it was left in Elena's car." I pointed to the screen.

I took a deep breath and thanked Carey for his assistance. "I have a feeling Ms. Sullivan won't be back for a while. But if she or anyone else pulls into her spot, please call me."

I wobbled back to my car, wondering about the timing of the inci-dent. As I paid for the short-term parking, Mickey told me that the guy I'd inquired about left a while ago. No surprise there—Elena and Luke left in separate cars.

I took my time driving back to Newport. I was in desperate need for sleep, but I also needed to plan my next move. There was no way I was heading back home now. I wanted the bastard who bashed my head.

As I crossed the Newport Bridge, the afternoon sun dazzling and fierce, I wondered if I ought to sleep before catching up with Detective Jackson.

But then JR called.

His usually steady voice rattled on. As he slowed his pitch, becoming more coherent, I realized I was right about McKenzie.

"McKenzie wasn't the target: He was the source."

I thought about the documents I'd begun reviewing in the garage. "You sure?"

"As sure as my mother's name is Maria Gonzalez-Greco. My source at the Justice Department is always solid. I can't go into details, but we got to talking about McKenzie and his supposed Medicare fraud scheme. My deep-throat guy was certain McKenzie was feeding some reporter information." He paused. "I told him the reporter and his assistant were missing, but he knew nothing about that."

"So Luke and Elena were working *with* McKenzie?" I said, almost to myself. "JR, I'm guessing Chewy wasn't part of the investigation. His motives were obviously personal."

"My source didn't know anything about him."

When I reached the other side of the bridge, I stopped at a light. "What if the target found out about the investigation and considered Luke and Elena too risky to keep around?"

JR said, "We won't know until they surface."

"They did surface." I told him about my incident in Boston. "Looks like they grabbed their information and took off again. They must be running scared."

The light turned green. I checked my rearview. "If what you're saying is true, Chewy might not have killed McKenzie after all. The target's henchman could have done his dirty work." I mentioned my encounter with PI Sexton at the pub. "He claimed he hadn't told Elena's boss-slash-lover about her relationship with Luke at the time, but he could have lied to me."

"PIs lie? Never." He laughed sardonically.

"If McKenzie wasn't the target, it had to be Elena's boss. Remember, he was McKenzie's competitor. Maybe the PI was tailing her not because her boss was jealous, but he was concerned she might be the leak."

"Instead, Sexton stumbled onto a romantic fling," JR added.

"Or both. What if Sexton was also a hitman? Maybe that's why they're running scared."

I hung a right on Farewell Street, passing Common Ground cemetery and turning left on Warner Street, working my way toward the Newport Police Department. "Whoever popped me obviously knew I was there, but they were so damn quiet it was too late for me to react. I touched my crown and grimaced. "The information, along with a piece of my skin, was taken. I have to believe those files were part of the investigation."

"Could be the condo is their headquarters," JR suggested.

"Was, anyway. I have no idea where they're running to." I then told JR about Chewy being in Boston.

"The parking attendant identified him with a photo I showed him. He's still a person of interest in my book."

JR asked, "Did you mention to anyone you were heading back to Boston?"

I thought a moment. "The parking attendant, but I can't believe he had anything to do with it." I stopped. "Wait a second. The only person who knew I was searching Elena's condo was the security guy at the lobby. I told you he's a retired cop."

"Could be he was very protective of her and knew about the investigation. Which meant whoever surprised you was already in the neighborhood. Like the guy at the front desk."

"Hold on." I put JR on hold and punched the last incoming call. Carey picked up.

"Hey Carey, I just wanted to thank you again for the first aid help."

"Hey, anything for a member of the tribe. Good luck."

Right, good luck.

Back to JR. "The last incoming number came from the security guy. He tried getting in touch with me just before the incident. Doesn't make sense that it would be him."

And then it hit me.

"The sole purpose for the trip was to confront Luke. When I arrived, his car was still parked, but when I returned, the attendant claimed he left."

"Well now, there's your answer."

At six that evening, I arrived at the Newport station house and found Detective Jackson, feet elevated on his desk, sipping coffee. He waved me in. His sullen appearance told me his day wasn't going well.

"Hank, I'd offer you a cup of coffee, but you'd probably sue me afterward." The tone of his voice belied his humor. He pointed to the chair opposite him.

I sat and watched him take another mouthful of coffee, scrunch up his nose, and then place the mug back on his desk.

"I wish I could offer you some positive news, but we're at a stand-still." He sat back and tented his fingers. "The only certainly is McKenzie's murder. Your missing people are still missing. The Coast Guard brought back McKenzie's yacht. It was found tied up at the marina on Goat Island, just across from us." He shrugged. "Still dusting for prints. Maybe we'll get lucky." He nodded with his chin. "So how long do you expect to hang around in Newport? Not that I mind you being here." He lifted his cup in my direction, peered inside, then placed it back on his desk.

I pressed my lips together and told him Patrice had left for Paris. I turned my head and showed Jackson my lump. "As for me, I'd like to find the bastard who left me with a big headache."

He leaned forward to get a better look. "Damn, I'm assuming it wasn't an accident."

I told him it probably had to do with the whistleblowing case and the missing duo. I didn't go into details as to where, what, or when. He seemed to buy it.

"I'll stick around a while and promise not to overstay my welcome."

He nodded. "Much obliged, but if you do find anything related to my investigation, I'd appreciate a heads-up."

"Of course."

He kept my gaze, and after an uncomfortable silence, his phone rang. I got up to leave, but he gestured me to stay.

He spoke, nodded, listened, and then hung up.

"So far, the only prints identified from McKenzie's yacht were his. There were two other sets but weren't in the system." He shrugged. "Sorry, Hank, I can't help you."

I probably should have told Jackson he was looking in the wrong direction and that Luke and Elena were working *with* McKenzie. But I needed him to use his resources to find the missing duo. I certainly couldn't do both. I wanted to rule out Chewy as the killer, and so I called Nick Parisi who, when he looked a little harder, found the kid's Newport address.

I pulled up to a small white Tudor with a side entrance, where I assumed Chewy lived, and knocked on the door. A minute later, a short, gray-haired man around seventy with a weather-beaten face answered.

I smiled, showed my out-of-state shield, and asked about his tenant.

"Haven't seen him in a few days. Is he in some sort of trouble?"

Some sort for sure.

"Person of interest," I said. "I'd like to see his apartment."

The guy squinted at me. "I won't get in trouble, will I?"

"For helping the police, no way," I promised. "Hell, you'll probably become a hero."

The guy smiled, apparently happy with the idea of becoming a celebrity. "Follow me."

He opened the door and swore. "What a pig!"

My same sentiments.

Chewy must have been in a hurry, because his work clothes were strewn about. Otherwise, the place was bare: nothing hanging on the white, worn-out walls. An old, torn, brown-leather sofa sat in one corner facing an equally ancient Zenith TV set on a wooden stand.

I asked the landlord, who introduced himself as Joe, if he'd noticed any noise coming from the apartment. "A party perhaps?"

He shook his head. "Nah, Chewy was a quiet guy. I never had a problem with him. He always kept things neat—until now."

"He fill out a rental application?"

"Yeah, it's back in my house." He thumbed toward the door. "You wanna take a look?"

"If you don't mind. I'll stick around here and go through his... things in the meantime." While the landlord was gone, I searched the apartment, rummaging through Chewy's clothes (seems rummaging through people's clothing was all I did these days). There wasn't much else in the apartment. The only things in the fridge were a few bottles of Bud. The cabinets were bare. I checked the bathroom medicine cabinet and removed a prescription made out to Tyler Bryant for Xenazine, 12.5 mg.

Tyler Bryant, Chewy's real name.

I Googled the drug on my cell, and when the definition hit the screen, I thought I had typed in the wrong word. I hadn't. Xenazine was used for treating symptoms of cholera associated with Huntington's disease.

I scrolled down and read that Xenazine helped reduce the brief, repetitive and jerky or uncontrolled dance-like movements. I scratched my head then searched for Huntington's disease.

I'd always associated Huntington's with middle age, but evidently juvenile onset Huntington's was a thing. There weren't any treatments to alter the course of the disease, and at some point, Chewy—or rather, Tyler—would die from it. Could his affliction have prompted him to make risky decisions, like taking revenge on McKenzie for the real Chewy's suicide?

When the landlord returned, he handed me the rental application. I searched for a relative he might have included on the application. I soon got my answer.

If I took a chance and called Tyler's mother, she might tip him off, assuming she wasn't in the hospital from the alleged car accident. But given what he was up to, she might not even know where to find him. Was I willing to travel three hours to New York City on a hunch? After all, the job application information could be nothing more than bullshit. My only hope was that JR had more time for me.

He did. He confirmed that for the past twenty years, Missy Bryant, Tyler's mother, had rented an apartment on St. Nicholas Avenue in the Washington Heights section of New York. He offered to check with Tyler's mother himself.

"Hold off, JR. If Tyler were there when you showed up, he might get spooked, or, given his disease, even kill himself. I certainly don't want you involved in suicide by cop."

I was making the trip.

I hadn't been back to the Big Apple since JR had assisted me in John Hunter's murder investigation, and quite frankly, the city did nothing for me. It was too big. But Washington Heights, at least, was north of midtown and close to the George Washington Bridge.

I met JR a block from Missy Bryant's apartment, and we exchanged bear hugs.

"Good to see you, Hank. It's been a while." JR showed his trademark infectious crooked smile. He was dressed in jeans and a plain black collared shirt. At six feet tall, we were head- to-head, and our hairstyles matched, too.

"I can't thank you enough for helping me out behind the scenes."

"Yeah, well, I get bored easily. Besides, I nabbed the perp I was looking for, so my boss stopped breathing down my neck."

I pointed to a nineteen-story art-deco-style apartment building with a fire escape. "That it?"

He turned. "Yup. I'm thinking you might want to go alone, just in case your guy decides to get some air down the fire escape."

I nodded. "Good idea. He's sick, has Huntington's disease, so he probably won't give me a hard time when I approach him."

Missy Bryant lived on the tenth floor, but I wasn't about to ring her doorbell. Instead, I checked for the superintendent's bell. I was about to ring him, when a young guy in the lobby started heading my way. He flipped up his hoodie then stopped when he saw me. I smiled a small, cautious smile. Recognition or not, Tyler quickly pivoted and charged for the elevator.

My finger pressed hard on the super's bell, and when he buzzed me in, I took off after Tyler. The elevator hadn't arrived yet, so the kid raced for the stairwell. His Xenazine must've been working, because he wasted no time or effort scaling the steps two at a time. I dove for his legs at the fourth floor, and he went down hard.

He started screaming, his arms thrashing. "Leave me alone!"

"I'm not here to hurt you, Tyler, so take it easy." I put my hands up and stepped back.

His eyes darted about like a calf being cornered for slaughter.

"Think we could talk about Elena Sullivan and Luke DuPont?"

He gave me a blank stare. "Who are they?"

"Listen, I can call the local cops and have you arrested for the murder of Warren McKenzie."

He got that. "I have nothing to say to you," Tyler said to the floor. Then he asked. "You a cop? I saw you in Newport."

I nodded. "At McKenzie's place. That's where you guys were cutting his lawn. Chewy, I know about your Huntington's."

He sat up, placed his head against the wall. "Yeah, no big deal, I'm dying." His pained face belied his apparent flippancy.

"Meaning you weren't concerned about killing McKenzie for revenge because you might not make it to trial anyway. Look, I read the report about McKenzie. He was a bastard, and we both know he was responsible for your friend's suicide, but I still have a problem, Chewy— or can I call you Tyler? Those two people I mentioned are missing, maybe dead."

His eyes jumped about again. "I didn't kill them!"

"I'm not saying you did, but they're missing. They were helping McKenzie in a whistleblowing investigation. You might not have had a reason to go after them like you did McKenzie, but it doesn't look good. See what I mean?"

"He killed Chewy!"

"I know. I read the articles. It was never proven, but I agree with you. McKenzie's actions caused Chewy to do what he did. I might have done the same thing you did."

Tyler's eyes welled up. "He was my best friend. He wanted to be something. Not like me, I had nothing. So, the guy had to pay."

He gazed up at me, searching for sympathy.

I nodded. "I understand. You pushed him over the Cliff Walk, right?"

Tyler crossed his legs and bent over. "I'm not saying anymore 'til I get my meds. I don't feel so good."

"Your Xenazine?"

He nodded.

"I found them at your Newport apartment. Guess you were in a rush."

"I have some at my mom's place." He pointed upward.

"Okay, but let's take the elevator."

Tyler's mother's apartment was decorated sparingly. I figured his medical bills took precedence over luxury.

"Where's your mother now, Tyler?"

"She went out, probably shopping. I really need my meds." He pointed to a bedroom. "Then we can talk, okay?"

I followed him, but the front door opened behind us, and I turned at the sound. Tyler pushed me hard, ran inside the bedroom, and slammed the door shut. I heard the click of the lock.

"Shit!"

The panicked voice of Tyler's mother rose behind me. "Who are you? And where is Tyler?"

I slammed my body against the bedroom door. "Open up, Tyler. I just want to talk to you."

I heard another click, presumably on the bedroom window, and dialed JR. "The fire escape! Go!"

"I'm calling the police," she threatened.

I turned. "I am the police. Talk to your son, Mrs. Bryant, before he tries something stupid."

Her eyes widened, and in one movement she leaped to the locked door and started banging. "Tyler? What's going on? Why are the police here?"

"I love you, Mom," he called out.

And then there was silence. Ramming the door on adrenaline, I charged inside—but Chewy was gone.

Heartrending screams echoed behind me as I raced to the open window. I stuck my head out and peered below. Chewy was down there, sprawled on the street, blood pouring onto the concrete. JR leaned over him, then looked up and shook his head.

TEN

C hewy had never officially confessed. He didn't have to. He died on the street. But JR and I found a diary in Missy Bryant's apartment that detailed his resolve to avenge Chewy's death. McKenzie didn't have a chance. Tyler had plotted every facet of the murder, starting with changing his name to that of his best friend, Chewy. Then he would locate McKenzie's residences in Newport and Boston. Tyler wanted to be Chewy when he killed McKenzie. Very poetic justice.

Missy Bryant had no idea what her son had been up to. All she had known was that since Timmy Jerkens had taken his life, Tyler had become a different person. He'd become depressed and angry. And, despite his Huntington's, he'd eventually decided to start fresh and move to Newport, though he never told his mother why. His father, who was dying from the same disease, had been a tugboat captain who had taken his son on short trips when he was younger. Hence Chewy's knowledge of boats.

I contacted Jackson immediately for fear that he'd hear it on the news first. Scrambling to find an excuse for being at Chewy's mother's apartment, I told him I was on my way to the Big Apple when an informant contacted me as to Tyler's whereabouts.

He didn't seem too upset, given that McKenzie's killer was no longer a threat, but asked for a report just the same.

Sure, why not?

Even though Chewy was no longer on the run, I wasn't finished. I still had to deal with the missing couple. As far as Jackson was concerned, he no longer needed to use the department's manpower, and that didn't help me at all.

JR and I downed a couple beers at a local bar near Amsterdam and Ninety-Sixth Street, a place called Upper West—original. The place was dark and quiet, which suited my mood perfectly.

JR's wily smile told me he was up to something.

"A senior detective's position in my precinct just opened up, if you're interested. Be cool having you around."

I took a much-needed slug of my Corona and nodded. He informed me I had a week to think about it. One week. In that time, I needed to find the missing duo and decide whether to go back to my Suffolk County job. My boss was starting to become impatient.

The pressures!

"I'll let you know in a week. Promise."

After staying the night at JR's apartment, I left for Newport around eight in the morning. I drove without music from the radio; I wanted to think. With the window open, taking in the mild summer fresh air, I wondered for the umpteenth time whether I ought to just pack up my things, pay my bill at the inn, and head home.

The funny thing about driving under the influence of thought: you tend to forget your surroundings. But every once in a while, I'd check my rearview mirror and realize I kept seeing the same black Ford Explorer. I was being tailed, and I didn't much care for it. I continued north on I-95 in the slow lane for about two miles, and then punched the accelerator, pulling into the center lane.

It didn't take long before my shadow followed and pulled behind me again. My heart raced. Someone was interested in me. I signaled to the right lane again and continued at the speed limit. I exited at the Darien,

Connecticut, northbound service plaza in search of gas—at least, that's what I wanted the guy behind me to think.

My shadow stayed close and followed me to an Exxon station, waiting just beyond the pump area. Guess he didn't need gas. Okay, smartass. You'll have to wait until I grab a sub.

After ordering two turkey foot-longs on whole wheat, I stepped outside and approached the guy's SUV. I was about ten feet away when he started backing up, and then he ripped across my path, tearing out of the parking area. I dropped the bag of foot-longs, pulled out my phone, and snapped a picture of his plate number. Oh well, another sandwich for me.

New York State. It should be easy for JR to trace the number in the system.

"Jesus, Hank, we just finished one case, and already you're looking for more work." He half-laughed, half-scoffed. "Where are you?"

"At the Darien, Connecticut rest plaza."

"Okay, I'll have the info way before you reach Newport."

I got into my car, tapped the steering wheel a few times, then touched my head and grimaced. It was still pretty tender. A name suddenly came to me, one associated with box seven taken from Elena's storeroom. A name I was vaguely familiar with: Elena's boss and/or lover, Preston Hartford, III.

I took a bite of my sandwich then hopped back on I-95. I checked my rearview mirror for the next several miles, but my tail seemed to be gone. I couldn't help but wonder: Why was the guy interested in me? Maybe he knew I was searching for two people. Could be that Hartford, who'd already hired Sexton to find out if Elena was cheating on him wasn't satisfied with his nonperformance and hired another. Especially if he thought there was more going on than romance.

For a fleeting moment, I thought of Patrice, that maybe she'd hired the guy. But that didn't make sense. She had me. The tail did provide pause for encouragement, though: whoever was following me must have had reason to believe Luke and Elena were still alive.

JR's call came in as I reached the Wilson House.

"I have to tell you, Hank, your investigation is getting weirder and weirder. Looks like you have another PI interested in your investigation. Guy's name is Danny Stone, and he's from New York City."

I scanned the inn. Brady was standing near the window, and when he saw me, waved me in.

"I'd better find Luke before this Stone does."

ELEVEN

B rady swung open the door. "I see you got your name in the paper for capturing the Cliff Walk Killer. That's what I call 'im anyway. Nice work."

"Don't read too much into it," I said, stepping inside. "We got lucky."

"Newport hasn't had this much excitement since 1993, when Adam Emery and his wife supposedly jumped off the Newport bridge after he was found guilty of second-degree murder. Stories floated around: was it suicide or a scam?"

Theories abound.

"Can you do me a favor?"

"Anything for a hero."

"Ask Chuck the neighborhood security guy to keep an eye out for this car and plate number. Hold on, I'm going to text it to you." I sent Brady the photo I took at the rest stop.

After a ping, he grabbed his phone off the desk. "New York, okay. I'm guessing you can't tell me more."

I grinned. "Not yet, but the guy—or guys—in the vehicle could be dangerous, so make sure Chuck wears a Kevlar vest."

Brady shot me a look. "Hank, that's not funny."

"Just have him keep his eyes open," I said, and patted Brady on the back.

I entered my room and flopped down on the bed. What a day. I closed my eyes, but sleep was out of the question for me.

Damn you, Luke! Are you a good guy or not?

I thought of Chewy. He had been obsessed with killing McKenzie. To some, he would be considered courageous, fighting death while enforcing his own punishment on another.

And then Ana, the phony domestic, entered my thoughts. Who was she and what team was she on?

I rolled onto my side. God, I could use a drink. I assumed happy hour at The Nautical Pub was still going strong at six, so I washed my face and headed out the door again.

The place was jumping. Locals were mixing with tourists amid loud eighties music. I claimed the last stool on the corner of the bar and looked over at the bartender. He reminded me of Paddy from Salty's back home; his Irish accent was comforting.

Before I could snag a few pretzels off the bar, someone tapped my shoulder. I turned and was greeted by two bright eyes.

Maureen and I smiled at each other.

"Where's your partner, Hank?"

"Gone baby gone," I said too quickly.

"Too bad. I could tell she was into you."

I raised an eyebrow.

"Really, a woman can tell. Her eyes spoke, and they said you were special."

"Now you tell me." I sighed. "Kinda like that couple we asked you about?"

"In a different sort of way. I mean, yeah, they were chummy, but I got the sense it was false, more flirtatious. It seemed like she was seducing him, know what I mean? And like I said, the way she looked, it wouldn't have been hard for the guy to lose his way with her."

"You think she might have been playing him? Like she wanted something from the guy?"

"She was definitely the aggressor," Maureen started. "And like I said, she was real hot."

Right, hot.

It dawned on me then that Maureen wasn't in her server outfit. "You off?"

"Finally."

"Let me buy you a drink."

"Hank, I thought you'd never ask. Tonight's my night out, but my friend canceled on me. Hell, I wasn't about to miss a few hours out on the town. I've got teenagers at home. What about you? You have kids?"

My home in Eastpoint flashed in front of me and I sighed.

"Come on, Hank, what? You don't know?"

"Long story. What are you drinking?"

Maureen called over the bartender. "Brendan, a Guinness. Hank, what's your pleasure?"

"Guinness works for me. I took out my wallet, but Maureen shoved it back. "Working here has its perks. We're on the house tonight." She winked.

"Much obliged." I was about to offer Maureen my seat, but the guy next to me slid off his. "Quick!" I said.

She slipped in, and I said, "I guess you heard about the Cliff Walk murder a few days ago."

"Who hasn't? I also read that the killer died jumping off a fire escape in New York City? What the hell?"

"Yeah, it's a rough one. What's the gossip here?"

She shrugged. "Not much at this point. Sounded like the guy had it in for McKenzie." She leaned in to me. "At the time, I had my own theory. Wanna hear it?"

Brendan returned with our brew. I took a swig. "Always enjoy theories."

Maureen lifted her own pint and took a sip. "McKenzie wasn't a regular, but he'd come in occasionally, usually for a few drinks, though sometimes he'd grab a bite and then leave. I served him sometimes. Nice guy. And rich."

"Was he alone?"

"Mostly. About a week or so ago he came in with a woman, though. She was attractive, obviously younger than him. Latina, I think. He called her…Anne? Anna? Something like that."

I felt a twinge in my neck. I gulped some beer and wiped my mouth with my hand. "Go on."

"You could tell they weren't happy. Actually, she left without ordering." Maureen took another sip. "I don't pry in people's business, mind you, but I did ask McKenzie if everything was all right. He must have had a few drinks before he got here, because he asked me to sit with him a minute, then just started talking. Very loose tongue, if you know what I mean."

Maureen turned her head to scan the bar scene. The music had died down, so she leaned in closer. "He wasn't happy. He accused her of cheating, but it didn't sound like with another guy. He was slurring a bit. He said she was going to 'mess things up,' his words. He must have realized his tongue was wagging too much and told me to forget what I'd heard. Then he paid his bill, dropped a hundred in my lap, and left."

"Did you mention any of this to the police after he was killed?"

A deep sigh. "I was going to, but then I found out about the kid who killed himself." She shrugged. "I figured it probably didn't have anything to do with that night. Did I screw up, Hank?" Her face turned grave.

I touched her hand. "You're fine. But I'm glad you told me."

"Good. I think I need another Guinness."

———

Sometimes law-enforcement guys get lucky through happenstance, and in my case, with Maureen's minor confession about Ana and McKenzie, I now had a sense that Ana was a component in McKenzie's business or demise. Maybe she hadn't done it directly, but back at his place, Ana had misled me, pretending to be his domestic. I mean was that happenstance, too, that she'd been at the house when Patrice and I had pulled up?

Then there was her relationship to Elena. They knew each other; Ana had attested to that at the house. And the photo I'd discovered of them with McKenzie...she knew her, all right. According to Maureen, McKenzie said that Ana was going to ruin him. But how? And with or without Elena?

I left my favorite server at the bar, but not before slapping down a big tip for Brendan. Hell, I had to pay for something. I reached the inn in deep thought.

I'm going to find you, Ana.

Instead of climbing the steps, I went to my car. I drove in silence, tumbling ideas around in my head as I made my way across the bridge to Jamestown. When I reached McKenzie's driveway, I turned off the headlights, crawled along the gravel rocks, then shut off the engine. McKenzie's mansion was dark except for a small light emanating from one of the back rooms. About ten minutes later, the light went out. I knew it couldn't be McKenzie.

I stepped cautiously and quietly out of the car, Glock in hand, and kept low, all the time keeping my eyes glued to the house. No more lights appeared anywhere. Someone was either going to sleep or preparing to leave.

The front door opened, and I froze. The person who stepped through the door was short, and wore slacks, sneakers, and a hoodie. He —or she—was carrying a box and was now heading for the garage.

"Police!"

The shadow stopped abruptly, shot me a look, then dashed to the left toward the water. As I chased it, I heard a small craft engine rumble to life.

Shit!

The shadow outran me. By the time I reached the dock, the boat was jerking forward toward God knows where. The person removed the hoodie, exposing long, blond hair that blew wildly in the wind. She turned her head and stared at me.

"Elena, I'm not the enemy," I called out. "I want to help."

She turned her back to me again. I searched beyond her to see the driver—who appeared to be male—but his face remained forward, steering the speeding boat. I could only guess who he was.

I punched in Detective Jackson's number.

"I think I found my missing duo, but I could use your help. They took off from McKenzie's place in a small motor boat heading south. Can you call the harbor patrol? I'm heading over to Newport now."

"I'm on it, Hank."

"I doubt they're armed, but I wouldn't take chances."

I sprinted to the house and turned the doorknob. One by one, I went through the house and turned on the lights, hoping Elena had left something behind. I wondered where she could have stashed whatever it was she'd removed from the house. If McKenzie had a safe, I couldn't find it. Nothing else appeared to be out of place.

Elena had looked as though she'd been heading for the garage. I took off in that direction, but not before turning off the lights again. Reaching the garage, I opened the side door and turned on the overhead light. Two cars were neatly parked, which meant Elena and Luke had returned with them. The air-conditioned garage was neat. In one corner, I spotted a large, Bosch stainless steel French-door refrigerator stocked with beer, wine, and expensive champagne. I circled the cars, and then checked inside. I wondered whether Elena had been carrying the same box I had been sifting through when I'd gotten popped on the head. Then I wondered: If she had a boat waiting for her, why had she been heading here?

In the far corner, there was a large, white sheet neatly covering something squarish. I snapped it off, revealing McKenzie's third car, the sporty, light-blue Mini Cooper convertible.

I opened the glove compartment, shoved my hand underneath the seats, and finally, flipped open the trunk. There—a small box. I removed it, set it on the garage floor, and began rummaging through it.

Pay dirt!

Scanning through several printouts, it was clear that Elena and Luke were onto something big and had perhaps sensed danger, especially after McKenzie's murder. And then I realized: This had to be part of a bigger file, perhaps what Elena had been holding in her arms when I'd confronted her.

I had to find Luke and persuade him I wasn't the enemy. But unless Jackson found them on the boat, that was unlikely. After all, he and Elena had eluded us for almost a week.

I hustled back to my car, box in hand, and wondered about their destination. Luke—if it was Luke—had the boat. Was Elena just heading to the garage to remove the files from the Mini Cooper I now possessed? Or perhaps to take the car and meet up with Luke later? Either way, they were definitely on the run.

After opening Google Maps on my cell, I typed in Jamestown, Rhode Island, hoping to narrow down the southern route on which they were traveling on Narragansett Bay.

Then I checked car rental agencies, and, upon finding a Hertz location in Newport, I called Jackson and told him they may attempt to rent a car there.

There was no time to lose, so I took off for Newport. The evening traffic along Thames Street was maddeningly busy. I took a right on Wellington then slid down a few more local streets before hitting Fort Adams Drive. I took a right toward the state park, recalling the time I'd visited years ago for the Newport Jazz Festival. Right now, I was only interested in the Fort Adams Bay Walk. I pulled up and tore ass toward Brenton Cove, where the park's boat ramp stood.

A lone, small craft stood idle, tied up against a small dock. I ran over. The engine was still warm, but there were no signs of the duo or their booty. There were only a handful of people remaining in the park. I heard a car engine start up and turned. It was Danny Stone, the PI in the SUV, about fifty feet away. He flashed his high beams, taunting me. I couldn't let him get away from me this time, so I charged for my car. His tires screeched as he dodged out of the parking lot.

I jumped in my car, peeling out after him. It wasn't until I'd pulled out of the lot that I realized the bastard had flattened one of my tires.

I punched in Jackson's number again. No pleasantries this time—just a heads-up, including a plate number. I didn't want to tell him I already knew who it belonged to. Instead, I mentioned a possible kidnapping, topping off the conversation by including deadly weapon. I kicked the tire and swore as I hung up.

Soon after I changed my tire, Jackson called and told me Stone was stopped by a member of the patrol division on Thames as he attempted to jump a light, like an idiot. The guy must have realized I'd call the locals and had tried hammering out of Newport. The officer checked the vehicle, but the driver, an athletic fortysomething with a military cut, tried talking his way out of a ticket. When Jackson arrived, the guy became testy, unable to understand why they needed backup. He didn't resist, though, and was brought in for questioning—something about a missing couple last seen in an out-of-state black SUV.

When I arrived, Jackson had already checked Stone out, but had found nothing incriminating.

"Name is Danny Stone, a PI from New York City. He's got a clean record. In fact, he served a tour in Iraq."

That confirmed what JR had told me. I snapped a photo of Stone from behind the security window and whipped it off to Brady.

He called me back a moment later. "Doesn't look familiar, Hank. But I'll pass the picture on to Chuck."

When I got off the phone, Jackson asked, "Anything else you want me to ask Stone?"

I kept my eyes steady on the guy. He had a smug look about him, leaning back in the interrogation seat, arms crossed. He was obviously a pro.

"Maybe read him the riot act." I smirked.

"As far as the people on the boat, I called a few local car rental companies to be on the lookout. Nothing yet."

"I didn't think so." I nodded, thanked Jackson, and left.

Stone was on his cell the moment his feet touched the street. He didn't appear too happy, and abruptly hung up. I knew I was in store for a long night, and after tailing him a few miles southbound on I-95, placed a call in to JR.

"You've got company tonight, my friend," I said, keeping my eyes on the SUV.

"Please tell me she's a blond."

"Short brown hair."

"Let's see, you're on the highway tailing someone."

"You're good, JR."

"Where are you heading? I'll meet you."

"Beats me. I'm following the Stone fellow you told me about. The bastard sliced one of my tires. I wanna get even, so it doesn't matter where he winds up. I'll call when I get close to you."

Stone was easy to follow. He didn't speed, nor stop to take a pee, which I desperately needed. I was getting too old for this.

I assumed Stone was heading toward the Big Apple, so I figured I had time to call Patrice. She didn't pick up, and I realized it was the middle of the night in Paris. I called again and left a message.

"Patrice, I found Luke and Elena in Newport, but they eluded me. At least he's alive. Call me when you can. Sorry, I realize it's late, but thought you should know."

An hour went by, but no Patrice. I got antsy and called again. "Just in case you didn't get my last message, Luke is alive. I'll call your office and leave a message just in case your phone is down."

She called back within minutes.

"Hank, I was just thinking of you."

"Didn't you get my message about Luke?"

"Sorry, I was in the middle of something pressing. I'm working nights for a while." She added, "I had time to think on the plane. It's over between us."

"Us?"

"Me and Luke, silly. Certainly not you."

Did I hear right—on both accounts?

Patrice whispered into the phone; obviously she wasn't alone. "He broke my heart with…that other woman. We had plans for when the investigation was over. With his share of the reward, we were going to get married, maybe travel around the world, and possibly even move to an island to live. That's all dead now—sorry, I'm blabbering."

Strike recovered.

"I appreciate your concern, Hank. Actually, I figured you'd be back home by now."

"You know how cops are. One thing leads to another. I'd really like to see this through." I told her about Chewy, McKenzie not being the target, my mishap in Boston, the boat, and finally, PI Stone, whom I was currently tailing.

"I see you're a little busy, Detective Reed." She laughed wistfully. "Bad timing for me to head back to Paris. I keep thinking of that night." A pause that seemed as big as the Atlantic. "I miss you."

That caught me off-guard.

"I…miss you, too, Patrice. Maybe when this is over…"

I heard a sigh. "I'm still trying to get that transfer."

Just then, Stone exited the Henry Hudson Parkway at West Ninety-Sixth Street in New York City.

"Patrice, the guy I'm following just got off the parkway."

"Go ahead, we'll talk later."

Later.

Stone swung right and headed eastbound before turning north and finally parking on Central Park West, near an apartment complex on One Hundredth Street. I watched him enter the building.

Just another day at the office, honey.

While searching for parking, I called JR and gave him my location. I finally squeezed into a tight spot around the corner, near the Dive Bar. There, I met up with my buddy detective, and after another bear hug, I excused myself and took a much-needed whiz.

"You're in my neighborhood," he said when I returned, "so drinks are on me."

"I need sleep, so I'm nursing my beer tonight or you'll be chatting with yourself."

He grinned and patted my back. "The couch is yours as long as you need it. My apartment's just a few blocks away."

"Much appreciated," I said. I could feel my eyelids refusing to open all the way. I pointed in the direction of Stone's apartment building a few blocks away. "Danny Stone is my new person of interest. He's a freelancer, whatever that means in this case. It only makes sense that he's looking for Elena and Luke. But who hired him, and why?"

"Don't know, but apparently the duo eluded him, too."

"And slashed my tire, the bastard." I shook my head and put my fist in my hand. "I'm not finished with him."

"I'll order the beers."

The dark interior of the Dive Bar made me feel even more tired. We chitchatted about women and murder—in that order. He knew Susan and I were on our way to a divorce, and he wanted to know more about Patrice.

That made me perk up a bit. I took a sip of beer and smiled. "She told me her relationship with Luke is over. That makes me happy, obviously, but I'm still cautious. You know how these things work. Jumping into a new relationship right after a bad one…"

"I hear you."

"Plus, she lives in Paris. Unless she gets a transfer to the States…I don't believe in long-distance relationships."

JR held up his glass. "To transfers."

I grinned. "To transfers."

We remained quiet for a few minutes, and then JR removed a three-and-a-half inch BlizeTec survival knife from his pants pocket and handed it to me. "Look what I happened to find on the floor." He winked. "Might do some damage to a tire. You'll be even."

"Not if I slice all four."

After making a stop at Stone's car, JR dropped me off at his apartment building and promised not to call until six a.m. I let myself in and dropped on the bed, clothes and all.

Like clockwork, my cell rang out at the stroke of six.

"Rise and shine, amigo. It's a beautiful, cool morning in the Big Apple. Time to investigate."

I rubbed my eyes. "Good morning to you, too, JR."

"Sleep okay? You looked pretty peaceful when I paid you a visit an hour ago."

"It's too early to tell, but yeah, I feel okay."

"I just stopped by Stone's apartment. He was outside, didn't look very happy. Pissed off is more like it. He was on his cell barking at someone—probably Triple-A." He snickered.

I stood and started out of the room. Bathroom was calling.

"Hope you're not looking for food, because there isn't any." He laughed. "There's a deli around the corner on 100th Street, not far from Stone's apartment—Mandel's. Meet me in fifteen minutes."

Nothing like a New York bagel and coffee first thing in the morning. The commuter crowd had lined up, waiting to order, so I decided to hold off until it died down. I caught JR's wave and threaded over to his table.

"I ordered you a toasted whole-wheat bagel with cream cheese and coffee. You don't look like a lox guy to me." He pointed to my breakfast.

I put up a hand. "Right on that." I sat and took a much-needed gulp of coffee.

"You can't beat a good neighborhood deli like Mandel's."

I took a healthy bite of my bagel and another sip of coffee. I had to agree.

"So," he started, "your friend won't be too happy with you, assuming he discovers you were the culprit. Four tires are kind of costly." He raised his eyebrows and pursed his lips. "I'd say you probably have a leisurely hour to enjoy your bagel and pay him a visit. Want me to join you?"

I thought about JR's involvement with Stone and decided I'd feel better if he fed me information rather than get directly involved. Hell, I shouldn't get directly involved myself! "I have your number in my favorites, so if I'm in a jam, I'll call you."

He winked, downed the rest of his coffee. "I'll be close by. And if you need another night on the couch, it's yours."

I removed his house key from my pocket and held it out in my open palm. "I'm hoping Stone will lead me back to Newport."

"Just in case."

I slipped the key back into my pocket, somehow knowing I'd be using it again tonight. I swallowed the last bite of my bagel and stepped through the deli's tinkling glass door into the bright morning sunlight. I could see Stone in the apartment lot, apparently waiting for roadside. His face held a scowl that could kill.

Must be a busy morning for tires.

"Damn," I said, walking up to him. "I thought this was a safe neighborhood."

Danny Stone glanced at me and then glared at the car. It seemed he didn't recognize me. "Fucking animal. When I find out who did it, he's a dead man." Stone kicked a rear tire then checked his phone. "Where the hell are they?"

"If you gotta be some place, I can drive you." I gestured in the direction of my car.

He shook his head. "Thanks, but you don't wanna drive to Newport, Rhode Island."

"No kidding? That's where I'm heading. Two friends of mine are missing there." I smiled.

His head jerked up and he looked more closely at me, narrowing his eyes under his bushy, graying brows. "You fuck!" Stone jumped up and charged after me, but stopped short when he heard a siren heading our way.

"What's going on, fellas?" JR asked, lowering the tinted window of his unmarked car. "Christ, what happened to your tires?"

Stone put up a hand. "A misunderstanding."

"Everything is good here, officer," I said.

"It's 'detective!'"

I stopped myself from giggling. "Detective."

"Don't make me come back. I mean it."

After JR left, I stepped close into Stone's space, speaking evenly and with a calmness that intimidated even myself. "We're both looking for the same people. I want them alive. The Newport locals know about you, Mr. Stone. A dead body or two is on you."

Stone snorted. "You think I'm tailing you to knock off your friends? You're wrong, Detective Reed, or whatever your title is these days. Unlike you, I'm trying to keep them safe."

The tow truck company called Stone to apologize for the delay, claiming there had indeed been a rash of car problems in the city.

"Another half hour," Stone whined.

"Hey, I have nothing going on right now. I'll hang out."

"This was your fucking fault, Reed."

"You're forgetting you slashed my tire first." I shrugged. "Tit for tat."

"Fuck you."

"Look, let's not get into a pissing match. If you're telling the truth, we're probably on the same team. Who's your client?"

He snorted. "Right. You know I'm not about to reveal my client. What about you, Reed? What's a Long Island detective doing working in Newport for a pretty French woman?"

I held off on the banter then. Stone obviously knew some things about me, so if I wanted a little quid pro quo, I'd have to offer him something.

"It actually has nothing to do with my police work. I'm doing her a favor, making sure Luke DuPont doesn't wind up like McKenzie."

"She's hot. I totally get your involvement." He sneered then looked at his tires and shook his head. "You're still a prick."

"Fighting won't get us anywhere."

Stone set his frigid gaze somewhere beyond me before finally meeting my eyes. He let out a frustrated sigh. "I was hired to keep Elena Sullivan safe from whoever wanted her harmed. Nothing more, nothing less. I knew you were searching for Luke DuPont, so I hoped one of us would find them, and alive."

"Then why did you slash one of my tires?" I protested.

"Okay, that was kind of dumb on my part," he admitted. "I guess I just wanted to find them before some idiot cop did." He shrugged. "No offense."

I glanced at his tires and smiled. "None taken."

"By the time I arrived at the park, they were gone. Shit, they were quick." He checked his Apple Watch and huffed. "Where the hell are they?"

I didn't trust Danny Stone, and probably wouldn't until I found out who hired him. Maybe I never would find out.

Stone offered, "In case you don't already know, your French friend's fiancé has been screwing Elena Sullivan for a while already. That's how he found out about the whistleblower investigation." Stone rested a hand on my shoulder. "Hell, you might get lucky whether we find DuPont dead or alive. It's worthwhile sticking around." He threw his head back and laughed.

I didn't much care for Stone's remark and shrugged off his hand. "I don't work that way."

When the tow truck revved up, I pulled out my cell. "If you decide to share real information then give me your number now."

Stone hesitated.

"Else you're on your own."

The slender white driver in his thirties emerged from his truck and whistled when he got a look at Stone's SUV. "Someone's having a bad day."

Stone rattled off his number to me, and I called it. His cell went off —the ringtone was a patriotic tune. Typical.

He picked up the call, and I said, "Hurry up and get some new tires."

"Fuck you, Reed. And you're paying for them."

"Fine, but only three—and that's *after* we find Luke and Elena."

TWELVE

I f McKenzie wasn't the target, it had to be Elena's boss and lover, Preston Hartford, III, the CEO of Fox Reynolds. And its headquarters was located in New York City. How convenient.

I had a few hours on Stone, and with no particular lead, decided to pay Hartford a visit. I Googled the company. Turned out it was located here in Manhattan, on Park Avenue and Forty-Eighth Street. I called hoping Hartford was in, and that he would take my call.

He was, and he did. He sounded concerned after I told him I was hired to find his missing assistant.

"Elena's missing? How can that be? She left on a vacation less than a week ago."

That was convincing.

"Who did you say hired you, Mr. Reed?"

Good try.

I patiently explained the client confidentiality privilege to him. He wasn't feeling it.

"I mean, come on, she hasn't been gone that long."

I'd thrown Hartford a small Pinocchio, since I wasn't actually getting paid or hired by anyone. "According to my client," I replied, "Ms. Sullivan was supposed to meet up with someone, but never showed up.

I'm sorry, Mr. Hartford, I can't divulge much more than that. I was hoping you might have information that would help me find her."

"My God! This is crazy. Yeah, of course, I'll do everything in my power to help."

It sounded like PI Sexton was still milking his investigation, because Hartford's tone would have been less concerned otherwise. Then again, his 'My God' might have meant, 'My God, I'm going to kill her when I find her.' Regardless, he was good. But the fact that Elena was missing —and that I was searching for her—might have complicated his plans.

"There is one thing you can do, Mr. Hartford."

"Please."

"I'd rather discuss it privately. I'm sure you understand."

"Of course, where can we meet?"

"Actually, I'm in your building now," I lied.

"What, you're…here? I—"

"I know you're a busy man, but it shouldn't take long. Especially since your help could save Ms. Sullivan's life."

A pause.

"Mr. Hartford?"

"Yes, of course. Can you give me fifteen minutes?"

"Perfect." Which was, considering I was on the other side of town. "See you soon."

He hung up in the next beat. No doubt in my mind, he was definitely hiding something.

I found a subterranean parking garage east of Lexington Avenue on Fifty-First Street. I practically had to max out my credit card to park there for a few hours. When I emerged from the garage, the smell of barbecue wafted over my senses. A parked food truck—Pigs on a Grill —painted in bright blue, stood on the corner. I hustled off to Hartford's building before being tempted by the pigs.

While climbing to the fortieth floor in the elevator, I imagined what it would be like working next to JR in the Big Apple with all its grittiness. I wasn't sold yet. For me, I still preferred my beloved Eastpoint, Long Island, and its tranquility. Nonetheless, I was sure JR would help me acclimate. Maybe starting with a Pigs on a Grill dish.

Upon entering the Fox Reynolds' lobby with its white marble floors, double glass-top reception desk with silver tones, and midcentury aqua waiting area chairs, I was greeted by a brunette in her early thirties with light brown eyes and a friendly smile.

I added my own grin to the mix. "Hello, I have an appointment with Mr. Hartford."

"Mr. Reed?"

"Yes," I said, somewhat surprised. Hartford must have put the word out about my impending arrival.

I followed her to a deep cherry door down the hall that was cracked open just slightly. "He's expecting you," she said to me as she knocked lightly, and then opened the door to a large office with ceiling-height windows covering two of its walls.

Preston Hartford, III, was haggard and nervous, and that was before I'd even started asking questions. He had a light brown, three-day stubble beard, which helped balance out his receding hairline. He wasn't handsome or ugly—just plain, and in his late forties. If looks were a priority for Elena, Luke was the winner, hands down. As I surveyed the office, my eyes steadied on the modern, Danish rosewood and chrome desk behind which Hartford was seated. It screamed of wealth. I guess money soothed all blemishes.

Hartford stood quickly and approached me. "Elena's disappearance, that's terrible." His grim expression looked genuine, but it was probably more for him and his company than for Elena. "I can't imagine where she might be. I mean, I know where she was heading, but…" He shook his head.

"Thanks for seeing me on such short notice," I said, shaking his hand, which dripped with perspiration. "I've been investigating the whereabouts of Ms. Sullivan for almost a week now. That's when a… concerned person hired me. No one seems to know where she is." I looked out one of the grand windows, surveying the view. "Apparently, Elena was supposed to meet her boyfriend in Newport. They were supposed to be vacationing together." My eyes turned back to Hartford's. "That's the story, anyway."

"Her boyfriend?" He lifted a brow.

"So I'm told. Can you add any more to that, Mr. Hartford?"

He shook his head. "Her boyfriend…," he answered absently.

Apparently, Sexton hadn't reported back to Hartford after all. "I'm sure you can understand, Mr. Hartford, it's rather frustrating. I realize Ms. Sullivan—Elena—is your employee. Do you know if she had problems at work, maybe working on something sensitive or perhaps something in her personal life? Did I mention the boyfriend is also missing?"

Hartford cleared his throat, his arms folded. He stood up a little straighter. "Elena did mention Newport, but never said anything about a boyfriend."

Not to him.

"You did say you were from Long Island, right?"

"Correct."

He stood in thought for a moment. "So this interested party who hired you must live there, right? I mean, otherwise, he or she would have hired someone closer to Newport."

I smirked. "I'm the best at finding missing people. At least, that's what I've been told."

Hartford put up a hand. "Don't take offense, Mr. Reed. I'm a layman at these things. I just figured it would be natural…"

"None taken. I wish I could tell you more, but as I said, the client privilege is sacrosanct. But, again, she and the boyfriend were supposed to meet in Newport. Lovely city. The Cliff Walk is a must."

"Yes, so I'm told." Hartford's eyes suddenly darted around the room. They stopped at the far end of a long, glass and metal table.

I followed his eyes to a picture frame.

His eyes shot back to me, and he feigned a smile. Apparently in his haste, he'd forgotten to remove all the necessary picture frames from the office.

"Married?" I asked breaking the silence.

"Divorced."

I nodded. "Since Ms. Sullivan worked closely with you, I was hoping you knew her boyfriend's name."

He looked at me, and I could have sworn he was about to blurt out his own name but then recovered. "Um…Ben something-or-other."

I gestured towards the door. "An employee?"

He shook his head. "I believe they met at MoMA."

"I'm sorry?"

126

"MoMA. Oh, right, you're from out of town. The Museum of Modern Art." He pointed behind him. "On Fifty-Third Street. If you have time, it's worth spending a few hours."

Odd timing for a piece of cultural advice. "Wish I had the time. Maybe after I've found Ms. Sullivan." I searched Hartford's face, which was stoic.

Hartford obviously knew I wasn't about to hand over any more information, so he shot a glance at his designer watch and announced he had a meeting. He offered his hand. "I'm sorry to be abrupt, but I do have to go. If there's anything else I can help you with regarding Elena —Ms. Sullivan—don't hesitate to contact me." He reached onto his desk and removed a silk laminate business card from a high-gloss mahogany and silver holder and handed it to me. Chairman, Fox Reynolds Corporation.

I stared at the card and hoped he wouldn't ask me for one. I shook his still-clammy hand before making my way slowly past the picture frame. I blinked a few times to be sure I saw it right. The photo had been taken at an event, probably a company extravaganza. I turned back to Hartford. "Lovely couple."

That picture.

Ana Lucía stood smiling with Preston Hartford for the camera.

Gathering my thoughts at the elevator, I couldn't help but wonder about the smiling couple, dressed to the nines and toasting with champagne glasses. Who the hell was Ana to Hartford? Clearly, not his domestic.

Did I get it wrong? If Ana and Hartford were a couple, why would he hire Sexton to follow Elena around? Unless the purpose of hiring the PI was to find out what she was up to regarding the whistleblower investigation. Could be Sexton just took it upon himself to add something more to the investigation. The pervert.

The elevator door opened, and I was about to step in when a woman exiting stopped in front of me.

"Sorry."

I smiled. "Ana." Her eyes jumped up to mine, wide. "What a coincidence! You know, I was just thinking of you."

Apparently, Hartford hadn't managed to contact her quickly enough, because she was clearly taken aback. Haltingly, she stepped back onto the elevator then realized her mistake. She plowed past me.

"You must've mistaken me for someone else," she assured me in perfect English.

I turned, my eyes following her as she sped toward Hartford's office. "Elena and Luke told me to say hi."

I let the elevator door close and went back to the receptionist.

"That woman who just got off the elevator, I met her at a recent event, but, I'm embarrassed to say, I can't remember her name. Ana, I think?"

The woman followed Ana's path and then turned back to me. "You're right. Ana Martinez. She's Mr. Harford's administrative assistant."

"Oh, right, Ana Martinez. Funny, I thought Elena Sullivan was his administrative assistant."

Her mouth twisted to one side. "It's complicated, actually."

"Did you know Elena is missing?"

Her light brown eyes widened. "Missing? No, when?"

I put a finger to my lips and searched her nametag. "Lisa, it might be nothing, so please don't let the word get out. Okay?"

She nodded rapidly.

"Do you know her boyfriend by any chance? Ben? They were supposed to be meeting in Newport for a vacation."

Her eyes narrowed. "Ben?"

"That's what Mr. Hartford thought it was. Apparently they met at MoMA."

She shot a glance toward Hartford's office. "I…if that's what Mr. Hartford told you, it must be true. He knows Elena quite well." Her eyes held mine.

I nodded. "Much appreciated, Lisa."

Pressing the elevator button, I turned my head toward Hartford's office and wondered what he and his assistant were discussing now that they knew I was on to them.

I picked up my car and drove across town to Stone's apartment building. He and his SUV were gone, and I assumed he'd be looking for me. News travels fast.

I figured Elena and Luke had found a safe place for now, so I grabbed a cup of coffee back at Mandel's. While I sipped, I went to findme.com on my phone's browser. I knew the results would be limited, but I was curious about Ana's age, family members, and past and present cities of dwelling.

I found her. Ana Martinez, age thirty-nine, was associated with a few other surnames—all Spanish except one. It didn't mention the types of relationships she'd been in. Her past and present residences included New York City, Austin, and Los Angeles—nothing and no one I was interested in. I took another sip of coffee and called JR.

"I should be getting paid extra for all this information I'm supplying you." JR laughed. "You still in the city?"

"Yep, at my favorite deli, sipping coffee and doing research. And by the way, I'll pay you half of what I'm getting on this non-paying gig." Now it was my turn to laugh.

"I'm sitting around the precinct doing my own research, but I need a break. Give me her name and age, and I'll do the rest."

"Are you looking over my shoulder?"

"I'm a detective, too, remember? Besides, I figure you're on one of those sites that offer little more than that. Okay, maybe a city and relative."

"You got it. I'm on the FindMe site. The 'she' is Ana Martinez, McKenzie's phony domestic I told you about. I just happened to bump into her at Hartford's office. Turns out, she's his administrative assistant. Apparently, she moonlights as McKenzie's domestic. Besides the usual information, I wanna know how she's tied to McKenzie, if at all. I mean, she was in his house, so there's something."

"You're kidding, right? Okay, let me see if I can find a connection. I suppose you're heading back to Newport."

"Not sure. I kinda like Mandel's coffee. I'll hang around a bit. Who knows? Your information might keep me in the city."

"Well, like I told you, the couch is yours as long as you want it."

At noon, a line formed at the entrance of Mandel's deli. I'd last spoken to JR an hour ago and was wondering whether I should have taken off for Newport.

My bladder was full, and I was about to get up and flush out my system when my cell beckoned.

Great timing.

"Sorry it took so long, but I wanted to be thorough. Turns out Ms. Martinez has a clean record, been living in the city a few years, and divorced."

I stepped inside the men's room, found a vacant urinal, and negotiated my predicament as the splashing sound echoed off the ceramic tile walls.

"Too much coffee, eh?"

"Sorry, I'll put it on mute next time."

JR snickered.

"Where did she live before moving here?" I asked.

"Get this: Boston."

I stopped the flow. "Say again?"

"You heard right. That's where she hooked up with McKenzie."

"Boston didn't show up on the FindMe site."

"Well, those sites aren't perfect."

A quick shake before zipping up. "How'd you find this out?"

"Don't ask questions and I won't tell you lies. I can say that Ana was McKenzie's administrative assistant for a few years before she took a job with Hartford's company."

"Damn."

"Right."

I washed my hands, my phone stuck to my ear. "Don't tell me she was married to McKenzie."

"Close—his lover. I told you she was divorced. Well, it was quite messy. Her ex-husband, a guy by the name of Randy Wolfe, also worked for McKenzie's company. Evidently, he found out McKenzie and Ana were working late a lot, if you know what I mean. Wolfe was canned after making threats to McKenzie. He found himself a good attorney, sued McKenzie, and got an out-of-court settlement. I couldn't find the payout amount."

I began trying to connect the dots in my head, but the din from the deli forced me outside. "What was Wolfe's position at McKenzie's company?"

"Hold on."

I searched the street and headed west, finding a quiet area halfway down the block and waited for JR to continue.

"He was head of accounting."

"Do you have any idea where this Wolfe guy is now?"

"Best question of all. You'll never guess."

"Just tell me."

"He works for Hartford's company."

"You're not serious."

"Very. And guess what else? He's in charge of Hartford's accounting department."

"Jesus Christ—this is nuts! So Ana and her ex used to work for McKenzie, with pretty sweet positions. She hooks up with the boss and a messy divorce ensues. She then moves on to Hartford's company, and brings her ex with her? I'm thinking this has got to be some kind of scam."

"Sure sounds like it, Hank."

"Except…Hartford and Elena are a couple—at least, that's what Sexton claimed. And the receptionist at Hartford's office alluded to it, too. Actually, her exact wording was that it was 'complicated.'"

"So maybe he's doing both women."

"A *ménage à trois*." I laughed.

"Works for me," JR said. I could hear the wicked smile in his voice.

"So, what do you think?"

"About the *ménage à trois*?"

"Funny," I muttered. "What I think is that both Ana and Elena are into more than just Hartford. I'm wondering which one set off the whistleblower investigation."

"I'll check into it a little more, try to see whether Mr. and Mrs. Scammer worked the same game with prior employers," JR said.

"Okay, but my main concern isn't infidelity. It's about finding two people. For all we know, the foursome are on different teams, which might not bode well for the losing two."

I was in my car just outside the city, more or less following the speed limit, when JR called.

"There's been a shooting."

My car surged forward. I exited at Riverdale Avenue in the Bronx before heading south. According to JR, a neighbor called in a disturbance coming from the apartment of Randy Wolfe. When the police arrived, the place was empty except for a puddle of blood on the bedroom floor connected by small rivulets to the front door.

Entering the city, I exited at West Ninety-Sixth Street, then turned north on Riverside Drive. Due to gentrification and high rents in the lower parts of the city, more professionals were moving above Ninety-Sixth Street.

At 110th Street, I turned right and drove to Amsterdam Avenue, where I met JR. Even though he wasn't the detective on the case, professional courtesy got me closer to the crime scene.

"It's preliminary," JR started, "but no one has seen Wolfe and we have no idea who the other party was. It doesn't appear he took the elevator, because the only blood was on the stairwell. Wolfe's apartment is on the third floor."

I peered up at the brick and stone prewar building then looked around. A crowd had gathered beyond the crime scene tape. Typical for New Yorkers to think movies and probably assumed a big-time film-maker was in town setting up a Hollywood scene. Not today.

"What about his ex-wife, Ana Martinez? Has anyone seen or contacted her?" I asked.

"I passed her name on to the lead detective. He was surprised when I offered that information. I told him about you. Should be okay."

"I'd like to see her face when she discovers her con-man partner might be out of business."

"Assuming she wasn't the other party."

A detective in his mid-thirties (I assumed, although his soft facial features made him look like a teenager) with short, black hair and a shield hanging around his neck headed our way. JR introduced me to Detective Connors. His deep, baritone voice was a quirky contrast to his baby face.

I told the detective I'd been looking into two missing people, and Randy Wolfe's name had surfaced along with that of the ex-wife.

He nodded. "This a Long Island case?" He asked innocently.

"Long story, but the short answer is no."

Connors searched my face a moment, then JR's. "We'll leave it at that for the time being. Anyway, it's too early to assess the incident, other than Wolfe's next-door neighbor calling the cops after hearing yelling and then what sounded like a pop. Outside of a few pieces of furniture knocked over—and the blood—it doesn't look like the place was touched."

I asked, "Has anyone called the ex-wife?"

Connors pointed to the crime scene tape. "One of my guys found her business card on the desk and tried her cell. She's not picking up."

I searched the crowd, which had risen to around fifty now. I was interested in a particular female face, but didn't see her. I took out my phone, stepped a few feet away, and called Hartford's office. JR stood next to me. "Yes, Lisa, this is Mr. Reed from this morning. I forgot to ask Mr. Hartford a question, shouldn't take long."

She hesitated. "He's left for the day."

I stared knowingly at JR. "Oh…well, I guess Ana, his administrative assistant, can help. Can you patch me through to her?"

She cleared her throat. "I'm afraid she's gone for the day, too."

"Ah. Okay, thanks."

I hung up. "We have a problem. She and Hartford have left the office."

I decided to fill Connors in with the pertinent information for his investigation.

"So you're saying they're a couple for con purposes only?"

I shrugged. "Looks that way. My guess is that Ana Martinez and Randy Wolfe discovered some kind of impropriety with Hartford's company. They and another employee began feeding a reporter damning information. It has to do with whistleblowing. Something must have gone wrong."

"Maybe one of them got greedy and decided not to share," Connors said.

I nodded. "I thought of that."

If Preston Hartford, III, had known about the whistleblowers, he would have taken action to thwart it. Maybe Randy Wolfe was the first of several on his hit list. PI Sexton claimed that Hartford had hired him to follow Elena Sullivan around, but maybe it had nothing to do with cheating. And maybe since Sexton hadn't found Elena and Luke, Hartford had to hire a second PI, Danny Stone. Were Stone and Sexton PIs, or hired killers?

I left my business card with Detective Connors, hoping he would have better luck dealing with Ana and Hartford. I entered my car and drummed on the steering wheel. With Hartford and Ana out of the office, I tried Lisa once more.

"There's been a terrible accident at Randy Wolfe's apartment." I let it sink in a few seconds, then said, "Ana needs to know what happened, and she's not picking up her phone."

"Oh, God, that's terrible."

"Where did she go, Lisa? Was she with Mr. Hartford?"

"They're at a medical device conference at the Hilton Millennium on Church Street. It's downtown."

A quickie, perhaps?

"Lisa, you intimated that Mr. Hartford and Elena Sullivan might be involved. Where does Ana fit in?"

"Oh, God," she repeated.

"It's okay. It stays with me. Was Mr. Hartford involved with both women?"

"'Course not."

"So the conference is strictly business?"

"As far as I know. Look, Mr. Reed, I don't feel comfortable talking about this. I could lose my job."

"Okay. But Lisa, the police will be paying the company a visit before long, and they'll be asking much tougher questions about Mr. Wolfe. Just tell the truth."

The Hilton was near ground zero, and I assumed the traffic and parking would be difficult, so I opted for the subway.

It was a good choice. I emerged from the subway after twenty minutes. Upon entering the Hilton, I surveyed the lobby, and then headed to the front desk. I asked the tall, dark-haired clerk where the Medical Device Conference was being held.

"One flight up. You can take the elevator if you like." He pointed.

The meeting room door was open, and I stuck my head inside. A sea of heads were pointed at the speaker standing at the podium in the front of the room. The topic of the meeting sounded too technical for me, but I wasn't there to learn about medical devices. As I surveyed the room, I noticed a familiar face listening in front of the dais: Preston Hartford, III. I searched the crowd for Ana, too, but apparently, she wasn't interested in this gibberish. Who could blame her?

At least Hartford had an alibi. Not sure about Ana. I turned and gazed down at the lobby behind me and smiled. There was Ana—blabbering into her phone and slouching against a hotel column. She didn't look too thrilled. She was less happy when she saw me approaching. She gave me a 'God, not you again' look, and immediately slipped the phone in her bag. She made to scurry away, but then stopped. She spun around to me, her face beet-red, and pointed an angry finger.

"This is harassment. I know who you are, Detective, and I told you before, you have me mistaken for someone else."

"It's just that you look so much like McKenzie's domestic. Oh, by the way, someone killed him, Ana."

"Well, I certainly didn't—"

"I'm not accusing you of anything yet." I tilted my head and grinned. "But you were pretending to be his domestic. I should have realized right away from your soft skin and French nails that you were an impostor. I can call the Newport Police department and tell them where I last saw you, unless you want to tell me what you're up to."

Her eyes darted around the lobby before stopping at the conference room doors above. "It's complicated," she said, and her tone was softer.

"But you can't charge me with anything." She met my eyes. "It could be dangerous."

"It already is. There was a disturbance at your ex-husband's apartment a few hours ago. Somebody was shot, maybe killed. The locals are looking for him. Know anything about that?"

Her face blanched. "What are you talking about?"

"If you'd picked up your phone this morning, a detective would have been able to inform you."

She closed her eyes. "This can't be happening." Catching me by surprise, she grabbed hold of my shoulder for support. "Please," she said in a low voice, "get me out of here."

Ana had a room at the Hilton on nineteenth floor. We rode the elevator up and when the doors opened, she peeked out in both directions, grabbed my wrist, and pulled me inside her room. The suite consisted of a king-size bed and two windows that overlooked the East River. Not bad, considering Hartford's company was paying for it.

She bolted the door and turned to me. "He must have found out," she said, fear registering in her eyes. "Especially if what you said is true about Randy."

"Oh, it's true, all right. But if you want me to keep you safe, no more lies."

Ana nodded quickly. Then she crossed the room, peered out the window, studied the street below, and then returned to me. "Look, it was supposed to be easy. All we needed to do was gather enough information to put him away and claim the whistleblower reward." She met my eyes but remained silent.

"I know about you and Randy conning McKenzie out of a chunk of change," I told her. "I have a detective looking into your past as we speak. What will it reveal, Ana Martinez?"

She held up a hand. "Okay, yes. It's true about McKenzie. But Hartford is different. This is legitimate." Then she mumbled, "I guess it doesn't pay to go legit."

"I'll know if you're telling me the truth."

A quick glance. "After our falling-out with McKenzie, Randy and I needed to find work. I knew Preston Hartford from the business world and asked for a position in his company. He knew Randy and I had worked for McKenzie, so he hired us both. I could tell by his questions that he wanted the scoop on McKenzie and his business." She paused. "There really wasn't much to tell him, and he dropped it after a while."

She took a breath. "Then one day, out of the blue, McKenzie called me. He knew Randy and I were working for Hartford's company now, and he told me he had reason to believe my boss was scheming to defraud the government. It had to do with some phony medical device gimmick, some kind of drug test for treatment centers and sober homes —a lot of that was going on in Florida." She stopped, her eyes flitting out the window again. "McKenzie wouldn't say how he knew, but claimed there'd be a substantial whistleblowing reward if Hartford was convicted. He told me all he cared about was that Hartford went down. They'd been bitter enemies for years."

"Enemies?"

"Yeah, well, business stuff, you know, stealing secrets from each other." Ana sighed as though she were purging her sins. She met my eyes. "I hope Randy's okay."

"It might be nothing," I said, to keep her going.

It worked. She nodded and went on. "Once we agreed to join him, McKenzie said we'd have to split the reward money four ways. He said Elena and this new reporter boyfriend, Luke DuPont, were also going to be a part of the investigation. Randy and I were fine with that, and given what'd happened with us and McKenzie, I kind of felt we owed him."

Right, owed him.

I paced the room before coming back to stand in front of Ana. "I can understand you might need a reporter, but where does Elena fit in, other than being Hartford's lover?"

"It's not like that. She was playing him to gather information, but they were never lovers, though not for Hartford's lack of trying. Honestly, the man's a creep, insanely jealous. He thinks he owns his employees, especially the women. He was crazy over Elena because she's beautiful."

"I know. I've seen photos. But what about you? You're beautiful."

She smiled. "Are you hitting on me?"

"No," I said, maintaining my hard-shelled cop expression, "and that's not an answer."

She shook her head. "Hartford thinks Randy and I are still married, so I guess that's why he never pursued me. And like I said, he's crazy over Elena."

"That was good for McKenzie, at least until Luke came along."

"What do you mean?"

"Well, if she wasn't involved with Hartford, McKenzie didn't have to worry about her cheating on him."

"What? No, you have it all wrong. Elena is Warren McKenzie's niece."

"His niece?" Ana must have noticed the confusion on my face.

"I should know, Hank. I worked with her at her uncle's company. Though, I must admit, at first, she wasn't too happy with Randy and me for obvious reasons. But now we're working together against Hartford."

The confusion remained on my face. "You obviously didn't know. Elena worked at McKenzie's company before she moved to New York. Hartford hired her on the spot, not knowing she'd worked for his competitor. He liked the way she looked and must have figured he'd have a chance with her."

"He didn't ask her about her prior employment?" I asked, trying to piece the story together.

"Like I said, he was smitten. I don't think he cared what her background was. So, no, he didn't ask for a résumé. Elena started searching for incriminating information almost immediately. Then one day she's at a bar in the city and meets Luke, strikes up a conversation with him, finds out he's a reporter." Ana made her way to the window again, fidgeting with the hem of her blouse. "After she got to know him a little, she told Luke what she was up to. As an eager reporter, he wanted in." She looked at me and shrugged.

It made sense, for the most part.

"What I don't get is your whole fake-domestic appearance."

She waved a hand. "That's a story for another day. It was really just a coincidence that you popped up on the same day the files were in the house. I needed to keep them safe."

Ana's answers appeared to be honest, but I still didn't trust her.

"Okay, so you agreed to split the whistle reward four ways. Well—three maybe, in case one party wasn't around to collect his or her share."

She glared. "That's not funny. I hope you don't think I had something to do with that. I was here all morning."

"So was Hartford. It doesn't mean you guys couldn't have put a hit on Randy."

"Oh, please. Why would I do that?"

"More money?"

She shook her head and began pacing the room, stopping by the window each time she passed it. Her fingers slid down the curtain. "I just want you to know, Randy and I had nothing to do with McKenzie's murder. That…kid, I have no idea who he was, but he did it. The papers said it was about revenge."

"The kid was McKenzie's landscaper. Apparently, he'd ask to use the bathroom when he cut the grass. Seems he did on the day you were there."

Her eyes widened. "That kid? True, I let him use the bathroom, but he left right after he was done. He even thanked me. That's scary."

I thought a moment. "What do you know about Hartford hiring a PI to follow Elena around in Newport? He thought she was cheating on him."

She nodded. "Like I said, they weren't lovers, so she couldn't have been cheating on him. I guess he wanted to find out who she was sleeping with. Creepy, huh?"

"I happened to bump into the PI in Newport; his name is Sexton. Tall, a little overweight. Not good at pretending to be an FBI agent, but he is a good photographer."

"All I know is Hartford was upset that Elena all of a sudden took off on vacation. He was suspicious and wanted to know who she was with."

I asked Ana about Danny Stone then.

"Who?"

"Another PI, and a former Navy SEAL. I met him, too. He claims to be protecting Elena."

Ana shrugged. "Can't help you there, Hank."

"Well, if he is working for Hartford, I wouldn't be surprised if he was Randy's morning visitor."

She abruptly turned to me from the window. "Shit, Hartford's downstairs." Her eyes pleaded with me. "You have to help me."

The connecting room door flew open. Randy Wolfe rushed in, directing a Walther P22 handgun at us.

"This isn't playtime, Ana. The boss is looking for you." Wolfe's lips held a sneer. He wagged the gun in my direction. "And what are you doing in here with this guy?"

She ran over to Wolfe, but he put up a hand. "What's going on?"

"Oh my God, you're alive! I thought something bad had happened to you." She turned and glared at me. "You said he was dead."

"Actually, I said something like he *could* be dead." I nosed Wolfe. "Apparently, I was wrong."

He smirked, then gave me a curious look. "Hey, you must be Detective Reed. I heard about you." He gave Ana a wink. "What are you doing here?"

I kept my eyes on his weapon. "We were just making funeral arrangements. But it looks like that won't be necessary."

"Guess not, asshole. "He waved his gun at me again. Wolfe stood about five-eight and looked to be around forty. A ridiculous comb-over attempted to deny the fact that he was balding badly. His slender frame wouldn't be a problem to overpower—except that he had that Walther in his hand.

"You do know NYPD is looking for you," I said, keeping an eye on the gun, which he held steadily in my direction. "I think they'd be interested in hearing your side of the story."

Wolfe's expression softened. "I'll get around to telling them soon. Right now, there are more pressing issues."

"Seriously?"

"Here's the thing, Detective. We're almost finished with our investigation, and then we'll hand over everything to the authorities. We need to do this without distractions, like the guy who broke into my apartment this morning. He was hired by the enemy."

That was a pleasant surprise. Wolfe had just handed me his defense for whatever had happened in his apartment.

"I'm not your enemy," I said. "And I wasn't following you, or Ana. I'm here because I promised a friend I'd find Luke. She was concerned that something unfortunate had happened to him. Once I find him and let her know he's okay, I'm gone."

Ana said, "Randy, he's a cop, not some thug trying to stop us. Let him go before we get into trouble."

"She's right, Randy. My purpose here has nothing to do with your whistleblower investigation."

Wolfe squinted his eyes, musing over my response, but then shook his head. "Luke doesn't wanna be found until *after* the investigation. And as for your friend, Luke's not interested in being found. You get what I'm saying?" He grinned.

"Fair enough." I started for the door.

"Get back here," he threatened. "I'm not a fool. I don't trust you, cop or no cop. You're gonna have to stay put until we're gone."

Ana, who had distanced herself from Wolfe a couple feet, stepped back even further. She must have been reading her crazy ex's unhinged demeanor, because her eyes begged me to do something.

"Randy, please," she said, "this is not a good idea. Just leave."

"Without you, dear? I don't think so. You're coming with me, just as soon as we take care of the detective here."

"Goddammit, Randy, stop this!" She started in his direction, and he shifted the barrel of his gun onto her.

"Don't you make me, Ana."

She stopped in her tracks.

"He'll be fine," Wolfe said, his voice syrupy sweet. He removed a pair of plastic zip-tie handcuffs from his jean pocket. He looked at me with beady, bloodshot eyes. "Turn around," he demanded.

I glanced over at Ana and gave her a slight, reassuring nod. Then I turned my back and stuck out my arms.

The last thing I heard before being cold-cocked was, "Have a great day, Reed."

THIRTEEN

These head bumps were becoming a workplace hazard. At least Wolfe had been good enough to slam the other side of my skull. The way I was going, another blow might put me out permanently. For some reason, Wolfe hadn't cuffed me after all—small favors—so I crawled over to the bed and, with difficulty, lifted myself up. The room was spinning out of control, so I leaned against the bedframe for a few minutes. When I felt I could safely walk a few feet, I trudged to the bathroom, where I soaked my head and face in the sink. At least there were clean towels.

Slogging back into the room, I found the minibar and removed a bottle of water.

Bill me.

The end-table clock flashed three-ten. I assumed it was p.m. In that case, I'd been out about an hour, which meant Wolfe and Ana were long gone.

I searched my cell for incoming texts or calls. I'd missed a call and a text from JR. The message read, simply: *Checking in. Call me.*

"I was distracted for an hour," I said when I returned the call. "Another love tap."

"Christ, Hank, anymore of those and you'll be wearing a nametag that says 'Hi, my name is Hank.' Want me to pick you up and take you to New York-Presbyterian? It's close by."

I thanked him, declined the offer, and filled JR in on events leading up to Randy's Wolf's love tap.

"And you're sure it was Wolfe?"

"Ana just about leaped on the guy and called out his name. He was insistent that she leave with him. He knew I was a cop and that I wasn't interested in stopping their investigation—"

Then it dawned on me. "JR, I think Randy Wolfe is changing sides. I'll bet Hartford found out about the investigation and offered him more money to put it to bed. He doesn't want me anywhere near Wolfe or Ana." I paused. "Wolfe is a true con artist: his allegiance is only to money."

JR added, "If that's true, Wolfe wouldn't have to split the reward with the others, including Ana."

"Right. But that's only if he finds the others before I do. He already has Ana." I pressed my tender skull and winced.

"I'm driving back to Newport ASAP."

My head pounded, and I hoped Ana had pain reliever somewhere in her room. I noticed a cosmetic case sitting on the bathroom vanity table and opened it, hoping to find anything for my headache. I removed lip liner, lipstick, perfume, and a compact before removing a bottle of Tylenol.

Christ!

I flipped off the top and tried shaking the pain killers into my hand. It was empty. At least I thought. I peered inside then noticed a matchbook cover stuck in the bottle—odd. I pulled it out and unfurled the cover. The front showed a picture of a charming New England inn surrounded by a winter scene, and a sign hanging out front that read "Wharf Inn, Newport, Rhode Island."

Huh?

I tried keeping my headache in check and called the Wharf Inn's phone number listed on the cover.

"Ana Martinez's room, please," I said steadying myself before struggling over to the bed.

"Sorry, sir, there is no one here by that name," said the middle-aged-sounding woman on the other end.

"That's strange, how about Elena Sullivan?" I asked, sitting.

"Sorry, sir. Are you sure you have the right inn?"

"Oh, I'm so embarrassed. You're right—they're staying at another place. For Wharf Inn, I meant Luke DuPont."

"Okay, let's see. Hold on."

I heard some taps and then, "Sorry, sir, they must all be staying elsewhere."

I hung up and stuck the matchbook cover in my pants pocket, then struggled out of the room. Downstairs, I checked the lobby, then the conference room. The meeting was still going on, but Hartford was no longer in attendance. Surprise, surprise.

Outside, I flagged a taxi to the parking garage. After paying an ungodly rate for my car's short stay, I shot out for Newport. On the Henry Hudson, I checked in with JR.

"I was just about to call you, Hank. There's been an accident on the Major Deegan in the Bronx. Seems your friend PI Stone hit the median. The paramedics took him to Bronx-Lebanon off the Grand Concourse."

"He was the driver?"

"Apparently. There wasn't anyone else in the car."

I came upon a highway sign. "JR, I just passed the George Washington exit on the Henry Hudson. I need directions."

The Bronx-Lebanon Hospital stood on the Grand Concourse, a major north-south thoroughfare in the Bronx less than ten minutes from Yankee Stadium. I doubted Stone was in the mood for a game.

I found parking several blocks away and surveyed the community. A few abandoned buildings littered the area, and I prayed my car would still be standing on all four tires when I returned. It crossed my mind as I walked that I might be going on a wild goose chase. Had some poor sucker stolen Stone's SUV and driven off? He obviously hadn't made it to his destination.

I entered the emergency room and flashed my shield at the triage nurse. "The guy the medics brought in from a ten fifty-three, do you have his name?"

A middle-aged black woman eyed my shield then shrugged. "You'll have to ask them." She pointed to two blue uniforms.

After a quick exchange, they directed me to surgery, where I found two more officers standing around, chitchatting. As I approached, one put up a hand. "Where are you going?"

I opened my jacket, revealing my shield. "I think I know the guy in surgery. I need to speak to him as soon as possible."

They met each other's eyes. "You're too late, detective. He was DOA," said the taller, white, male cop. He pointed inside.

"Looks like he hit the underpass wall head on," suggested his partner. Latina, female, cute. She continued, "It doesn't look like he died from the crash, though. More likely from the gunshot wound. At this point, we can't tell you where or when he was shot."

I could.

"What about a name?"

"That we have." The white officer pulled out a pad and read it off to me.

Danny Stone. He must have been taken by surprise or hoodwinked by Randy Wolfe.

"Is that the guy you thought was driving?" the officer asked.

I nodded. "Yeah, that's him. He was a PI, and former SEAL."

"Those guys are pretty instinctive. He obviously didn't see this coming, though."

That was an understatement.

"One of the paramedics said Stone kept repeating he had to 'find her' before he died. Or words to that effect."

"Did he say who, or where?"

"Not according to the medic. Wanna take a look to make sure he's your guy?"

They brought me inside the emergency operating room. I glanced down at Danny Stone, who looked peaceful. At least Wolfe hadn't shot him in the face.

"Where's the wound?" I asked, turning back to the cops.

"Seems he took it on the right side here and bled out. He must have thought he was going to make it wherever that was."

I handed both of the officers my card.

"If you hear anything."

"So this Stone guy wasn't in your jurisdiction?" the Latina cop asked after she'd read my card.

I kept the explanation simple. "Stone was working on a case. I just happened to run into him one night. He was concerned about something, but that's all I know." I shrugged. "I hope you guys find out who did this."

———

I sat in my car, whose tires were intact. I tried to piece together what had happened to Stone. There were a lot of moving parts. First the disturbance inside Randy Wolfe's apartment and now Stone dying from a gunshot wound? Coincidence? Not a chance.

And the paramedic had said Stone needed to find her. I assumed he meant Elena, but that didn't make sense given he'd had no idea where she was. Or had he? And had he planned on find *her* before bleeding out?

My hands squeezed the steering wheel. Why wouldn't Stone have gone to a hospital first? Was he hoping to reach someplace or someone who might take care of his wound, no questions asked?

I tapped JR's name on my phone and called him.

"What's the prognosis?"

"Stone's dead from a gunshot wound. He bled out."

"Gunshot wound? What the hell was he doing driving on the highway?"

"Good question. He must've had a destination in mind. Far away from Randy Wolfe, that's for sure."

"You think it was him?" JR asked.

"No doubt. Wolfe alluded to it in the hotel room. I think Stone was telling me the truth that he was trying to protect Elena. And I'm sure it was *from* Wolfe. It's beginning to make more sense that Wolfe is working with Hartford to eliminate everyone associated with the investigation." I massaged the bridge of my nose. "It also sounds like not all the parties are in agreement with Wolfe's decision to change sides. Which is great for him: fewer people to collect whatever Hartford was willing to pay out."

"And great for Ana?"

"Don't know yet," I replied. "She didn't want to leave with Wolfe at the hotel. Christ, this guy is bad news."

"I'll fill Detective Connors in on your theory, Hank."

"Thanks. Where would the police have impounded Stone's car after the accident?"

"The closest precinct. I'm guessing the forty-fourth, over on 169th Street. Stay where you are. I'll make a call."

I started up the engine, turned on the radio, and searched for a classical station. I stopped when *The Blue Danube* flowed softly through my speakers. I closed my eyes.

JR got back to me within minutes. "Right, the forty-fourth. I spoke to a Detective Manny Hernandez. He's expecting you. The car's impounded because it's considered a crime scene, so you'll be at Hernandez's mercy. I know him; he's a good cop."

I pulled out of my spot and worked my way out of the neighborhood, arriving at the precinct in ten minutes.

I met Hernandez inside. He was forty-something, tall, handsome, and muscular, with a full head of brown wavy hair. I tried not to feel jealous of his good genes. He shook my hand when I introduced myself.

"JR gave me a heads-up you'd be coming." He smiled—nice teeth, too. "So this Stone guy was looking for the same missing people you were, is that right?"

"That's what he told me when I last spoke to him." I shrugged. "He kept telling the paramedics he wanted to 'keep her *safe*' or something to that effect, but then he lost consciousness."

Hernandez nodded, waited for me to continue.

I wanted to keep it short, but said, "I think I know the perp. Your locals are looking for him. I'm hoping the victim's cell phone is in the car. It might help me figure out where he was heading."

Hernandez beckoned and turned. "Follow me."

He pointed to Stone's SUV, demolished on the front end. "There it is. We'll have to wait until the CSU guys process the vehicle, but they oughta be here any minute. You understand, I'm sure."

"Of course."

Two members of the CSU team arrived moments later. They, too, shook hands with Hernandez. Both of them wore blue jackets with NYPD Police Crime Scene Unit lettering on the back. Hernandez introduced us. One was white, the other Latino, both in their early thirties.

"Stay close, and point or ask questions. No touchy," the Latino said with a grin as he snapped on latex gloves.

"Got it," I assured him.

Hernandez said, "Detective Reed is interested in the guy's cell phone, so if you come across it, holler."

I hoped they'd get lucky. There'd be his final calls, both incoming and outgoing, and any text messages. And, if he'd activated GPS, possibly his destination.

Hernandez asked if I wanted some coffee.

"Sure, thanks."

I watched as the team dusted about carefully so as not to screw up the scene.

Hernandez returned with my coffee. "Good luck." I think he was referring to the coffee.

It didn't take long before one team member pulled his head out from the SUV, waving a cell phone. "Detective Reed, take note of these numbers." I pulled out my phone and opened a new dictation.

When he finished reading them off, he scrolled through the phone some more, and then eyed me. "Looks like the victim was heading to Riverdale."

I thanked Hernandez and his CSU team, and told them I owed them one. I now felt guilty I'd sliced Stone's tires. He hadn't been the bad guy. His GPS showed he'd been attempting to reach a woman in Riverdale by the named of Kelly Rule. Cool name.

I was already on my way. I didn't want to call ahead, for fear I might spook this Ms. Rule. Then again, I'd be the one who would have to break the news—assuming Stone meant anything to her.

Riverdale was an upper-middle-class residential neighborhood in the northwest portion of the Bronx. I was taking a chance. For all I knew, the address from her cell phone could prove fruitless. Ms. Rule could be anywhere.

I passed Manhattan College and parked twenty feet away from Kelly Rule's seven-story brick apartment building. Then I dialed her number. After she picked up, I identified myself, then asked her relationship to Stone. She was silent at first then asked the standard, "What is this about?"

"There's been an accident. Danny's at Bronx-Lebanon Hospital."

"Oh, God. Is he okay?"

"I'm afraid it's not good. May I ask your relationship to Mr. Stone? He had your phone number in his contacts list."

She mumbled something inaudible, and then, "Look, I can't talk right now." The line went dead. Within minutes, the door to the lobby flew open and a thirtyish woman with long, auburn hair and wearing jeans and sneakers ran toward a black Honda parked in the lot. She tossed in a small bag, started the engine, and shot out of her spot, tires squealing.

I followed her, staying close as she whizzed by several cars and entered the northbound entrance to the New York State Thruway. There, the traffic was light, so I gave her a five-car-lengths lead. I wondered: If Danny Stone was lying dead in the Bronx, which was south of here, why was Kelly Rule driving north?

After two hours of driving, she hooked a right off Exit 28, West Onteora Trail, and then hung another right onto NY-375 N to Mill Hill Road. She stopped at a Cumberland Farms gas station and convenience store in Woodstock—the one and only.

Thank God! I pulled in to the pump behind hers. She got out, her head darting about nervously, then hustled inside the store. I tried not to stare, but she was stunning. I followed her inside and watched from the candy aisle as she purchased a bottle of water and a ripe red apple—healthy. I settled for coffee and a Snickers bar.

While pumping gas, I munched on the candy bar and steadied my eyes on Kelly, who kept checking her surroundings. When her eyes met mine, I gave her a friendly smile. It wasn't returned.

"Great afternoon for a ride," I said.

Kelly looked impatiently at the digital gas display. It was clear she was desperate to leave.

"A long way from Riverdale, Ms. Rule."

Her eyes shot back to me. She pulled the gas nozzle out of the tank and aimed it at me. "Don't come near me."

Thank God it wasn't loaded.

"I'm a detective. I'm the guy who called you. My name is Hank Reed. We're on the same team, Ms. Rule." I held out my shield. "Why did you race out of your apartment after our conversation?"

Her silence gave me an opening and I stepped closer. "I was at Bronx-Lebanon and saw Danny. He said something about finding *her*. I know who he was looking for. I'm looking for her and another friend, myself, and want them safe. Like I said, we're on the same team."

She stuck the nozzle back in place then broke down. I tossed the Snickers and coffee cup in a trash can and approached her. "Who are you running from?"

She leaned her body against her car, head in her hands. "I don't know."

This was not what I wanted to hear. I put a hand on her shoulder. "I'm really sorry about Danny. It wasn't an accident; he'd been shot."

She wiped her eyes. "I know. He told me what happened."

"He was driving to you?" I raised my eyebrows. "Why didn't he attempt to go to a local hospital?"

She shook her head. "I begged him to, but he didn't think the wound was that bad."

Until he did.

"I'm a nurse. He thought I could fix him up. Oh, God, Danny, why?"

"Did he tell you who shot him?"

She shook her head again. "Only that he had an altercation with a guy in an apartment building in New York City."

I looked around the gas station. We were alone. "The name of the guy who shot him was Randy Wolfe. Does that ring a bell?"

"No." She was crying and pressed against me for support. I hesitantly put my arm around her and patted her back. "I knew he was supposed to find and protect a woman, keep her safe. That's all."

I thought a moment. "Why were you driving up here, Kelly?"

She pointed northward. "I have a cottage. Danny told me to drive there if anything…happened to him. When Danny didn't call me back, and then *you* did, I feared for my life."

That made no sense. "Why were you fearful for your life? I mean, it was Danny's investigation. Are you his wife?"

"His sister. He had information at the house that would eventually be made public."

"Up here in Woodstock?"

She nodded, then wiped her nose.

"Okay, let's get out of here. I'll follow you."

Kelly's house was a few miles from the gas station. I followed her along Tinker Street. With its lush, pastoral views and patches of forest, it reminded me a bit of Sound Avenue back home on Long Island. When we reached Wittenberg Road, she took a right and drove about a quarter mile before turning onto a long, narrow, asphalt driveway a hundred feet off the main road. I peered up at an early-twentieth-century, white clapboard house with gray shingles and black shutters. The closest house was half a football field from here.

Great getaway.

Kelly approached me, her eyes checking the street and then returning to my face. She gave a nervous half-smile. "We're home."

I could tell by the red around her eyes that she'd been crying in the car.

"A long way from Riverdale."

"It's been in the family for decades. We used to summer up here. Now, just occasionally." She trailed off and sighed, then scanned the street again.

"I was checking my rearview mirror the whole way from the Bronx. We're safe," I assured her.

"For now." She turned, and I followed her to the back of the house. Inside, we stepped into an open area where the living room met the kitchen and where a pipe stove stood next to the chimney. Wooden stairs presumably led to the bedrooms upstairs.

To my right, two sets of French doors led to a patio and a back yard —lots of land back there. The place was modest, but private. About two

151

hundred feet beyond the house was a one-car garage with a wooden door in need of a paint job.

"Cozy," I said. "We have cottages like this back home."

"Where's that?" Kelly said somewhat absently as she surveyed the back yard.

"Eastpoint, Long Island."

"Never heard of it," she said, returning her attention to me.

"That's the way we like it." I drew a smile.

She feigned one in return. "Well, I'm in your hands, Detective Reed. There's no one else I can..." She paused. "Danny mentioned you. He said you could be trusted."

My expression slid from one of comfort to confusion. "I don't understand."

"In spite of you slashing his tires." She rolled her eyes and grinned with just the left side of her mouth. "He wasn't thrilled about that, but he did say both of you were trying to keep people safe. Believe me, I wouldn't have brought you here if I didn't think it was true." She pulled in a lungful of air. "He never told me about the case he was working on, only that it was important and could be dangerous. I managed to get *some* information out of him, but like a good PI, Danny was close-mouthed."

I thought a moment, rubbing the two-day stubble that seemed to have just sprung up. "Did Danny say why he thought it was dangerous?"

She shrugged. "Like I said, he was pretty close-mouthed, but I do know it had something to do with a whistleblowing investigation."

I remained silent, wondering how dangerous a white-collar crime could possibly be.

She crossed the room and leaned against the kitchen counter, facing away from me. Her manicured fingernails drummed on the Corian. "Danny was also working on something connected to finding this person he was hired to protect. He said the investigation was becoming...complicated."

She turned back to me. "I guess he was right."

Kelly was holding back tears. I could see she was struggling to keep it together. I moved toward her and placed a hand gently on her arm.

"You must have been close, you and Danny."

"It was just us," she answered. "Our parents died a few years ago in a car accident." She paused then resumed drumming on the countertop with her fingers. "I was married once but it didn't work out. Luckily, it was a clean break, no kids." She smiled wistfully, that same cute, unbalanced grin. "Between Danny going into the military and then his PI business, he was always too busy for a wife and family."

I smiled back at her. Kelly was more than just attractive: she had an ethereal beauty, her features soft and perfect.

"I'm really sorry for your loss, Kelly. I liked Danny, though at first, I wasn't a hundred percent sure what team he was on. I'm glad he was one of the good guys."

"Me too."

"I'm going to find the person responsible, I promise. The couple Danny and I were trying to find are somewhere in Newport, Rhode Island. At least, they were. That's where I started my investigation. Danny ever mention Newport?"

Kelly shook her head. "Sorry." Then a tiny spark illuminated her eyes. She gazed past me and pointed out the window. "I just remembered, it might mean nothing, but Danny spent some time in the garage."

I followed her finger. "Let's go see what he was up to."

The tiny, peeling one-car garage was as old as the house. Kelly unlocked the side door and we were instantly hit with a dank odor.

"Sorry about the smell," Kelly said. She walked over to the garage door and pulled it open, letting in a gush of fresh air. I surveyed the area. Without a car, the place was bare except for a beach chair, lawnmower, and a few garden tools.

"I come up here as a retreat. I love gardening. Too bad the season's almost over."

Looking around, I couldn't imagine what Danny would have been up to in this garage, unless he worked on his car. Against the back wall, a wooden ladder was leaning. "Did your brother do work around the house?" I turned to Kelly. "Maybe use that ladder in the back?"

She laughed. "No way, not Danny. My dad used that ladder occasionally. Except...now that I recall, Danny did use it to climb up to the attic sometimes."

I gazed up at the garage ceiling.

"Not here. In the house."

I grabbed the eight-foot ladder, then followed Kelly into the house and up the stairs. She stopped at a small, cozy bedroom. The door was open and I glanced inside. A few military photos were perched on the dresser, along with some mediocre sports trophies. I assumed this was Danny's bedroom.

Kelly pointed to the ceiling. "There."

I steadied the ladder against the wall and climbed a few rungs until I could reach the small, black metal handle screwed into a square indentation on the ceiling. I pushed the scuttle panel up into the attic then stuck my head in. I pulled back quickly, met by a waft of the same musty smell as the garage. I shook my head and looked down at Kelly.

"You wouldn't happen to have a flashlight? It's totally black up here."

"Oh, there's a switch to the left of the opening," Kelly told me.

I felt around, and when I found it, flipped it up. A dangling, naked bulb lit up one side of the attic. "Have you been up here lately?"

"Me? I've never been tempted. I'm afraid of heights." Kelly laughed lightly. "What's that, nine feet up?"

Something like that.

"Danny use this place for anything besides storage? There're a few cardboard boxes stacked up here, but that's about it."

After a moment, she answered, "Not sure. I remember one time I boosted a few boxes up to him. I climbed up about halfway and stopped. That's my limit." Kelly laughed again, but this time her voice was hollow.

"Hank, I think there's another switch for the ceiling fan near the light switch. I suspect you'll need it."

"Much obliged." Negotiating the last few rungs, I climbed inside the attic and turned on the much-needed fan. The ceiling couldn't have been more than six feet high. I kept my head carefully bent down to avoid any further damage to that much abused region.

"I think you might have to crouch most of the time. Danny did. You guys are about the same size." A pause before she softly corrected herself. "Were."

I disappeared from her view. The boxes were labeled in thick Sharpie with people's names I wasn't familiar with. Stone's previous clients? I had hoped to find the names of Elena Sullivan, Warren McKenzie, or Preston Hartford, but none of those were here.

I sighed in the stale, dank air. Oh well. "Nothing here," I called down.

"What about on the other side?"

I peered into darkness. "Think there might be something back there?"

"Maybe. Danny might have a desk and small chair up there. I think there's another light switch somewhere on that side. Sorry I can't be more helpful."

Christ.

"I'm sure you'll find it."

Or fall into a big black hole.

The unpainted walls angled, wooden beams jutting out. I hated A-frame construction. I began sweating, and it had little to do with the heat. The walls felt like they were closing in on me. I closed my eyes, took a deep breath, and then stepped tentatively on the creaking floor, my hands extended.

Having fun yet?

"Feel around on your right side, Hank."

Thanks, said the blind man.

"Be careful."

How sweet.

I assumed the switch would be at the same height as the previous one, so I felt around and after another two feet, found it. Flipping it on, the rest of the room was illuminated.

"Found it."

I surveyed this side of the attic. Like Kelly said, there was a desk and tiny chair.

"You okay up there?"

I turned my head toward the opening. "I'm good."

"Want a glass of water?"

I smiled. "Not right now, thanks."

"I'll be right here if you need me."

Very comforting.

"When was the last time Danny climbed up here?"

"I don't really know. He'd been coming to the house more often the past few weeks."

I sat tentatively on the chair and had a flashback to Mrs. Kleinbub's seventh grade classroom. I was about to get up and leave when I noticed a two-foot, glass-enclosed wooden square frame on the wall over the desk, two curved metal handles attached.

I pulled back on the handles. Inside, photos and index cards were thumbtacked to a cork board. Cognizant of the low, angled ceiling, I stood slowly and peered over. Danny Stone's latest case stood in front of me. I scanned the walls of the area again, and found another opening, one that could fit several boxes. Bingo!

"Any luck?"

Kelly's head popped into the attic, and she waved. "That wasn't so bad, actually. Find anything?"

Oh, yeah.

We sat at the kitchen table, sipping coffee. I told Kelly her brother had been a great PI.

Stone had strung together the investigation. He had the characters and the motive. From the info I'd found in the attic, I now knew that he'd been hired by McKenzie. Protecting Elena had been the utmost part of his contract, but his mission had also included acquiring and putting together the information Elena gathered from Hartford's company—sort of as a backup for what Elena and Luke were doing. That piqued my interest. Why two sets of information?

Stone's investigation had begun soon after Elena started collecting incriminating evidence on Hartford's company. And at the same time, McKenzie had been filling Stone in on any information he had on his competitor.

According to Stone, Elena had started to get suspicious of Randy Wolfe. Whenever she and Wolfe had connected, he'd hinted that Hartford would probably be willing to pay twice as much to bury the evidence against him.

Evidently, Wolfe, the ultimate conman, had decided that Hartford's job would be more lucrative and less work. Elena had passed her concerns on to McKenzie and Luke, and they'd all agreed to play along with Wolfe—and Ana, who would go along with whatever her ex asked her to. Elena told Wolfe she wanted to gather all the incriminating information first, to make sure they had enough evidence to go either way. Wolfe agreed.

But McKenzie knew what Wolfe and Ana were capable of from his past dealings with them and became alarmed. Soon after they figured out what the two hustlers were up to, Luke and Elena took whatever information they had gathered and went into hiding. Even her protector, Stone, had no idea where they went.

I let Kelly absorb my revelations, then said, "At some point, Wolfe must have discovered Danny was spying on them."

Kelly's fiery eyes weighed heavy on mine. "He set my brother up!" she cried.

I touched her hand. "I don't know for sure at this point, but I'm leaning that way, too. Which means he's probably been to Danny's Manhattan apartment."

Her eyes widened.

"Do you know if Danny had any files there? Similar to the ones I found in the attic?"

"I don't know."

I pulled out my cell phone and called JR.

"Where the heck are you?"

Such a concerned parent.

"I'm in Woodstock."

"Say again?"

"The one and only. I'm with Stone's sister."

"Oh yeah? How is she?"

I met Kelly's eyes. "What you'd expect. I need your buddy Connors to check Stone's apartment. Wolfe might have already been there."

"He did check it and it was ransacked. Anything important in the apartment?"

"Good question. I'll tell you one thing: I found a treasure trove up here. What started as an exposé was turning into extortion. And that makes at least two of the players guilty. I'm not sure yet about Elena and Luke."

"Assuming they weren't, Hank, how come they hadn't gone to the authorities?"

"Good point, don't know. From what I can tell from Stone's collection of information, they were in the final stages. After McKenzie was killed, the information he was feeding them dried up. I can tell they were very close. I'm hoping they have the final pieces somewhere safe. I need to find the two of them before Wolfe does."

I stood and walked into another room. "We know what the guy's capable of. I'm afraid if he finds Elena and Luke, he won't hesitate to kill them."

"And Ana? Where does she fit in?"

"She's Wolfe's protégé. Whatever he says, she'll go along with. For all I know, that scene at the hotel room where she thought Wolfe was going to harm her was a ruse."

"Unless it wasn't. Wolfe might have decided the same fate for her."

"True. Guess we'll see."

I ended the call and walked back inside. Kelly had been weeping softly. "I need to see my brother."

With all that was going on in the attic, I'd forgotten about Stone. He wasn't going anywhere but the morgue, awaiting his next of kin to identify his body.

I placed a hand on hers. "I'll take you. I'll call ahead and tell them we'll be there in a few hours."

She shook her head. "Thanks, Hank, but I need to do this alone. I need some time by myself."

I smiled at her encouragingly. "I understand."

"You can stay here if you want. Danny's bedroom is—"

"The couch is fine. Thanks." Then I told Kelly I needed a favor.

A big one.

FOURTEEN

K elly's Woodstock house would become my headquarters until at
least one of the players popped his or her head up. While I was
two and a half hours from New York City, and more than three from
Newport, I felt more comfortable here. I wasn't familiar with my
surroundings, but the community was peaceful and reminded me of my
beloved Eastpoint. And in this place, I could hear anyone pull into the
long, gravel driveway.

While Kelly was on her way to ID her brother, I studied Stone's
extensive notes; he was good—there'd been nothing too small to over-
look. Unfortunately, his only contact, McKenzie, had been killed, and
all information had dried up afterwards. Still, Stone continued on,
hoping to find Elena and keep her safe.

That objective—and finding Luke—would continue to be my
mission.

With plenty of time to spare, I remained at the kitchen table,
drinking more coffee and reading. At around eight in the evening,
having eaten nothing since my bagel that morning, my stomach began
roaring like an angry lion. I checked the refrigerator—empty. Made
sense. Kelly wouldn't have made the trip up here if it wasn't for me.

I opened a few kitchen drawers, finally finding several local menus.

Funny, everyone keeps menus. After perusing them for a couple minutes, I settled on the Catskill Mountain Pizza Company on Mill Hill Road, in Woodstock. Kelly had written ballpoint on the cover: *Best pizza this side of Brooklyn*. Quite an endorsement. I'd let her know if I agreed.

The late summer evening breeze was perfect for driving, and I opened my windows and breathed in fresh air. I reached a single-story frame house with a steep-pitched red roof, once a residence but now a restaurant. A green door and fence complemented the building. Homey.

Inside, an enticing aroma swirled about, the air filled with the evidence of a good Italian kitchen: fresh mozzarella, ripe tomatoes, hand-tossed dough. Thank God I didn't have to wait. I was seated at a small wooden table, and when my server approached, I was ready to order, thanks to the menu back at Kelly's place.

A woman in her late forties with salt-and-pepper hair and a delicious smile—okay, I was really hungry—greeted me. Her name tag read "Petal." Interesting name.

I started with a mug of Rogue Dead Guy Ale craft beer—don't ask—and a white Popeye pizza, which came with ricotta, Romano, and mozzarella cheeses, fresh garlic, tomatoes, basil, and, of course, spinach.

"You must be a regular," Petal said.

"I'm not, actually, but I did have a chance to review the menu back at a friend's house. She recommended the pizza."

"You won't be disappointed." She pointed at me and promised.

I sat back, took in my surroundings. Happy faces everywhere, eating the best pizza this side of Brooklyn. I suddenly felt lonely. I missed Patrice and wondered what she was doing right now, though quite frankly, with our six-hour time difference making it after two in the morning in Paris, I doubted she was doing or consciously thinking anything.

Petal brought my Rogue Dead Guy Ale and said with a wink that I'd just die for the flavor of it.

"I might want to die a few more times before the night's over." I made some small talk with Petal, found she'd been born and raised in Woodstock. I figured if her parents had attended the lovefest in 1969—which had been held in the nearby town of Bethel, there'd be a good chance Petal was an offspring of that weekend. I mean, her name *was* Petal.

She delivered my Popeye pizza piping hot. "Watch your tongue," she warned.

I devoured the first slice, gulped down my beer to put out the fire on my tongue, then went for a second slice. Oh, Popeye, you're the best!

It had been several hours since Kelly left for the Bronx, and I tried to imagine how she was dealing with seeing her brother at the morgue. I'd advised her to drive directly to her Riverdale apartment afterward. But as I gazed up from my beer mug, there she was, standing in front of me.

Christ!

"What are you doing here?" My tone was a little too rough. I tried again with a playful smile in my voice. "Did you fly to the Bronx?"

Her swollen, red eyes told me she had been crying. She pulled up a chair and sat across from me. "I couldn't go. I mean, I drove halfway there, then turned back. I cried all the way."

I touched her hand. "Kelly, I'm so sorry." I suddenly felt guilty enjoying my meal, and asked, "Can I get you something?"

She shook her head.

I thought a moment. "How did you find me?"

She forced a smile. "You left the menu on the counter. I figured you might be here." She pointed to my Rogue Dead Guy Ale. "What are you drinking?"

Oh, boy.

I called Petal over.

She and Kelly exchanged quick greetings.

"Two more of these," I said, not mentioning the Rogue Dead Guy.

"Sure, and another place setting?"

Kelly put up a hand. "Just the beer, thanks."

Petal returned with our brews, and I watched as Kelly gulped hers down.

I leaned forward. "I really wish you had taken my advice and stayed in Riverdale tonight."

Kelly glared. "Sorry, Hank, my plans have changed."

Outside, Kelly said, "I'm sorry for being difficult before. I made the call like you asked and left a message. But you have to put yourself in my place."

I knew what she meant. Kelly obviously had a little bit of her brother's toughness in her. "Okay, but you have to listen to me now."

She nodded. "I'll meet you back at the house. I want to pick up some ice cream. Comfort food soothes me." She pointed to the Cumberland Farms store where we first met pumping gas.

That sounded like a good idea. I could use a few items myself. "I'll go. You drive directly to your house. If you notice anything off, keep driving and call me."

"Yes, father." Kelly scrunched up her nose.

"I'm serious. I'll be there soon."

I watched her drive away and shook my head. She was one tough woman.

Inside the store, I picked up some junk food, a six-pack of Bud, a toothbrush, soap, and deodorant. I placed the items on the counter, and the cashier, a young, pimply kid around nineteen, asked if that was everything.

Oh! The ice cream.

"I'll be right back," I told him. I found the freezer and peeked inside, then realized Kelly had never mentioned what flavor of ice cream she wanted. I took out my cell and dialed her number.

Bruce Springsteen's *Born in the U.S.A.* sang out, followed by, "I'm tied up right now." Not funny.

I tried again, and this time left a message inquiring about her ice cream of choice.

Back at the counter, I gave it another try, but still she didn't pick up. The store was empty so I wasn't holding anyone up.

"Damn." I hung up on Springsteen. I turned. Looking back over my shoulder, I told the kid, "Hold my items, I'll be back," and rushed for the door.

I hoped Kelly was either on the phone with someone more important than me, or her battery had died. I stepped on the gas pedal and reached her bungalow in less than five minutes. The house was dark and the driveway empty. Where was she?

I passed the house and parked a hundred feet from the end of her property. After surveying my surroundings, I darted out of the car and skulked my way through thick brush and trees on the side of her house. That sucked. I reached her back yard and took cover behind an oak. The closer I got the better view of the driveway.

That's when I noticed Kelly's black Honda nosed against the garage. She had made it home. I stepped closer to the garage and took out my cell. I dialed again. I heard the faint tones of Springsteen. I walked slowly around the car, following the sound and arriving, finally, at the trunk.

No way.

No wonder she hadn't picked up. I placed my ear against the garage door.

Quiet.

Gazing up at the house, I thought I saw a brief wave of a flashlight moving about on the second floor.

Crouching down, I put my face close to the trunk. "Kelly?"

A muffled sound.

I popped open the trunk release and there she was, her mouth wrapped with duct tape, her hands and legs bound behind her. She looked like a pretzel. I pulled her out and removed the tape as gently as possible.

I put my finger to my mouth and she nodded.

"Who?" I whispered.

"I don't know. He was too quick."

"A man?"

She nodded. "He had a deep voice. He came out of there." She nodded to the garage. "His car must be inside."

The garage.

I remembered seeing garden tools inside, so I snapped up Kelly and carried her over to the side entry door. The perpetrator had broken in. Inside sat a late-model white BMW X5 with a New York State license plate. I found shear cutters on top of a garden table and snipped off the plastic zip-ties to release her.

Wolfe's trademark.

"It was him, wasn't it?" she said, shaking her hands and rubbing the circulation back into them. "The guy I called and left a message for?

The bastard who killed my brother?" She was about to bolt out the door, but I grabbed her arm.

"Listen to me." I looked firmly into her eyes. "This is not the time to be a hero. We have to do this right, so I want you to stay here."

She started to protest, but I put a finger to my lips. "I need you to call my detective friend from NYPD. Can you do that?"

She nodded.

I texted Kelly JR's number. "Tell him I asked you to call. Give him the plate number. He'll know what to do." I pointed to Wolfe's car.

"Okay."

"And stay here until I return. If I'm not back soon, jump in your car and drive to the nearest police station."

She grabbed my hand. "Please come back."

I had every intention.

———

Darkness enveloped the house. The light from the second-story window disappeared, which meant Wolfe—or whoever—was either sleeping or found the ladder to the attic. I could wait outside and surprise him, but that could take hours. Besides, the attic was the last place I wanted him to find.

I removed my service Glock and crept into the kitchen. Though I could use my cell phone's flashlight feature, I held off not wanting to use up my power. I recalled seeing two flashlights in one of the drawers. Feeling around, I found one, flipped it on, and aimed the light close to the palm of my hand. Plenty of juice.

The downstairs was eerily still. I sneaked halfway to the second floor, following the light rays up the stairs, and stopped. I wiped my brow. Wolfe was being too quiet. At least, I believed it was him. I had to assume he was armed and dangerous—or desperate, which could be worse.

Was he alone? I mean, Ana was an accomplice—unless she was dead. When I reached the top of the stairs, I killed my light.

Where are you, Randy Wolfe?

The ladder stood a few feet away where I had left it, still angled against the wall leading to the attic access. I peered up and saw that the attic light wasn't on. If he wasn't up there, where was he?

Then, from the bathroom down the hall, I heard the toilet flush. At least the guy was courteous.

As he stepped out, I said, "All employees must wash their hands before leaving the bathroom." My flashlight and weapon rested at his chest. "Now would be the time to drop your weapon."

"Fuck."

"Weapon first."

He hesitated.

"Trust me, I'm a good shot."

Wolfe appeared to weigh his options.

"Okay." He tossed the gun at my feet and for a brief moment, I flinched. He took advantage of it, charging me. We were both knocked to the floor, and Wolfe jumped on me, swinging his fists wildly, and connecting one good shot to my jaw.

My gun was still clutched in my hand, but the flashlight went flying and suddenly we were literally shadowboxing. I swung the butt of the Glock down hard and smashed his nose. In the dimness, I saw black liquid spurt onto his face and he groaned, but his adrenaline kicked in, and he slammed his fist into my mouth.

"Damn you, Wolfe!"

"I should have killed you at the hotel!" he ranted, yanking my arm and grabbing for my weapon.

I landed a blow to his skull. More groans, but the bastard wouldn't give up. Pissed, I rammed my fist into his nose, triggering more blood splatter. He screamed, but his rage continued as his fist caught the side of my face. I pulled back, and he kicked me in the balls.

As my hands dropped to my groin, we fought over the gun. A shot blasted the floor. Wolfe pulled hard and scrambled to his feet, gripping my gun. He scooped up his flashlight and spit out a mouthful of blood, then aimed my gun at my head. "You're fucking up my retirement plan, Reed."

I wiped my lip with my sleeve and raised my hands. "Take it easy, Randy. You don't want to kill a law enforcement official. That would really screw up your golden years."

He spit out more blood. "You broke my fucking nose."

"Sorry, that's what happens when I get carried away. My jaw hurts."

"Asshole."

"Randy, let's get real here. Who do you think told Kelly to call you? Stone never had a file," I lied. "I set you up. If you had all the files you needed, you wouldn't have rushed up here, would you? You're still looking."

He threw me a menacing look.

I nodded. "The cops know you killed Stone and are on their way here. Now would be a good time to hand over my service revolver and give yourself up."

He snarled. "You're conning me, shithead. No one's coming."

"You should know about conning, but I never took you for a killer. Why did you kill Danny Stone?"

Wolfe elevated his head slightly, touched his nose, and grimaced. "I knew McKenzie hired him, and when McKenzie was killed, I told Stone his services were no longer required, that we had everything under control against Hartford. The bastard wouldn't take no for an answer."

"Because he figured out you were extorting Hartford instead of trying to nail him legally as a whistleblower. He also believed Elena wasn't part of your scheme," I said, not knowing if it were true. "So Stone had to find Elena and confront her."

Wolfe wiped his nose, didn't respond immediately. "Stone got in my face, said I didn't hire him, and that his contract wasn't finished." He shook his head. "We got into a pissing match and...look, he wasn't supposed to die, Reed. I swear. I'm not a killer. If I was, I would have killed you at the hotel."

Should I believe him?

"Look, Stone could've gone to the nearest hospital and had his wound taken care of. That's on him."

"But you shot him, Randy. You should have helped him."

"Are you kidding? He charged out of my apartment. I couldn't stop him. That's the truth, Reed."

"Did you know Stone was a former Navy SEAL? It's hard for those guys to get killed unless they're waylaid. Sounds like that's what happened."

When Wolfe didn't respond, I said, "What I don't get is why you changed sides all of a sudden. I mean, you were part of a whistle-blowing investigation against Hartford. You could have collected your reward and been a good citizen. Now, you can forget about the reward and retirement. You're screwed."

He waved my gun. "You really are naïve, Reed. The whistleblowing business isn't what it's cracked up to be. If they got a conviction, and that's a big if, it could take years before any money came our way. I don't trust the Feds; they'd find a way to screw us out of the reward." He sneered. "Besides, extortion is easier."

I needed to tread lightly with Wolfe. "I get that, Randy. I really do. But what if Hartford reneges on his promise to pay you? McKenzie's dead, and from what I hear, you don't have enough evidence against Hartford yet."

"Don't worry about me, Reed. He'll pay up."

"I don't know, Randy, it sounds like a bad investment to me." I pointed. "Like your dying flashlight."

He felt around for a wall light switch and flipped it on. "Better, asshole?"

"Much better," I said. "Now I can see the blood on your shirt." I smiled. "You're right. Your nose is broken."

He sneered. "Yeah, well, fuck you. Enjoy the lights, because you won't be seeing them for long. And when I'm done with you, I'll be gone and begin my retirement."

"You just told me you're not a killer."

"Ever hear of self-defense?" He snickered.

I wondered if Wolfe had persuaded Luke and Elena to turn. My guess: he'd rather not split the extortion money. Which meant he was still on a mission to eliminate everyone in his way, including me.

"What's going through your head, Reed? How you're going to sweet talk me out of giving myself up?" He shook his head slowly, spat out more blood. "That's not going to happen."

I was beginning to think he was right. I wiped my forehead. "Randy, I believe you're not a killer, even though you have a gun pointed at me. Why not just take what you need and leave? You could probably claim self-defense with Stone. But killing a cop, they'll hunt you down…"

The stairs creaked behind him, and for a second, Wolfe turned his head. I shot across the room and tackled him around the legs. He fell over, slamming his head on the floor, and my gun flew toward the top of the stairs.

He cried out and held his nose. "Shit, shit, shit. You're a dead man!"

I pummeled my fist into his face. "This is for Danny Stone, you bastard!"

Kelly rushed in, a Ruger GP100 revolver staring down at a dazed Wolfe. "You killed my brother!"

He blinked.

"Get off him, Hank."

"Kelly, don't do this," I begged. "He's not worth it." I got up to calm her, but she dropped to her knees and rammed the gun deep into his mouth, chipping off pieces of Wolfe's enamel.

I touched her hand and tried to find her eyes with my own. "Kelly, don't. We have enough on the bastard to put him away for a long time. You don't want to pay for his sins."

She eased the hammer forward, shoving the gun deeper. Wolfe's eyes widened and sweat streamed down the creases of his forehead. He brought his hands to his mouth, gagging on blood and broken teeth.

"He's not worth it," I urged again.

She wiped her own brow and eased the hammer forward, yanking the revolver out of his mouth. She straightened up and kicked him on the side of the head.

The Woodstock police arrested Wolfe, broken teeth and all. Attempted murder, kidnapping, assault, breaking and entering—and that was just locally. He refused to talk without his attorney present. Woodstock was a long drive from New York City.

I left the station around midnight and stopped back at the Cumberland Farms store. Hoping Kelly liked Moose Tracks, I picked up a half-gallon of Dean's Country Fresh. The pimply-faced kid, who was still working, asked if I was okay.

I smiled, then grimaced. "You should see the other guy." I glanced down at the stuff I'd left on the counter. "Thanks for holding these for me." The kid just stared at me, mouth slightly agape.

I drove back to Kelly's house and parked behind her Honda. The interior lights were on, so I assumed she was still awake. "Hey," I said, entering the living room. "I hope you're up for ice cream."

She turned and offered a thin but genuine smile. "This is a perfect time for comfort food. I've been watching old home videos." She sunk back into the couch. "Great times."

The TV screen showed images of two happy teenagers at the beach. I guessed they were Kelly and Danny. They were all smiles for the camera.

"Nice. Sorry I interrupted."

"No, not at all. Scoop us some ice cream. I want to reminisce tonight."

"Got it."

After finding two soup spoons and bowls, I joined her.

"How did you know I love Moose Tracks, Hank?"

"Seriously?"

She smiled. "It doesn't really matter right now, any kind will help, but yeah." She took a big spoonful and smacked her lips. "Thanks."

I wanted to thank Kelly for saving my life, but I had already done so numerous times. I only wished I could have reciprocated for Danny. I told her I had a few calls to make and that I'd join her for more ice cream and videos in a few minutes. Then I stepped outside.

Getting the word out that Luke and Elena were safe to surface was my priority. As for Ana, I didn't know if she was dead or alive. It was almost one in the morning, and I had no idea if JR was working. He answered on the first ring.

"I see you're up," I said.

"I never sleep, Hank. Actually, I'm sitting in a local pub with a few buddies."

"I would've gotten back to you sooner, but I've been having one hell of a time up here in Woodstock."

"You finally get laid?"

"Hardly. Randy Wolfe is sitting in a Woodstock jail cell. He has quite a bloody face and will need some teeth capped."

"Now, that does sound like fun. I got a message from Stone's sister telling me Wolfe was in the neighborhood, so I figured you'd call when you could."

"Right, the neighborhood. If Wolfe had had more time, he would've made his way to the attic and found Stone's files."

"So tell me about the broken teeth. I want details."

I chuckled. "Always one for drama. Okay, well, he tried to kill me. Kelly saved my life, and in the process, rammed her pistol in his mouth."

"Ouch. In Woodstock, of all places? The home of the flower children?"

"I guess her parents hadn't gotten around to telling her about love and peace. Anyway, you and Connors should be hearing from the locals soon."

"No one's called me yet. I'll check with Connors. So the sister knocked out a few teeth? Nice payback."

I looked back at the house. "Not enough of one. She's going to ID her brother this afternoon. I was thinking of going with her, but I need to get back to Newport and get the word out that Wolfe is in custody. I wanna make sure the missing duo is safe and sound so I can get back to my real job."

He laughed. "Right, you finally need to get some real work done."

"I'm committed until Luke surfaces, anyway. I'm not sure Patrice cares anymore, but I want to finish what I started."

"Ah, Patrice. Anything new in that department?"

"Still in Paris."

"I mean between the two of you."

I knew what he'd meant, but I didn't want to go there, not yet. After Luke returned—assuming he did—there'd be time to sort things out. I was hoping that would happen sooner rather than later.

I slept on Kelly's sofa—Danny Stone's bedroom felt sacrosanct—and was awakened pleasantly around six a.m. by the scent of strong coffee.

I lifted my head, rubbed my eyes. The sheets were hanging off the sofa and my pillow was on the floor. "Morning," I said, half asleep.

Kelly turned. "I hope I wasn't too loud. I couldn't sleep so I got up and made us some coffee. You drink coffee?"

"Probably more than I should."

"I don't have milk, but you can always add Moose tracks." There was a sad tint to her smile.

"Sounds tempting, but I'll stick with black, thanks." I watched her pour. Her eyes were unfocused, which made sense, given the circumstances. She handed me a mug with the words *I Love You* on it.

"Sleep okay?"

"Perfect," I lied. I hadn't slept more than a few hours, all of which were nightmarish. Thank you, Randy Wolfe.

"Thanks for the hospitality. With Wolfe in jail, I think it's safe to keep Danny's files here in the attic. I also have some files in my trunk I found at Danny's client's garage. At some point, I'll return for them."

"Yes, of course. Anything you need."

"I brought the ladder from upstairs back to the garage last night." I paused. "Danny did a great job following his instincts." Without going into detail, I assured Kelly we had enough information to nail Hartford.

A wistful smile tugged up her lips. "Danny was a pro."

I nodded. "I wish I could be with you today, but I have to get back to Newport. I can ask JR to meet you, if you like."

She waved me off. "Thanks, but I prepared myself last night. I'll be okay."

"All right, then." Finishing my coffee, I rose. "I'd better get going soon. I'll hop in the shower and be out of your way in no time."

"Consider this place yours until you finish. I'll put a key under the potted plant near the back door." She stepped across the kitchen and gave me a warm, heartfelt hug. "Thanks for everything, Hank."

I wrapped my arms around her and patted her shoulder. "Of course," I said. Kelly Stone was the kind of woman any man would vie for—beauty, brains, grit, the whole package—and I was not the exception. Right now, however, my heart was with Patrice. "Call me anytime you want to talk." I kissed her forehead and then pulled myself back from her at arm's length, my hands on her shoulders and my eyes on hers. I smiled an everything's-going-to-be-okay smile and she nodded. "I'd better go fix myself up for the day," I said.

———

I entered the New York Thruway to I-90, toward Boston. The traffic was typical for a weekday morning, and after adding a few more main roads to my trip, I arrived in Newport in just over three hours. Brady was happy to see me until I told him I'd be checking out soon. That was my intent, at least.

"Nothing personal, but my tab is running up way beyond my budget, even with your weekly discount rates."

He drew a broad grin.

"What?"

"This happens to be your lucky day, Hank." He pointed a finger at my chest. "You have a benefactor. Your bill is paid in full."

"What? Yeah, right."

"Swear to God."

"I'm not that religious," I said, my eyes narrowing on him. "You serious?"

"Very. And this *person* included a few additional nights if needed." Brady paused furrowing his sizeable brows in my direction. "You don't seem too happy about it."

"Confused is all. What do I have to do for this benefactor, sit through one of those timeshare presentations? Because I'd rather pay than to hear those guys——"

"You're too much."

"Seriously, who's my admirer? Or is that a secret?"

"I promised not to tell."

"Even if I threatened you with deadly force?"

Brady thought a moment. "How deadly?"

I shook my head and puffed a silent chuckle. Had to be Patrice. "I'm going to my room. I expect an answer before I checkout."

As I left the lobby, I thought about the inevitable: going back to Eastpoint, the Department, and Susan. Susan and I had become more estranged than ever. We hadn't spoken since I left for Paris. Space was what we both needed. Or, as Susan put it: "Going on with my life." That phrase suggested she was no longer in love with me, and that she was either looking for a replacement or she'd rather live alone. Personally, I'd rather her be in the alone camp, but that was my ego talking.

"Interesting."

I turned back to Brady, whose eyes were checking out the TV screen. "What's going on?"

"They just found an abandoned boat off the coast of Florida."

I went back and stood behind him. A CNN reporter was telling his anchor about a capsized boat. Then the cameraman panned in on the back of the vessel.

I brushed Brady aside and got up close to the screen, staring intently. The craft was listing on its port side. I squinted as I struggled to read the name.

It couldn't be. I gave my eyes a good rub.

Could McKenzie have owned a second boat?

The camera again homed in on the aft of the sailboat.

Pretty Diagnostic II.

"I think that's Warren McKenzie's boat."

Brady turned to me, confused. "I thought he was dead."

FIFTEEN

McKenzie was dead, and yet the *Pretty Diagnostic II* was listed on its side off the coast of Florida, with no one on board.

I immediately called JR.

"Please, no more favor requests." He laughed.

"Listen, I'm at the inn, watching cable news. The Coast Guard found a capsized sailboat off the coast of Florida. Where it was headed is anyone's guess. They found no one onboard." I walked away from Brady and found a quiet corner.

"I'm guessing the party on board didn't get to its destination." He chuckled then said, "But considering your call, the situation is probably more ominous."

"The name of the sailboat is the *Pretty Diagnostic II*. McKenzie's Newport yacht is called *Pretty Diagnostic*."

I went silent to let JR come his own conclusion.

"I've got a source at the Coast Guard. Stay close to your phone."

I had my own thoughts as to who the passengers were and wondered if Luke's sailing days were over. Then I recalled the tropical setting on Luke's computer. Apparently, it looked like paradise would elude him.

Back to Brady, I asked, "Anything new coming out?"

His faced remained on the tube. "Only that they extended their search. They identified the owner as Warren McKenzie, deceased."

"Brady, I'll be in my room for a while. Ring me when you find out more."

It was nearly one p.m. when I entered my room. I opened the closet door and pulled out Luke's laptop. I sat at the desk, switched on the little tabletop lamp, and fired up the computer. I studied the beach scene again. White sand, palm trees, crystal-clear turquoise water. Hell, it could be anywhere in the Caribbean.

If it was you onboard, Luke, where were you heading?

I opened a browser page and headed to Facebook—because everyone's on Facebook, right? Either Luke was the exception, or he'd opted not to stay logged in. I clicked on the Windows app icon and scanned the ones Luke had installed. Along with Netflix and a photo editing app, I saw one called Fast Runner. The icon was a guy running down a country road. I remembered Patrice mentioning that Luke was in great shape, ran in marathons. Too bad his running days were probably over.

Personally, I'm not much into running. For that matter, I'm not fond of any type of exercise. But the icon of the guy running down the road sparked my curiosity. I clicked on the icon, and Luke's personal page popped up, showing his stats, running friends—of which he had a few, all from different states. Looked like Mr. Fitness walked or ran at least ten thousand steps a day. Hell, if I wanted to impress Patrice in a bathing suit, I'd have to move my ass a bunch more steps than I was currently in the habit of doing.

Then I noticed something odd. Was there a glitch with the program? My eyes focused on the step movement. The numbers were climbing, as though Luke were running more than…four miles? A map icon was positioned next to the ever-increasing distance tracker. I clicked on it, and now I could see a little dot moving along a map along with the ticking numbers. I followed that little dot until it reached five miles. How could that be?

The room phone rang.

"Hank, there isn't anything new. Station's just telling viewers to stay tuned. I've got to get back to work."

I rubbed my eyes. "Sure, I understand. Thanks." I stuck my hand in my pocket and pulled out Ana's matchbook cover. "Say, are you familiar with the Wharf Inn?"

"Here in Newport? Sure, the place belongs to the Bassons—Marty and Anne. Their place is a few blocks away. Why, you're not happy here?" He laughed with caution.

"Brady, you're my favorite innkeeper, but I wonder if you could check out something for me—surreptitiously, of course. Promise not to get you in trouble."

"Aw, I like trouble. What can I do for you, Hank?"

———

JR called back a half hour later, his voice rushed. "The Coast Guard retrieved one passport inside a safe onboard the boat. It belongs to Luke DuPont. At least we know who was aboard."

"Only one passport? What about Elena Sullivan?"

"Nope, only his."

That surprised me, obviously. I'd assumed since Luke and Elena were a couple, she'd be onboard with him.

"They're still searching for his body. The news isn't official, so keep the information close to the breast. Though you might consider calling Patrice."

"Thanks, JR, I think I will."

I paced the room, putting together a new theory. The room phone rang again.

"Hank, it's Brady. Anne Basson from the Wharf Inn just got back to me. She provided me with the names you asked about, but begged me not to let you leak out the information."

"Of course not."

"Okay, the reservation was made by the Fox Reynolds company. That's Preston Hartford's company, I believe."

"Correct. Did Ana Martinez check in under the company name? She worked for Hartford. And it was her matchbook cover I found in her hotel room."

"The only person who checked in was a guy by the name of Trevor Burke. Anne described him as having thick salt-and-pepper hair, late forties. She recalls him wearing sunglasses, so she has no idea what color eyes he has."

The name Trevor Burke meant nothing to me.

"This might not mean anything, but Anne said the maid mentioned that the 'Do Not Disturb' sign was hanging on his outside doorknob, so she hasn't been able to clean up yet."

"Christ! I need to enter that room. Tell Anne it's a police matter." I hung up and hustled over to Brady's desk. He was on the phone, presumably with the proprietor. He nodded and hung up.

"I'll give you directions."

I snatched the paper out of his hands and raced for the door. "Keep this between us."

I trotted three blocks east and noticed a woman standing outside the inn. She introduced herself as Anne Basson. She was an attractive woman in her mid-fifties, with grey hair in a classy bun. Her blue eyes held a nervous look.

"Could be nothing." I tried to assure her. "But I need to get inside and find out for myself."

She spun on the heel of her flats. "Yes, yes. Follow me." When we got to the door, she knocked then called out. She shrugged when no one answered.

"I'll take it from here, Anne. Thanks."

She dropped the key card into my hand and stepped back.

I slid the key into the lock, dropped the handle and pushed the door forward.

"Oh my God!" Anne yelped.

Not good. "Go back to the office and call 911. And tell them to inform Detective Jackson," I said, keeping my eyes on a female lying fully clothed on the floor, her arm extending into the bathroom.

I could have called Jackson myself, but I needed time to look around. Besides, the individual lying on her side on the floor wasn't going anywhere. From previous photos, I had no doubt it was Elena Sullivan. She was dressed in black jeans and a draped V-neck top. I knelt down beside her and observed neck bruises, indicating strangulation. Absent of a rope, I knew she'd been murdered. Her nails were shattered, so she must have fought off her attacker.

I immediately thought of Preston Hartford, III, the CEO of Fox Reynolds, the company registered to the room. There was one problem: Hartford didn't fit Anne Basson's description of the person who checked in.

So who was Trevor Burke?

Close to Elena's hand was a man's open double-edged razor, its blade sitting next to her fingers, and small droplets of dry blood on the floor. Other than a small prick from her right index finger, there were no traces of blood on her. My eyes surveyed the bathroom and stopped cold at the mirror.

Something was scrolled there in blood. Elena's right-hand fingertip had been cut by choice. I stood in front of the mirror and followed the smeared letters. *SEX.*

SIXTEEN

The frantic roar of a fire and rescue truck approached the inn. Within minutes, a team of first responders entered gear in hand, followed by a gurney.

"She's dead," I said, putting up a hand and identifying myself. "It's now a crime scene. Detective Jackson from the station house is on his way."

When Jackson arrived, I informed him that the deceased was Elena Sullivan, murdered by strangulation.

He stepped inside the room and looked down at her. He then touched her body. "Very stiff." He looked up at me. "Based on the stiffness of the body and before the pathologist takes a peek, I'd say she's been dead for at least twelve hours, though closer to twenty-four."

I counted in my head. "Or somewhere in between. The killer could have placed the 'Do Not Disturb' sign anytime last night, but certainly before the maid had a chance to make up the room this morning."

Jackson thought a moment. "My guess: sometime after dark." He shrugged. "Just a guess."

"She was one of the missing duo I'd been looking for," I told him. "Looks like she fought hard."

"This her room?" he asked, sizing up the place.

"A company she worked for reserved the room for an employee, but not her. A guy by the name of Trevor Burke checked in. The proprietor vaguely remembers him. Apparently, he returned to his room only after dark. And the 'Do Not Disturb' sign was hanging from the doorknob today."

Jackson turned to me. "So there's a connection."

"That would be my guess." I was about to tell Jackson I needed to find out who and where this Trevor guy was, but reminded myself this wasn't my case.

"I can tell you her boss hired a PI to follow her around. I met the guy. Bit of a creep. He showed me some sexy photos of her with the man I'd been looking for, Luke DuPont. My guess is if the PI reported back to his client, the guy might have a reason to do this to her."

Jackson remained deadpan. "I'm assuming you're still looking for DuPont."

I held off on the full details. "I think he drowned off the coast of Florida."

He narrowed his look. "You know this how?"

I told him it was all over the news. "It's a timeline issue. I don't know how long the victim's been dead, nor when Luke DuPont left Newport. The boat belonged to McKenzie. Not his yacht in Newport: he owned a sailboat somewhere else. My guess is Fort Lauderdale."

Jackson nodded, obviously trying to piece together the events. "He could have killed her and taken off. Maybe they had an argument and things got heated."

I shot a quick glance at poor Elena. "I thought of that, except neither she nor Luke was staying here. Only Trevor Burke or whoever he was."

He nodded, not looking at me.

"There's something else strange about the scene," I said. "Did you notice the razor blade by her hand?"

Jackson knelt down next to Elena. "She doesn't have any lacerations, except for a small cut on her finger."

I pointed with my chin. "Check the bathroom mirror. I'm assuming she wrote 'SEX' with her finger. Unless her killer wrote it and wanted to tell her in death it had only been about sex."

"Crime of passion," Jackson intoned, standing and stepping into the bathroom. "That would make Luke DuPont a person of interest."

Jackson was close. Preston Hartford had the real motive, and I suggested that to him.

He smiled wearily. "You must believe in this Luke guy. Okay, I'll get my crime unit on it. In the meantime, I'll call Hartford's office and find out who this Trevor guy is." He paused. "What about you, Hank? Are you sticking around a while?"

I hadn't had time to think about my next move. I was now between strangulation and drowning. "Not really sure."

I started to leave.

"Hank, I don't mind you sticking around, just in case. If not, I understand. Thanks for your help. I hope we catch this guy soon."

Me too.

We shook hands. Heading back to my room, I couldn't help but think that Elena was no longer a threat to Patrice. Then again, with Luke likely dead, it wouldn't matter.

Back in my room, I splashed cold water on my face and watched the drops fall into the sink as thoughts tumbled around in my head. Hartford's potential involvement in Elena's murder kept gnawing at me. He was my prime suspect. But this wasn't my case. So I called Jackson and asked him to contact JR and have him pay Hartford an unexpected visit.

But several hours later, Jackson called back and told me JR met with Hartford—and found no apparent indication of an altercation. In fact, Hartford seemed totally caught off-guard and dismayed by Elena's murder. He admitted he'd hired a PI to tail her, but claimed the guy hadn't finished the assignment—which annoyed him, since he felt the guy had been padding expenses. And as for his company registering a room at the inn, he hadn't done it, nor did he know anyone named Trevor Burke.

That threw a wrench into the whodunit. Luke was missing and presumably dead, Ana was also possibly dead, and Wolfe was sitting in a jail cell. If not them, who had a reason to kill Elena besides Hartford?

I decided to return to the inn. When I got there, I called Jackson again.

"Having a hard time staying away from murder, huh?" Jackson laughed. "Okay, I'll meet you at the inn in twenty minutes."

I arrived sooner. The door to the room was slapped with crime scene tape. Anne Basson must have been watching and dashed over to me.

"Business dropped off almost immediately," she complained. "I guess the M-word got out. Please get that off the door as soon as you can," she pleaded then trudged back to the office.

Jackson arrived with an update. "For sure, she'd been throttled by asphyxiation, but outside of her blood, the room was clean. Trevor Burke, or whoever he was, cleaned out the place. We're still waiting for the results of his fingerprints."

Inside the room, I stood in front of the mirror, head cocked to the side, analyzing the cryptic *SEX* message. After several minutes of staring, whatever fog had been in my brain began clearing, and information started registering. As I gazed at the *X*, I saw a small smear of blood trailing off to the right of the letter, and realized Elena had attempted to continue writing. She must have fallen before having a chance to finish her message.

She'd been attempting to write the name of her killer.

"Sex had nothing to do with the smeared inscription on the mirror," I told Jackson as I approached him in the living room. "Elena was attempting to reveal her killer's name, and my guess is that Trevor Burke is actually Everett Sexton, as in S-E-X." I raised my eyebrows. "And Sexton is Hartford's PI, the one I told you about."

I could see the light dawning in Jackson's eyes as he looked at me. "Let's talk to the proprietor," he said.

When we entered the office, Anne Basson stared at us, wide-eyed, obviously freaked out.

Jackson asked her a few questions, answered by nods and head shakes. I remembered the selfie I'd taken with Sexton in men's room of The Nautical Pub's, and showed it to her.

She gave a slow, lingering nod and peered back up to me.

"You're sure?"

"Yes, yes. But…he doesn't look like a killer."

Yeah. Those were the ones you had to watch out for.

I was about to slip the phone back into my pocket, but then thought to search for a photo of Elena. I wished I had one of Ana, too.

"Did this woman check in?" I asked. "She's the deceased."

Anne stared at the photo. "She's the one who was killed?" Her voice both rose in pitch and lowered in decibels. "I mean, I didn't recognize her…that way."

"You mean dead?"

A nervous nod.

"But she *was* here at the inn?"

"Yes, yes. She was with the other woman who checked in. I can't remember her name offhand. She had dark hair, very pretty. Actually, both of those ladies were very attractive."

"Was it Ana Martinez?"

"No, no. I don't believe that was her name."

She walked over to her desk and checked her computer. "Alicia Ramos, two adults." She glanced over at me questioningly.

Huh. No wonder Ana's name never showed up as registered; she hadn't used her real name.

I pulled Jackson aside. "I can't tell you why this Alicia woman checked in under a false name, except that maybe she didn't want to be found. Her real name is Ana Martinez, and she was working with the deceased to nail Hartford for Medicare fraud."

I let Jackson take in the situation. "It sounds like Sexton's job description included murder," he said finally.

"Makes sense. Except why didn't he go after Ana?"

"Could be he never had the opportunity," Jackson said. "Maybe he's still looking for her." He gave me a grave look.

Jackson's theory had merit, and I might have agreed with him. Only Jackson didn't know that Randy Wolfe, who was now sitting in jail, admitted to...an agreed extortion. My gut was saying that Ana, if she wasn't dead, was part of Wolfe's extortion scheme. Which meant Hartford wasn't interested in harming her. On the other hand, Wolfe, before he was taken in, might have decided he didn't want to split the extortion money with anyone.

SEVENTEEN

As far as I was concerned, Sexton was Jackson's problem. I texted him the selfie I'd snapped and reminded Jackson that I was the other guy.

That got a laugh. "All right, I'll call you when I have something."

We shook hands, and then I headed back to the inn. With Luke missing for the last time and Elena dead, I had no reason to stick around. Ana might be dead or guilty of some crime, but she wasn't my problem, either. Patrice was the only person I needed to get in touch with before I drove back home.

As I approached the inn, I saw Brady looking idly out the window. He waved when he saw me.

"It's too quiet here. I hope the murders aren't going to cost us too much business."

Same concern Anne Basson had expressed. People had to make a living, I guess. I told Brady I didn't want to be disturbed for a while, that I had some pressing calls to make.

Inside, I pondered the call to Patrice. I wanted to soften the blow about Luke as much as I could. I tapped her name, and she picked up on the first ring.

"Hank, what a coincidence! I've just been sitting at my desk thinking of you." She chortled.

Definitely not a good time to bring her up to date.

"It's been a while," I said, my voice constricted in spite of the pleasure I got from hearing her voice.

"Is something wrong?"

There was no easy way.

"Patrice, the Coast Guard discovered McKenzie's second boat off the coast of Florida. They believe Luke had been on board. They're still searching..."

The silence was severe. Then, "Was he alone?"

"As far as I know. There's something else: Elena was murdered at a Newport inn. The two incidents aren't related," I said. "It appears our friend, PI Sexton, strangled her."

More silence.

"You okay?"

"I don't know what to say, Hank. There's a lot to digest."

I was about to reply when she said, "Look, I really need to go. Please keep me apprised."

Apprised?

That didn't sound like Patrice. She was always probing for more. Perhaps she just needed time to digest the inevitable.

I tossed my clothes in my overnight bag then checked the closet and chest of drawers one last time. Luke's laptop was sitting on the bed. I couldn't decide who should collect it. I reached to grab it, then remembered the Fast Runner app I'd been looking at before I got called away.

I clicked on the icon to open it, went to the map, and noticed the dot was moving again. Yesterday, the program had accumulated six miles; today, there were four miles so far. I watched it move, and after four minutes it hit five miles. What the hell! To me, movement meant action, so something was very off.

Unless...

EIGHTEEN

Either Luke was running in the afterlife, or someone had stolen his tracker watch. I thought a moment then called JR for his assessment.

"Hank, do I look like I run? I eat and struggle to keep my weight down. *Pssht.* Definitely *not* a runner."

"Anyone in your precinct healthy? There's got to be a least one cop who doesn't fill up on donuts."

"Let me think. Well, maybe there's one guy. He's young and has one hell of a healthy wife. He's always working out. I'll ask him if he's familiar with this app. If you don't mind, why are you interested? Looking to get in shape for someone special?" He laughed.

"That too, but right now, I need to find the person wearing the watch."

"Say again?"

I told JR what I'd found on Luke's laptop.

"I thought he drowned. I can't imagine some shark taking his tracker after swallowing him alive."

"Unless Luke made it to land."

"Hank, they found the boat twenty-five miles off the coast of Florida. He'd have to be one helluva swimmer. Besides, by now, the Coast

Guard would have gotten the word out that he was rescued. Maybe he lost the watch or gave it to someone."

I hadn't thought of that. JR was right. Someone had to be wearing Luke's smartwatch. But who? And how did that person obtain it? More importantly, where the hell was the watch beaming from?

"JR, there's got to be an explanation. The thing must have GPS built into it. I mean, I can see movement. I need to know where it's tracking from. Can your buddy with the healthy wife help me out?"

"Hold on, he's here somewhere."

I glanced back at the screen. Whoever was moving was doing it fast. Over six miles now.

When JR returned, he said, "I'm not a computer guy, but here's what Kenny told me."

"Kenny, the active guy?"

"Right, him. There's an internal GPS in some smartwatches that homes in on their location. So whoever's wearing the watch, beware. Kenny said to check the app on the computer. In your case, Fast Runner."

"I'm on it."

"Look for a map icon."

"Got it."

"Let's see. Okay, click on the map and enlarge it. It should show the location, like New York City. Then you'll see a black dot moving. That's the actual location, like Forty-Second Street. See it?"

"Yeah, I've seen this before. The dot has been moving fast, today and yesterday."

"Okay," said JR. "Like I mentioned, click on the map, and you can enlarge it, see the details up close."

I did. "Damn."

"You got it?"

"Oh, yeah, someone's wearing Luke's watch in Bimini."

"The island? No shit?"

"No shit. Tell Kenny I owe him a piña colada or margarita or whatever he drinks."

"Kenny's a craft beer guy, I think." After a pause. "So what are your plans now?"

I had to make a quick decision. What if the activity on the app was some electronic fluke? Then again, what if it wasn't? What if the person wearing Luke's watch was responsible for what—fraud? I'd been chasing a ghost too long not to be interested. And, more importantly: I was a cop.

"Never been to Bimini."

I'd never been to Fort Lauderdale, either, but here I was, sitting inside the airport terminal waiting for a six p.m. flight on Silver Airways to the South Bimini airport. The Saab 340 twin-engine turboprop aircraft seated thirty-four passengers. The thirty-minute trip suited me, given I had just gotten off a three-hour flight from Providence, Rhode Island.

I tossed a pair of sandals, a few pair of shorts and several tropical-looking T-shirts I'd bought at the airport into my carryon. I wanted to blend in with the tourists, and glimpsing the gate area, I did—except for the laptop I held in my hand. My fellow passengers were on their iPhones or iSomething-elses.

I was lucky to still have my passport with me from my trip to Paris. I would have hated to ask Susan to overnight it to me. Course, she'd probably be ecstatic if I promised never to return.

Bimini was part of the Bahamas, fifty miles east of Miami. It was the westernmost district composed of a chain of islands—North Bimini, South Bimini, and East Bimini—that formed a hook shape and had little more than sixteen hundred inhabitants total. I was heading to Alice Town, in North Bimini.

After getting through immigration, I sprinted to the exit and picked up a taxi van to the ferry dock. Waiting for a water taxi, I couldn't help but appreciate the crystal-clear, blue-green water and the white sand beaches, breathe in the briny scent of the sea, and hear local gulls shrieking overhead. It really was a paradise.

Big John's Hotel, my living quarters for a day or two, was a cozy inn located about a ten-minute walk to the Bimini Big Game Club Resort & Marina. That's where I'd last tracked Luke's watch that morning. I hoped the person hadn't checked out yet.

Nope. After I checked in, I fired up the laptop and found the dot still moving. The person wasn't running or even walking fast; it appeared to be more of a stroll. Great—I had time to grab a quick bite.

My stomach growled. I'd only eaten a few pretzels on the flight earlier in the day, so I walked north past a few shops, bars, and restaurants, until I found Sherry's Place, a popular casual seafood restaurant. A nondescript concrete path led in from the street, leading to a rustic bar on the beach. Sherry's was known for its apparently spectacular piña coladas. It wouldn't be difficult at all to whittle away a few hours on the nearly deserted beach; unfortunately, I didn't have that luxury.

I ordered fried lobster, cracked conch, and a beer.

"You have to try our piña coladas. They're the best on the island," said Damien, my server. He had a natural, exuberant smile, and I would have taken him up on the offer, but I knew myself—if I had one piña colada, I'd probably end up staying for a few more.

I smiled back at him and put up my hand. "Next time."

Damien left to put in my order, and I glanced around the place. A sign above the bar read, "You can't get bored in Bimini. Swim, eat, drink, work, read, talk, fish, and sleep." That was a great mantra, and it reminded me that Patrice had mentioned Luke being into fishing and scuba diving.

While I waited for my meal and beer, I opened the laptop. Hopefully, whoever was wearing Luke's watch was taking a nap or a shower, because the damn thing had stopped registering movement. My heart sank. Please don't tell me the watch battery had died.

"Hey, people come here to relax, friend," Damien said, nodding to the laptop. He placed my beer and food on the table. "You're 'sposed to eat, drink, fish, and—" he looked around over his shoulders and then whispered, "screw. You can't do any of them with that thing." He smiled.

Damien was a friendly guy with a wide smile, and an easy talker. He gave me a quick history rundown. Bimini was the westernmost district of the Bahamas. English was their official language, which was a mixture of Queen's diction, African influence, and island dialect.

He was obviously proud of his island, so I nodded with interest every once in a while, in between slugs of beer.

"Hey, sorry, friend, I get excited. I better let you eat."

As he turned to walk away, I said, "I'm actually looking for an old friend. It just occurred to me that maybe he's been here."

I pulled my phone out of my pocket and flipped to my photo library, scrolled down, and brought Luke's picture into view. "He was supposed to arrive a few days ago, but I lost his cell number."

Damien held the phone away from the sunlight. He grinned. "Good-lookin' guy. But sorry, can't say I 'ave," he said, his accent singing through. "Could be in the water somewhere. I'd be."

Bad response.

"Y'know, snorkeling and scuba diving."

"He's a runner," I offered.

Damien leaned back. "Drugs?"

I chuckled. "No, running shoes, you know, jogging."

He nodded, though seeing his scowl, I wasn't sure he was convinced.

"Seriously, he's got one of those smartwatches." I lifted my hand, pointed to my wrist. I'm going to get one soon."

"Yeah, we have plenty of people wearing those around here. Me, I'd rather screw." He winked and pointed at my phone.

Horny little bastard. I liked him. "I'm with you. Running tires me out. Can't screw afterward."

Damien broke up in a high-pitched cackle and put out a fist for a fist-bump. I bumped it. "We're in agreement there, friend." He glanced at my meal and nodded. "You better eat before it gets cold. I'll keep an eye out for your friend."

"Much obliged. I'm staying over at Big John's Hotel. Name's Hank Reed."

He nodded and turned to leave. "Okay, Mr. Hank, but don't forget your priorities while you're here." He called over his shoulder, "Work is last."

I thought about what it would be like to share this paradise with Patrice. I did kind of like Damien's priorities.

Sudden movement.

I finished my second beer, dropped a generous amount of cash on the table, and charged out of Sherry's place. The dot was moving slowly, casually, as though the person wearing the watch was just out for a leisurely walk. I held the laptop open, cradling it in my left arm. Keeping an eye on the movement, I picked up my pace, passing several souvenir shops along the way. Then it stopped.

Dammit, I was out of Wi-Fi range.

The dot on the screen remained frozen. I closed the laptop and continued past the hotel to the public beach.

Where are you? Who are you?

Though the late August sunset was about an hour away, the beach was filled with vacationers. Maybe he or she went for a swim, but I doubted whether the watch worked in water. I felt like a voyeur, stretching my neck at every soul I passed. Scrubby old guys in fish-blood-stained shorts wearing boat shoes mixed with tight bodies in bikinis, shorts, and ball caps.

To blend in, I took off my shirt and covered the laptop with it. I glanced at the glassy water, where gentle waves teased swimmers, and I kicked up soft, white sand until I reached the end of the beach. I reversed myself, returning slowly, deliberately.

Show yourself, ghost!

But my quest for a familiar face proved fruitless. I slipped my shirt back on then headed beyond the beach, where I found Alice's souvenir shop that advertised free Wi-Fi.

The search was back on. The tracker was within a few blocks, and was stationary. I found a shopkeeper outside adding local crafts to tables, so I approached and pointed to the dot on the screen, asked if she knew where it was.

"Looks like where Merle's Restaurant is," she said, and pointed up the block. "Good food, mon."

She might have been right about that, but when I got to Merle's, only one table was occupied, far in the corner. I told the hostess, a young black woman with striking green eyes (*contacts?* I wondered), that I was with the person in the corner and I'd call over the server when I was ready to order.

I sauntered quietly across the room, squinting at large loop earrings poking out from behind a book.

"Is this seat taken?" I glanced down and noticed flawless French nails.

I'd obviously startled her, because she slammed the book shut and jerked her head upward. She scowled at me then went back to her book. "I dine alone."

"Come on. I'm far away from home and could use some company."

"Sounds like a personal problem," she said, turning a page. But then something must have clicked, because she glanced up with moon-round eyes.

"Oh, shit!"

"I get that sometimes. Hello to you too, Ana."

Her eyes registered fear as they darted about.

"I'm alone," I assured her, removing my sunglasses and offering a friendly smile. "By the way, you look stunning in that blue sundress. It complements your curly red hair well—though I do recall your hair being straight and black in the States. Oh well, changing hair color does wonders when you're on the run."

She'd recovered now and glared. "What do you want?"

"Is that any way to treat an old friend who tried saving you from your crazy ex-husband?" I turned and pointed to a small existing bump on my skull. "Like I said, crazy."

She sighed, closed her eyes, and shook her head. "Sorry, it's just that you startled me. I wasn't expecting anyone. And sorry about the bump. I have no idea what he was up to." She shrugged.

Right. I took a seat opposite her and placed Luke's laptop on the table. She glanced at it, but showed no reaction.

"No, I guess you were hoping no one would find you. Especially here in paradise, away from murders, fraud, extortion, and kidnapping. I mean, I guess technically Randy kidnapped you." I leaned closer. "How did you manage to get away from that nut job? He was pretty upset."

She waved me off. "A misunderstanding is all."

"Well, don't worry, Randy's not going anywhere. He's sitting in jail, accused of killing Danny Stone. Know anything about that?"

She scanned the restaurant, then ducked and whispered as though the place was filled with patrons. Or enemies. "Look, all I know is what I heard on the news. I didn't know Stone or what he was up to in Randy's apartment. And I haven't heard from Randy." She shrugged.

"You probably won't. He was entitled to only one phone call." I grinned. "You weren't number one on his list."

"Funny."

I pointed to Ana's cell phone sitting on the table next to her warm piña colada. "The police are looking for you, so I'm guessing you've been pretty selective about answering phone calls, especially now that you're here in paradise."

She pointed a finger at me and raised her voice from a whisper to above what would be considered normal chat-level. "Look, Detective Reed, I have nothing to hide and I haven't done anything wrong, so don't come here badgering me like I'm some criminal. If you want answers about Stone or anyone else, ask Randy. Like you said, he's not going anywhere." She smirked. "In fact, why don't you leave on the next flight?"

"Me?" I said with a smile. "I'm not going anywhere. I kinda like paradise, too."

She shook her head. "Give me a break."

"Besides, I'm not working right now. Let the locals investigate the murders. Let's see, there was McKenzie, Stone, and now Elena Sullivan."

Her eyes widened again. "What are you talking about? Elena?"

I tilted my head. "You didn't know?"

"Don't screw around. I just saw her—"

"At the Wharf Inn, I know. That's where you registered under the name Alicia Ramos. What was that all about?"

She ignored my question. "Did they get the guy who killed her?" she asked, her face becoming increasingly drained of her Bimini tan.

"The cops are still looking." I glanced around the restaurant. "He's not here," I said flippantly.

"I think I'm gonna be sick." She grabbed her phone, leaped out of her chair, and charged for the ladies' room. She returned ten minutes later with a fresh coat of red lipstick and the color returning to her face.

I stood, helped her to her seat. "Sorry I had to be the bearer of bad news. I figured with Elena killed, you might need protection." I leaned into her. "Scary—almost everyone involved in the whistleblowing investigation has been eliminated."

I thought Ana was about to bolt for the restroom again, but instead she closed her eyes and sighed shakily. "This is not good, Hank."

Hank, a friendly sign.

"No, I guess not. You have to admit, there's only one person who wanted the investigation to shut down."

Her eyes met mine. She swallowed. "Hartford."

"Who else?"

"Why do you think I took off and landed here? Bimini's a low-profile place to hide. It's true, we were threatened by one of Hartford's goons. I don't know how he found us. The guy warned us that if we didn't burn the records, we'd wind up dead. I didn't wait around for a second warning."

Ana sounded sincere, but I maintained my vigilance. After all, she was part of a pretty good scam team. "Apparently, Elena didn't take the message to heart."

She scowled. "Not funny."

I leaned forward and showed Ana the selfie I'd taken with Sexton.

She pushed it back. "Oh, God, you're with him? Please don't tell me you're here to kill me. What do you want? Money—"

I touched her hand. "Relax. I took the picture in a bar after interrogating him. I'm sure you know he was hired by Hartford to follow Elena around. Apparently, Hartford was quite the jealous type. At first, I assumed it had nothing to do with your whistle investigation. But after Elena's murder, I'm beginning to think differently."

She stiffened. "Well, maybe he followed you here. He could be anywhere." Another sweep of the restaurant. Jesus, this woman was worked up.

I covered her shaking hand with mine. "Stop worrying. I'm here to protect you until Sexton's caught."

She blinked. "Okay, good, do I pay you now?" She pulled away her hand and began rummaging through her handbag.

I watched carefully, making certain she wasn't pulling out a gun. "Look at me, Ana," I demanded, but she kept searching. "Ana!"

"Yes?" She glanced up.

"We'll worry about fees later."

"Okay, Hank." She nodded rapidly, but then her expression turned grim. "We have to alert Luke."

NINETEEN

"Luke's dead. He drowned off the coast of Florida in McKenzie's sailboat. Could be Hartford had something to do with that."

Her expression didn't register either fear or concern.

"Did you hear what I said?"

She nodded, glanced to the side. She was too calm.

"New York cops are interrogating Hartford. I'm sure the FBI is involved. Between the murders and fraud, he'll be going away for a long time."

Her head shot back to me. "They're interrogating Hartford?"

"Sure. And if he gives up Sexton, you'll be safe, and I'll be out of here in no time." A smile.

Her face drained again.

"I thought you'd be happy. You look upset."

"Confused is all. I ran out of Newport with just the clothes on my back. As far as I know, Elena had the files…"

"Well, Christ, now Sexton has them—which means Hartford does. Not good, Ana. Without that evidence, Hartford walks."

She closed her eyes, and I was sure her thoughts about living the lavish life were rapidly dimming.

Her warm piña colada had gotten warmer. I called over the server.

"Two of these, please," I said with a smile. I looked around. The place was starting to fill up.

Ana opened her eyes. "Let's get out of here."

"I just ordered drinks."

"I think I'm gonna be sick again." And off she ran.

Our drinks arrived before Ana returned. When she finally got back, she sat down and just stared at her drink.

"Sip some," I said, lifting mine and taking a mouthful. "Smooth."

"I'm glad you're calm, but then again, you're not being hunted by a madman." She nodded at the laptop. "And what's with that?"

"This?" I opened Luke's laptop, checked the battery life and turned it around. "See that dot? It's not moving because the person who's wearing the smartwatch associated with it isn't. That person is probably sitting in a restaurant somewhere in Bimini, making small talk with a friend." I smiled.

She leaned in, studied the screen, and then shot a look at her left wrist.

"What the hell? So that's how you found me? But—"

"It's Luke's watch, I know. At least, it was his." I pointed to her left wrist, then took another sip and smiled. "Clever, no?"

"The hell!?"

I nodded. "What I don't get is how come you're wearing it."

Her lips turned up. "It's mine. Luke gave it to me as a present. I don't get how you tracked me on his app, though."

"Good question. Maybe he wanted to keep an eye on you, so he synced them before giving the watch to you." I shrugged. "Makes sense to me."

She scowled. "That bastard!" She removed the watch and dropped it into her drink.

Ana's burning stare at her piña colada, or its contents, told me she cursed the day Luke gave her the gift. And she had to be blaming him for me finding her, even though it was too late for that. Yet, at this point, I had nothing on her, even knowing about the extortion business. Perhaps I would in a day or two.

"I'm not going anywhere," I said. "At least, until Sexton is caught."

Ana came back to life, met my eyes. "Hank, Luke isn't dead. I just spoke to him."

"Here in Bimini?"

A nod. "He's up in the hotel room. I told him you were here, and he said he wants to meet you. He feels like he owes you an explanation, especially since you were trying to find him." She feigned a smile.

I shook my head. "What about this 'missing' business? He faked his death?"

"Long story."

"I thought he was working to nail Hartford for fraud?"

She sighed. "Another long story. True, at first, he had every intention, but then Randy had a heart-to-heart with him." She paused, held my gaze. "It didn't take much persuasion after he added up the numbers. I don't know what Luke's...ex-fiancée told you, but he isn't exactly a role model for honesty. Luke is interested in only two things in life: women and money. I kind of feel sorry for her."

"Patrice?" I asked, feeling my blood start to warm.

"Yeah. He's a womanizer. He falls in and out of love rather quickly." She stopped, sighed. "I knew not to get involved with him, but Elena thought she could change him. And she might have, except she wanted no part of Randy's plan."

"I'm not getting this. Where does she fit in?"

"She doesn't. Luke tried changing her mind, but she refused, said McKenzie was relying on her to go to the authorities. Luke did manage to sweet-talk her into waiting until after Hartford wired the money." She shrugged. "What can I say? Luke's a charmer."

"And now it seems Hartford might be in possession of the incriminating files. That sucks."

Her hands were trembling as she took a sip of her drink.

"When was Hartford supposed to be transferring the money?"

She was about to check her watch, then swore under her breath. "Later this evening. I have to get back to the room. You should come with me and meet Luke."

I wanted to, but felt I was heading straight into a shit storm. Ana had given away way too much information. Hell, she confessed about the extortion. I didn't trust her or Luke. And here I was ready to go into her room—without my service weapon.

We walked to her hotel in silence. But the street noise must have become unnerving to her, and she grabbed my arm for support. She must have been suffering from the Sexton syndrome. Once inside the hotel, we took the elevator to the fourth floor. She slid the key card into the door and pushed it forward.

I let Ana walk in first, standing behind her and surveying the room. A wall-to-wall window overlooking the Atlantic was breathtaking. She lived like a woman who was about to come into a great deal of money.

"Nice room."

She nodded indifferently. "We're here," she called out then headed for the bedroom. "Luke, we have company."

I braced myself for the unknown, and suddenly felt dangerously careless for not bringing my weapon. I watched her disappear.

"Oh, God, no!" she screamed. "Hank!"

I charged inside and found Ana backed up against the wall, trembling and staring down at Luke, who was wearing jogging shorts and a Gold's Gym workout shirt. He lay there, still. As I walked around and crouched over him, I saw what appeared to be a .22 bullet hole drilled through his forehead.

"Get me a towel," I demanded. But Ana stood frozen.

"Christ." I went into the bathroom, grabbed a washcloth, and knelt down to check his vitals. His body was barely room temperature. Then, with the wash cloth, I rolled him over. No shell casings.

"You said you spoke to him when we were at the restaurant. That was about an hour ago."

A blank stare.

"Ana!"

"Yes, inside the bathroom."

I studied the entry wound. "Did Luke have a handgun?" I turned. "Goddammit, Ana, help me here. Did he have a gun?"

She nodded rapidly then pointed. "In there."

I pulled open the night table drawer. "It's not here. You sure it was here?"

"Before."

"Before what?"

"Before I left for the restaurant. He said he might need it."

"To use on me? Was that it, Ana? Luke was going to kill me?"

"No, of course not. He didn't even know you were here. He thought someone..."

Someone.

He was obviously right.

"Who knew you were here?"

When I glanced over, she had slid to the floor, her arms wrapped around her knees.

Great.

"I need answers."

"Maybe Sexton!" she screamed, closing her eyes and burying her head.

It made no sense that Sexton would know about Bimini. Then I thought, "Ana, you couldn't have picked up Luke off the coast by yourself. Who helped you?"

"Oh, God!"

"That's not an answer." I grabbed her off the floor and shook her. "Who the hell was with you?"

"My brother." She pulled away from me. "But he wouldn't—"

"Kill for money, really?"

"We already paid him."

I shook my head. "Christ you're either naïve or part of the murder. How come Luke wasn't with you at the restaurant?"

"Huh?"

"You were dining alone. How come?"

She got that. "He didn't feel like eating."

"Or thought whoever was after him might find him," I said.

She glanced over at Luke's body. "I'm scared, Hank. I could be next."

Yeah, she could be, but I wasn't buying her story. "Where's your brother now?"

"I don't know. He lives in Miami."

"Call him now!"

When she hesitated, I said, "Or I'm calling the cops."

She pointed inside. "In my handbag."

I went into the living room and removed her bag from the sofa. I opened it and searched for her phone, then looked further for a hand-gun. There wasn't one.

"Here," I said handing it to her. "Hurry." I had to call the Bimini police soon, not that it made much difference. Luke was long dead.

She placed the phone to her ear.

"Put it on speaker," I demanded.

She did, but all we got was a male voice telling the caller to leave a message.

"Tell him what happened and that you're in trouble."

"He's in trouble?"

I pointed. "You—both of you are. Tell him the locals will be searching for him so he'd better get in touch with the Bimini police if he's innocent. And if he's not…"

She nodded.

"Tell your brother you're in the room and the police are on their way." I paused. "In case he doesn't know about the murder."

She left the message and hung up.

I did a quick survey of the suite, but didn't find a gun. When I returned, Ana was curled up in a ball. I stared back at Luke, the missing-reporter-turned-extortionist, now dead. I wondered if his life would have taken a different turn had he remained faithful to his profession and to Patrice. I'd never know.

Ana was still in shock. I picked her up and moved her to the living room sofa, positioning her upright. I placed a call to the Alice Town police station, identified myself, and reported the murder. While I waited for them to arrive, I called JR and told him Luke was no longer missing.

"I'll get back to you once the locals leave."

They got there twenty minutes later. I identified myself again—formally, this time, with my shield. I told the officer in charge—Sergeant Weech, a member of The Royal Bahamas Police Force uniformed division—about the deceased having been missing from a boating accident off the coast of Florida and now murdered in a hotel room. I briefly explained the disconnect between the two events. I also told him I had been actively searching for the deceased, but not criminally.

He nodded, seeming to buy my explanation, and looked around. "Nice place to wind up, mon," he said. "I mean, before being killed." He glanced over at Ana, who looked comatose. "Wife, girlfriend?"

Extortion partner.

"Just friends."

He nodded.

"I know her from the States. We were at Merle's the same time this happened. You can check on that."

He nodded again then asked questions only Ana could answer: what, where, and when? I was more interested in who, as in *who killed him?*

Bimini wasn't my jurisdiction, either, but out in the hallway, I asked Weech if he'd mind keeping me in the loop. I handed him my card.

He read it quickly and gave me a thumbs-up.

Sergeant Weech explained he would be calling authorities from the States and other parts of the island to help with the investigation. He took notes and informed me that he was leaving a uniform in the room until the crime scene unit arrived, and that I was free to go. He pointed inside. "I need to talk to her."

Good luck with that.

Weech made an effort to ask Ana a few questions, but she was still too out of it to be of any help. When he returned to me, he said, "She needs to stick around until I'm satisfied."

Weech walked away to speak to the uniformed officer, occasionally looking back at Ana.

The officer nodded, and I knew Ana wasn't going anywhere for a while. When Weech left, I went over to the suite's minibar and brought out a bottle of twelve-year-old single-malt Macallan.

Hell, I wasn't paying for it.

I waved the bottle of Scotch in front of her. She grabbed it, twisted off the cap, and took a gulp. After two quick hits, I pulled back on the bottle, brown liquid spraying out of her mouth.

"Answers first. Then you can get drunk. Right now, I need you sober."

She pouted like I had taken away her teddy bear.

I pointed behind me. "They want answers, Ana. I can't help you."

She looked over my shoulder at the officer standing by the door.

"You can't leave me here alone, Hank."

I could, and I would leave Ana to fend for herself. Like the local police, I, too wanted answers. I couldn't help but believe she had something to do with Luke's demise. And with her brother in the picture, it made perfect sense.

I envisioned Ana sipping her piña colada while her brother was eliminating another partner in their scam. Cold and calculating. And then I'd appeared. She couldn't have asked for a better alibi.

Ana continued downing her Scotch, her eyes pleading with me to stay. She slurred, "Hank, I'm begging, please don't leave me here alone. The money should be in our account by now. I'll give you twenty-five percent, no questions asked."

I smirked. "Twenty-five percent of nothing is nothing."

She tilted her head in confusion.

I pushed my eyebrows upward in mock surprise. "Oh, I forgot to tell you. Hartford reneged on the money. After Randy was arrested, he was entitled to one phone call. You know it wasn't to you, but you'd figure he would've called his attorney. That would have been my choice, anyway. Instead, he called Hartford."

A blank stare.

"Randy called off the wire transfer. I guess he figured if he couldn't spend the money, no one would. He probably told Hartford that Elena was going to the authorities in spite of their deal."

"You're lying."

"Have you checked your account?"

Her eyes dashed to the coffee table. She struggled off the couch and opened her laptop.

I watched her attempt to start it up. It was almost comical. It's amazing how booze can screw up the brain. When she'd finally accessed her account, she gave her head a good shake as she stared at the monitor.

"Shit."

"Sorry, Ana. Looks like you've been conned." Satisfied that the transfer hadn't gone through, I stood, took one lasting view of the Atlantic Ocean from the window, and said, "Have a nice life."

Ana steadied herself. "Wait a minute! You promised to protect me. What if Sexton comes after me? He could be on the island."

"I doubt it. Hartford has nothing to lose now."

Inside a taxi to the airport, I called Sergeant Weech and told him what I'd recently discovered, that Ana's brother had access to the hotel room. Reaching the airport, I called Patrice, and when it went to voicemail, left a quick message: "It's important, give me a call." I waited another twenty minutes then called again. Same announcement. I recorded another quick message, letting her know it was extremely important.

I began to get concerned after she didn't return my calls, and I finally contacted JR for one more favor. He got back to me in fifteen minutes.

The phone number he provided was for Interpol HQ in Lyon, France. A woman with an Italian accent answered. I identified myself, but hit a roadblock. I suggested she contact Detective JR Greco from NYPD.

The woman put me on hold. While I was waiting, I conjured up thoughts about Patrice and Luke. There was never a good time to convey bad news. And here I was doing it again—only this time, I'd witnessed his dead body.

"What can I do for you, Detective Reed?" Another woman said and identified herself in perfect English as Angela Truffaut.

I'd been vetted.

"I need to reach Patrice DuBois immediately. It has to do with her fiancé."

There was an awkward silence. "Oh, well, I really wish I could help you, but Ms. DuBois hasn't returned from the United States yet."

I lifted a brow. "Sorry?"

"Have you tried her cell phone?"

"Several times. Are you certain she isn't back in Paris?"

"Yes, that's what I was told. If I hear from her, I'll be sure to have her call you."

I watched a plane taking off and wished I was on a flight.

"Detective?"

"Yes. Thank you."

———

After landing in Fort Lauderdale, I ran for my connecting flight to JFK. I arrived there at midnight, and like a good soldier, JR met me at the gate. With slacked shoulders, I trudged over to him.

"Jesus, Hank, you look like shit." He laughed, but his face showed concern.

"It's been exhausting. Plus there's something weird going on."

"You think? The drowned guy is now the dead hotel-room guy. I'd say things are damn weird."

"Yeah, but more than that. I can't reach Patrice. My calls go straight to her voicemail. And when I called the number you gave me, I was told she'd never even returned to Paris."

He pulled back and squinted at me in confusion. "Let's talk in the car."

When we got there, I slouched back in the seat, my head leaning against the headrest, my eyes closed. "She could be in trouble."

JR stepped on the accelerator, and within twenty minutes, we crossed over the Triborough Bridge into Manhattan. "You're staying over tonight. It's not an option."

Pulling up to his apartment, he handed me a key. "We'll talk about it in the morning when I get off my shift."

I nodded wearily, opened the car door, and lumbered toward his building.

I was exhausted. I needed sleep.

And even more importantly, I needed to reach Patrice.

TWENTY

P*ing.*
      My eyes fluttered, and for a moment, I had forgotten where I was.

There was another ping.

I reached across JR's night table and grabbed my cell. Just after six a.m. I'd been asleep for a little over five hours.

Sitting up, I rubbed my eyes. Who the hell was texting me at this hour? When I opened the messaging app, the text read:

UNKNOWN: Miss you terribly.

Christ, wrong number?

I didn't reply. I put my head back down in hopes I could sink easily back into sleep. Then another text sounded.

UNKNOWN: Perfect life until she came along. Wasn't supposed to happen.

Me: Patrice?

UNKNOWN: Borrowed a phone. Kind of.

Me: What does that mean? And where are you?

UNKNOWN: Can't stay too long. Work to do. Wanted to say I'm OK.

Me: Patrice we need to talk!!! Where have you been? Why lie about Paris?

UNKNOWN: You are wonderful. Really care for you.

I got out of bed and walked over to the window, staring down at the traffic. I ran a hand through my hair.

Me: Me too. I can help. Not too late.

UNKNOWN: Almost done. Then we'll meet.

She wasn't making sense.

Me: What does that mean? Almost done?

My head was swimming.

UNKNOWN: Trust me.

I held off a moment. Then,

Me: Luke's dead.

After a delay,

UNKNOWN: Yes, I know. Heartbroken.

How would she know? Luke was killed less than twenty-four hours ago—in Bimini, no less. Either news travels fast, or…

Me: Were you there?

UNKNOWN: Be safe, my love.

She was being too evasive.

Me: Whatever happened you need me!!!

When she didn't respond, I called JR.

There was no time for informalities. "Track down this phone number. I have no idea whose it is." I rattled it off to him. "I'm sure Patrice is close by. I think she might have stolen a cell phone!"

I went to the bathroom and splashed some water on my face. Then I slipped on my shoes and paced the room.

Come on, JR.

Five minutes later, he called back.

"It's coming from inside Mandel's deli."

I charged out the door. The restaurant was less than five minutes away, but when I arrived and peered inside, she wasn't there.

Where are you?

I glanced around. Was she watching me on the street? Come on, Patrice, stop playing games.

Inside, there were fewer than ten patrons—again no Patrice. The place was calm and orderly, nothing out of place, except for a guy in a business suit sitting at a table and looking confusedly at his cell phone.

JR called again.

"You there?"

"Sorry, yeah, I was in a rush. Okay, I have my eyes on a guy who's looking at his phone, kind of irritated."

"Check and see if he goes by the name of William Neilson."

"Thanks." I approached the guy. "Mr. Neilson?"

His head jerked up. "Yeah?"

"Is that your phone?" I pointed.

"Who are you?"

I stepped closer, flashed my shield.

"Something screwy's going on," he said, waving his phone. "These text messages popping up aren't mine."

"May I?" I asked, holding out my hand.

He shrugged, handed it to me. I viewed the text thread. It mirrored mine. Somehow Patrice had cloned this guy's phone. She wanted me to know she was okay without having me find her.

"When did you notice something weird was happening?"

He checked the wall clock. "I don't know, maybe twenty minutes ago."

I sat down next to him and pulled up a picture of Patrice on my cell. "She look familiar?"

"That's her," he pointed. "She was sitting at the table next to me. Who is she?"

That's what I wanted to know.

"What can you tell me about her?"

He raked his thin hair. "I don't know. She was alone, smiled at me. Attractive, dark hair. Dressed in a casual outfit."

What was your real reason for being here, Patrice?

"I'll fuckin' strangle her." Neilson growled, then shook his head, realizing who he was talking to. "Just a saying."

Just then, I got another call from JR. "Hey, I'm out front."

I glanced through the front window. "Mr. Neilson, someone's hacked into your phone. You're going to have to find someone to fix it. Sorry, I can't help. Good luck."

"But…"

I exited the deli, hopped into JR's car, and told him about the cloning. I handed him my phone. "Read this."

When he finished, he met my eyes. "Not good."

"Did she just admit to killing Luke? She said, 'Wasn't supposed to happen.' What the hell was she doing in Bimini? And how did she even find out that Luke—?"

"She followed you, Hank."

My eyes swept the street. "I don't get it. We were looking for Luke together. Why did she suddenly stop then lie about heading back to Paris?"

"Good question."

"I need answers, JR. And why follow me into the city, text me, and then disappear? Is she taunting me? And why?"

"Could be she has business here. Know what I mean?"

"Elena's dead. The Bimini police have Ana in for questioning. Besides, if Patrice was in Bimini she could have killed Ana the same time she did Luke. God, I can't believe I'm saying that." I shook my head. "Who's left?"

JR leaned close to me. "Take a breather, Hank. You're jumping way ahead of yourself."

I nodded, then opened the text thread and read it again. I turned to JR.

"She's going after Hartford."

I hit Hartford's number on my speed dial. He answered on the third ring.

"Who the hell is this?" he said his gruff voice delivering undisguised arrogance.

"Detective Reed," I said my voice rushing. "I met you as Mr. Reed at your office. Listen. I know about the failed extortion. One of the parties is out to get you. You need to get protection now!"

Hartford held off a moment. "Do you realize what time it is, Detective?"

"Murder occurs at all hours, Mr. Hartford. And this one is calling on you."

"Detective, I don't appreciate you accusing me of being part of some extortion scheme. I've done nothing wrong, so why would anyone want to kill me?"

I pressed my fingers on the bridge of my nose and took a quick, deep breath.

"I know Randy Wolfe contacted you from jail. He told you to renege on the transfer. But by doing that, he put a target on your back."

A snort. "That's ridiculous."

"And there's something else. I've seen the incriminating files. They're damaging. So what you thought was safe from the authorities is now in the hands of the FBI," I lied. "They may be raiding your home and business soon—until then, you have a serious risk of being killed."

That stopped him. Of course, I had no idea where the files were. For all I knew, he had them. But his hesitation told me otherwise.

"Did you hear me, Hartford? Either way, you're going down. I'm trying to make it safer for you. A few years in prison, versus six feet under."

"I keep telling you there was no impropriety or extortion."

Delusional!

"You haven't been listening," I said, raising my voice. "You may think all the players are dead or in jail, but there's still one out there— and I'm not talking about Ana Martinez."

After another silence, I said. "And that PI you hired to follow Elena Sullivan around will implicate you as soon as the cops pick him up for murder. He won't go down alone, Hartford: he *will* implicate you in the murder."

I thought I heard a long sigh coming from his end. "That was unfortunate, Detective, but I don't know any Sexton."

Hartford wasn't budging.

"Okay, Mr. Hartford. Don't say I didn't warn you."

"Thanks, Detective, I'll sleep on it."

I turned to JR. "He hung up. The idiot doesn't believe me."

"He's not an idiot, Hank. Hartford is making plans to skip the country."

I cracked my knuckles.

"It's your call, Hank."

I shook my head in frustration. "Why should I bother? Let the cards fall where they may."

"Because you're a cop. And secondly, if Patrice is going after him, you might help prevent her from killing him."

I scrunched my shoulders. "Hartford could be anywhere." I checked my watch. "It's too early to call his office."

JR said, "I might know a way. Give me Hartford's cell number."

TWENTY-ONE

We remained in JR's car, waiting for his contact to get back to him. My stomached ached. I had to agree with JR: My pleas to Hartford had nothing to do with him. I needed to save Patrice from committing (another?) murder.

"Ever hear of the Stingray tracking device?"

I blinked. "You mean cell site tower simulators?"

"Right. It mimics cell phone towers into sending out signals to trick a cell phone close by into transmitting their locations." JR smiled. "So far, it's legal. Once my buddy gets back to me, we'll be able to track Hartford down—and hopefully alive."

Fifteen minutes later, JR's cell purred. He nodded, said a few friendly words, then, "Are you sure? Thanks. I'm keeping you on speaker." He handed me his phone. "My guy's name is Derek."

"Hartford's moving slowly inside the Fifty-First Street south subway platform on the Lexington Avenue line," Derek informed us.

We waited.

"He stopped, probably waiting for a train. He could be heading anywhere on the East side, or he could connect to the shuttle at Forty-Second. You're on the Upper West Side. You might want to head south."

213

"Right." JR stuck the strobe on the car roof, slipped into drive, and pulled out, his blue lights sending psychedelic beams bouncing off nearby buildings.

Pedestrians blurred by us.

"You'd never have this much fun on Long Island. It's like driving on a race track."

A BMW slid into our lane in front of us, slowing us down, unfazed by JR's blasting of the horn.

"Until it's not," I muttered.

"All part of the fun, Hank." He half-turned. "You'll get used to it, especially when you use the siren." He kept honking, skirting around cabbies.

"He's heading south," Derek said.

JR glanced outside. "I'm at Fifty-Second and Seventh."

"Drive to Forty-Second."

"Be there in a minute." More traffic building up, more horns blaring. "Respect the law, you fucking assholes," JR shouted. Then, to Derek, "I'm at Forty-Second."

"Okay, he's on the move inside. Looks like he's heading for the crosstown shuttle."

JR pulled over. "This area is getting too damn crowded. Why didn't Hartford just take a cab?"

"I'll be sure to ask him once we find him," I said, unmasked tension penetrating my voice.

"He's stepped off the subway car. Looks like he's heading in your direction on Seventh."

JR pulled up to a hydrant. "Let's go. Bring my phone, Hank."

I chased after him. JR was pumped.

"Shit, Derek, there are four exits here. Which one, quick?"

"He's stopped. Maybe he's deciding which one to take. Can't tell yet."

"Come on, come on," I said, keeping an eye on the subway entrances.

"Okay, he's climbing the steps on the southwest side now, and he's moving quickly."

JR pointed. "There." We scrambled around cars against the light and reached the other side.

"You see him, Hank?"

"No."

"JR, he's on top of you!"

"Hank!"

My eyes swept the sidewalk. "I don't see him." I called out, "Preston Hartford!"

No response from the crowd except a few strange looks.

"He's entering a building, JR," Derek said, his voice rushed in excitement.

I looked up. This was a convenience store. JR and I exchanged looks, then followed a six-foot-tall, twenty-something guy wearing a light fall jacket. He shoved his hand in his pocket and asked for a pack of Marlboros.

"Cigarettes will kill you," I said, forcing my voice to be friendly.

He glanced over his shoulder and gave a croaking chuckle. "That's what my mother tells me," he said, collecting the change for his smokes.

"I need to ask you a few questions." I flashed my shield.

He looked at it, then at JR's, which hung from his neck.

"About smoking? I'm old enough."

I smiled. "Nah, about the cell phone in your pocket."

His eyes widened. "I didn't do anything."

"Okay," I said, guiding him to one side. "But I need to see it anyway."

He stepped back. "Why?"

"Because it might blow up." This from JR.

"Are you shitting me?" He jammed his hand into his pocket then slapped the phone in my hand.

I said, "Stay here," and walked outside. I returned a moment later and said, "The other phone."

"What other phone?"

"Inside your windbreaker."

He shot a look of bewilderment to me, then to JR, and then he slid a hand inside his other pocket. He pulled out another cell phone.

"Whoa, this is not mine—and I didn't steal it, I swear," he said holding up his hands.

I showed him a picture of Hartford. "Know this guy?"

He shook his head. "Never saw him. Is it his?"

I nodded. "Were you on the Lexington Avenue train at Fifty-First Street?"

"That's where I live, but seriously, I don't know how that thing got in my pocket."

I did.

TWENTY-TWO

We took a statement, kept Hartford's phone, and let the perplexed guy smoke his brains out.

"What'd you think?" JR asked as we weaved through the crowd back to his car. "It's too coincidental that Hartford and Patrice used similar tactics with their phones."

I looked at him over the car roof. "In it together? I can't believe that."

"Maybe you don't *want* to believe it, but step back a moment and be objective."

I leaned against the car and rested my head against my arm.

Think, Hank.

I didn't want to believe JR's assessment. I slid into the car and sat back, discouraged.

"Let it go, Hank. You can't control the world. Something'll surface, and when it does, you'll get a second crack at it."

JR was right. Criminals mess up. I wanted to be around when Hartford did. I glanced out the window, my thoughts slipping into a dark place. Maybe Patrice would be the one to screw up. Could she have been part of the con from the beginning? Have me believe she was looking for a missing fiancé? And when we couldn't find him together, decide to search alone? She was obviously in a hurry. Without Luke, she'd get nothing: no money, no sipping fun drinks on some exotic island. Even if they were no longer a couple, she'd demand her fair share or else.

"What are you thinking, Hank?"

"Hartford has always been the money guy, right? What if Patrice told Hartford she was in possession of the whistleblower files and threatened to expose him if he didn't pay up?" I turned to JR. "Could be the reason he fled."

"I only know Patrice through you. Can't say what she'd do."

I kept JR's stare. "Me either, at this point. If you don't mind, I'd like to crash at your place another day or two before heading home."

JR smiled. "Just can't let go, huh? Sure, the place is yours for as long as you like. I'm with you either way."

I kneaded my hands. "Not only that, I've been delaying going home. I know Susan is ready for a divorce. I am too, but…it's so final."

"I understand."

I sighed.

"Listen, amigo, I need to get some sleep. Where can I drop you off?"

I thought a moment. "Where's MoMA?"

"Say again?" JR's eyebrows arched.

"Museum of Modern Art."

"I thought that's what you said. You some kind of art aficionado now?"

I grinned. "Not really, but Hartford suggested if I had extra time in the city, to check it out."

"You're kidding, right?"

"Honest to God. I hear it's quiet inside. My head's telling me I could use some of that right now."

"Okay then, MoMA here we come." JR started the engine and removed the strobe from the car roof. "We won't be needing this right now."

He dropped me off at Fifty-Third and Fifth Avenue, in front of an impressive granite-and-glass building. A few people were lining up, but I found out the museum wouldn't open for another half-hour. I instead decided to head for a calmer environment: Central Park.

I made my way over to Sixth Avenue then turned north, entering the park in less than ten minutes. I'd never been here before, but suddenly, after passing the pond, I reached Hallett Nature Sanctuary and felt at peace. I closed my eyes and took in the fresh morning air.

A few minutes later, a ping on my phone brought me back to turbulent reality.

Patrice: Wanted you to know I'm OK. Shouldn't be much longer.

I punched in a response.

Me: Longer for what? What are you up to?

Patrice: UR clever, Detective.

Me: I know you are going after H. Don't do it!!

Patrice: You think you know me Hank. Be patient.

Me: Whatever it is let me help.

Patrice: UR sweet. Not this time. He's bad and needs to be punished!

Oh Christ! How do I get her to stop?

Me: Bad as Luke?

Patrice: Strange comparison. Luke was bad in a different way. Unfaithful!!!

I made my way over to an unoccupied bench and sat. My eyes surveyed the large expanse of the park. It was much too pretty for such a dark day.

Me: Let the authorities do it. Your life will be ruined.

I waited for a response.

Patrice: Already ruined. Sad, lost, nothing!! Want to make things right.

Did she mean about killing Luke?

Me: We need to talk. I want to hear your voice!

Patrice: I thought we had a chance.

Was she talking about me or Luke?

Me: We do have a chance. Please don't blow it.

When she stopped texting, I called her. Not surprisingly, it went straight to voicemail.

"We need to talk, Patrice. Please call me."

After an agonizing few minutes, I called Hartford, but like my last attempt, it too went to voicemail. His office had to be open by now, so I called there.

"Is Mr. Hartford in?" I asked the receptionist after identifying myself this time as Detective Reed.

"Oh, hi. Mr. Hartford called earlier and told me he had a last-minute business meeting. He said he'd be gone a few days."

"Did he say where he was going?" I pressed. "It's very important. I tried his cell, but it went straight to voicemail. I'm afraid it's full and he's not getting my urgent messages." I took a breath. "He could be in serious danger."

"Oh no, that's terrible! I...I don't know what to say. He didn't tell me where the meeting was being held," she said, her voice cracking. "Wait, hold on a second."

She returned. "It's not here, Detective."

"Settle down. What's your name?"

"Jessica."

"Okay, Jessica, what's not here?"

"Mr. Hartford's passport. I checked inside his locked desk drawer. It was there yesterday. He must have taken it. Oh, this is so bad. Maybe he's flying out of the country."

Very possible.

"Mr. Hartford said he would call when he got settled. He hasn't yet, so I'm guessing he hasn't arrived at his destination."

"Okay, Jessica, one last question. Did Mr. Hartford make a notation in his daybook as to where he was going?"

"Hold on, I'll check."

Come on, Hartford, give me a clue, anything!

She returned. "It's blank. It just seemed so sudden. And he's not usually like that. He's very organized about informing his administrative assistant when he has plans."

"You mean Elena Sullivan?"

She choked into the phone. "Right. That was so horrible what happened to her." She stopped. "You don't think there's a connection between...?

"No, of course not," I lied, not wanting to send her over the edge.

"Might be nothing. If Mr. Hartford calls, have him call me. Better still, Jessica, you call me afterward."

"I will, I promise."

I'd done enough damage for one day. I wanted to tell her to take the day off, but that wouldn't help if Hartford just happened to call in. Hartford might very well have already left the country. Then again, I had nothing yet on the guy to stop him.

The park was becoming active. A few joggers passed by. I stood and stretched, and was about to continue walking north when I noticed a woman out of the corner of my eye, heading my way and smiling.

Patrice? But as she approached, I realized she was at least ten years older than Patrice, and shorter. She passed me and met up with a guy, and they embraced. Was I becoming delusional?

JR was right. I didn't need this. If Patrice was going after Hartford, it wasn't my concern.

Except it was, dammit!

Beaten emotionally, I trudged north past Sheep Meadow, then Strawberry Fields—saying a quick prayer to John Lennon. At 105th Street, I glanced back and took in the beauty of the park with a sigh.

I stopped off at a Starbucks for coffee and settled in a quiet place in the corner. No texts, no calls. JR was probably asleep, and Patrice was... hell, anywhere.

By one that afternoon, I returned to JR's apartment and let myself in. The room was dark, and JR was snoring up a storm. I smiled and shook my head.

I quietly grabbed my carry-on and headed out the door. I walked several blocks to where my car was parked and noticed a slip of paper on my windshield.

Great, a ticket!

I waited a few minutes before turning on the engine. I put my head in my hand. My brain felt like it was in a vortex, squeezing the life out of whatever mental ability I had left. I rubbed my face, and then bid goodbye to the city, started the engine, and pulled away from the curb.

TWENTY-THREE

T he noise in my head remained, so I turned on a local news station to drown it out. Same old news. As I crossed the Triborough Bridge into Queens, there was a breaking news alert.

Hold on—did I hear right?

The FBI had arrested Preston Hartford, III, at Kennedy Airport while he was attempting to flee to Morocco. The Feds got a tip from Interpol, something about Medicare fraud.

I pulled off at the next exit and parked the car in front of a consignment store. At least he was still alive. I texted Patrice, but she didn't reply. Was she upset that she couldn't get to Hartford before the authorities? Or that I didn't believe her?

I was about to call her when my phone pinged.

Patrice: Where are you?

Me: My car, why?

Patrice: Turn on the radio. You might be surprised.

Me: I did and I am. What just happened?

Patrice: I couldn't let him get away.

Me: You? How? And what about the files?

Patrice: Good question.

Me: I need a good answer.

Patrice: Safe. McKenzie had a basement.

Me: In his Newport house?

Patrice: Yes.

I was beyond relieved that she hadn't gone after Hartford after all. My heart thumped behind my ribs.

Me: Now we can talk. Call me. I hate texting!!!

A delay.

Patrice: This is easier for now.

Me: Why? It's over. It is, right?

When she didn't respond, I built up the courage and asked,

Me: Did you have anything to do with L? Yes or no.

Her silence confirmed my fears. But there had to be an explanation if she killed him. Accident? Self-defense? And yet, all she offered was silence. I wiped my clammy fingers on my shirt.

Me: Where do we go from here?

I waited what felt like an eternity.

Patrice: Need to sort things out. ALONE.

And then she was gone. I sat still, my hands tightening on the steering wheel. I felt sorry for her, and helpless. I wanted to do something, tell her we'd work it through.

Wearily, I started the car and eased back on the highway. Ten minutes later, near the LaGuardia airport exit, a call came in from Detective Jackson.

"Sexton confessed!"

I shouted into the air. "Yes!" Then, to Jackson, I asked, "Where'd you nab him?"

Jackson laughed. "We found him at a bar, drinking up a storm and talking to himself. One of the servers called. Said the guy was giving her the creeps, kept mumbling that 'it was an accident.' Plus, he looked like he'd been in a fight. When we got there, he was downing a shot of something and muttering to himself."

"Let me guess. He was at The Nautical Pub."

"Yup."

"And I'll bet Maureen is the one who called it in."

"Right, you know her?"

"Yeah, and she's a very reliable witness." I smiled to myself.

"We brought him in for questioning. You know how interrogation goes. At first, Sexton denied even knowing Elena Sullivan. Of course, that changed when we confiscated his cell and began looking through his photos. I told him if for nothing else, we could nail him for being a Peeping Tom. He protested, said his client had wanted dirt on his girlfriend." Jackson paused. "I told him I didn't care who hired him, it was against the law."

I could tell Jackson was enjoying himself.

"He turned red, used a few profanities, and begged me for a Coke. I brought him one, gave him a serious look, and then dropped the photo we took of the bathroom mirror on the table. He freaked out, but said the word 'sex' in blood didn't mean he did it.

"The admission came when I explained his DNA happened to find its way onto the victim. I pointed to his scratched face and waited for his denial.

"He broke down, swore it was an accident. He admitted attempting to blackmail her, and said she'd laughed in his face and told him to stick the pictures up his ass. She told him she wasn't Hartford's lover, never had been. She threatened to go to the police." He paused. "The rest is history, as they say."

"Jesus."

"Anyway, I thought you'd want to know." Jackson then asked about the other missing person.

"Luke? He's dead. Shot once in the head in a Bimini hotel room."

"Well, I can tell you it wasn't my perp. Do they know who did it?"

I hesitated a second. "Not yet. The locals are still working the case."

"And you, you heading back to Long Island?"

A twinge in my neck. "I'm on my way as we speak."

"Well, thanks again for your help. If you're ever up this way, stop by."

I continued in the right lane, feeling melancholy over Elena's murder. She'd been the only legitimate player in the group. When I reached the LIE, JR called. I was tired, angry, and apprehensive, but I took the call anyway.

"Hey, where are you?"

"Sorry. I didn't get to leave a note because you were snoring so hard." I laughed lightly.

"Yeah, I hear that a lot. Why do you think I sleep alone?" He chuckled.

"I'm heading home." I conveyed the latest about Elena and Hartford.

"And Patrice?"

"I can't figure out where she is or what she's up to. I'm getting the sense she's going off the rails, especially if she killed Luke."

"Well, maybe I can help. I just got a call from the Bimini police. They have a person of interest. Seems the idiot left his keys in the hotel room. He obviously wasn't a guest. They're searching for him now."

A guy?

"So it wasn't Patrice." I let out a breath. "Then why was she acting weird in those texts?"

"I don't know, Hank—maybe she needs time before having a real conversation. Anyway, the Bimini police let Ana go. They had nothing on her, especially since you vouched for her."

"So the guy left his keys in the room? That was dumb."

"Who said killers were smart? Anyway, the prints on the keychain belong to a Ricky Ramos, a small-time con from Miami. Never been arrested for murder though."

I immediately pulled onto the shoulder. "Did you say Ramos?"

"Right. Know him?"

I dropped the gear into park and turned on my emergency lights. "Not him, but Ana checked into the Wharf Inn in Newport under the name Alicia Ramos. That can't be a coincidence. She told me her brother helped her pick up Luke off the coast of Fort Lauderdale. Which means most likely he was in Bimini at the time of the murder."

"That's interesting."

"What?"

"If it's the same Ramos, how come he didn't kill Luke out at sea when he had a chance? You said her brother helped her pick him up from McKenzie's yacht. Ramos isn't an uncommon name."

"I can't explain it, but there had to be a reason."

"Well, there's a BOLO out on him. I'll keep you posted."

I hung up, confused yet relieved that Patrice was innocent. Then I thought of the calculating Ana, using Ramos rather than Martinez to check into the Wharf Inn. (I had to assume they had different fathers.) Surely, he wouldn't have acted alone. Hell, she probably planned it. When I'd arrived at the restaurant, Ana had been calm, reading a book, and all the while Luke was in the process of being killed. Conveniently, she had me as an alibi. And she played the scene perfectly, even acting like she was getting sick. In fact, she didn't even need me for an alibi; she had the restaurant employees.

That was one cold and deadly woman.

I texted Patrice.

Me: The authorities know who killed Luke. They're looking for Ana's brother. Great news!!! I'm calling you now.

She picked up immediately.

"Oh, Hank, is it really true? How did you find out?" I could hear her trying to stifle her soft sobs.

"From JR. He just called. I'm really sorry, Patrice. I know emotions toward Luke were constantly changing, but in spite of everything, I'm sure you did have feelings for him."

She sighed. "Thank you. I did have feelings. I loved Luke very much, but realized after his infidelity, it could never be the same. I guess at the time, I was holding on to our past." She stopped. "And then you came along. I know it sounds crazy, but I began having feelings for you. I know I shouldn't be saying this. Not now, anyway."

"My feelings are the same. I really need to see you. I'm on my way back to Long Island. I have to face Susan and the divorce. We both agree this is the only answer to a broken marriage."

"I'm sorry, Hank. I was hoping it would work out for you."

"Were you really?"

"Isn't that what I'm supposed to say?"

"But do you mean it?" I pressed.

"No. I want to get to know you better, if that's what you want."

"It is," I said without hesitation. "Where are you?"

"You really want to know? Think coffee and a bagel."

"Mandel's deli? Seriously?"

"Seriously." She giggled.

"I'm a little over an hour away. Wait for me."

"I'm not going anywhere, Detective Reed. Hurry or your coffee will get cold." She laughed breezily.

I darted out of the shoulder and made the first turn about exit. I felt like a kid going on a first date. I smiled to myself and picked up my speed, heading westbound, believing there was a good possibility a special relationship was brewing.

TWENTY-FOUR

Forget the coffee. Patrice and I agreed to meet at her hotel—a quaint boutique-type on the Upper West Side, with all the high-tech bells and whistles. She told me a remote would open and close the drapes with the click of a button. Turning lights off and on worked the same way. I wasn't interested in high-tech anything. I did want the drapes closed and the lights off, period. On the way, I called JR and told him I didn't want to be disturbed for a few days.

He laughed. "You devil. Go ahead, Hank, you deserve a vacation. Catch you on the far side."

I smiled into the phone and hung up. With the weight of the investigation finally behind me, I could use some R&R. Patrice's room would be our respite from the world, at least for the next few days. I wanted her and room service—in that order.

God, I was crazy in love.

When we entered her room, she grinned and said, "I'm going to show you a few interesting tricks." She raised a seductive eyebrow and lowered her voice, "And then, off to bed." She picked up a remote off the dresser and began to point it around the room. The drapes opened, then closed. Another tap on the remote and the interior lights turned on and off again. She finally shut the drapes for good and turned to me, a mischievous smile spreading across her face. "This one was made especially for us." One more click, and the lights went out. As they did, a splash of stars appeared across the ceiling as though we stood beneath a night sky.

"I want to feel you in the dark," she whispered, her voice breathy. "Or rather, under the stars." She giggled, then touched my face gently with her petite fingers, and kissed my lips hard. I swept her up in my arms and carried her over to the bed. She ditched the remote on the floor, then snaked her arms around my neck and held me tight.

"Love me forever," she begged, pulling me down on the bed.

I fumbled to remove her top. I wanted all of her, but my brain was working faster than my hands.

"Hurry."

She, too, reached for me, tearing at my clothes. We tumbled around, arms and legs entangled, tongues fencing, racing to strip each other bare. Finally in sync, we gasped, breathless in our frenzied passion, climaxing together.

I stayed longer, didn't want to leave her beautiful body.

She looked up at me and smiled. "I love you, Hank."

"Me, too."

I fell back in bed and settled my breathing as we lay in silence. Patrice kissed my hand. "This is for real," she said. "I want you to know that."

I turned, removed a few strands of hair from her face, and kissed her mouth with tenderness.

It was just us.

"It's just us," she said as though reading my mind. "I could stay here forever. Only other thing we need is room service." She laughed breezily and squeezed my hand.

We made love again, slowly and more sweetly, replacing our animal instincts with tenderness. Afterward, I rolled over to my pillow with sigh of satisfaction and let my eyes close.

I awoke smiling. This was real. I reached for Patrice, but the bed was empty and cold. I glanced around.

"Patrice?"

I sat up, my eyes straining to search the darkness. For some reason, the stars on the ceiling had disappeared. I fumbled for the light switch for a minute before remembering the remote. I pawed around on the floor until I finally felt it, and then pressed a button. The drapes pulled back.

Daylight streamed in.

I pressed another button and the lights illuminated the room. Something was seriously wrong. The closet was open, but Patrice's clothes were gone.

"Patrice," I called out again, though I knew I was alone. My gaze shot to the night table. My Glock and shield were still there, but my phone was missing.

The hell?

I slowly took in air through my nostrils, trying not to make a big deal of the situation. But then my intuition got the better of me, and I jumped out of bed searching for a note or any explanation for her sudden disappearance. I shook my head, grabbed the hotel phone, and called the front desk.

"Yes, good morning, this is Room 724. What time is check-out?"

A woman who introduced herself as Cindy responded, "Eleven o'clock, sir."

"Okay, thanks." I hesitated. "So I still have the room till then?"

Cindy probably thought I had dementia, because she replied haltingly, "Yes, sir, of course." Then she must have looked at the computer screen. "Oh."

"What?"

"Strange, it says the bill has already been paid."

"It was? When?"

"Let me see. It says...just after five this morning."

At least Patrice had been good enough to pay her bill.

"Interesting," she continued. "It says Ms. Dubois only checked in for one adult."

Patrice hadn't been expecting me.

"Oh, that. It's our tenth wedding anniversary, and I wanted to surprise her."

"Oh, that must have been romantic."

Until now.

"Well, take your time. You don't have to vacate the room until eleven. Is there anything else I can help you with?"

Find her.

"No, all's good. Thank you." I hung up.

What are you up to? And why?

I was embarrassed to call JR. He'd probably think I was a bad lover. Was I? I began wondering whether our lovemaking had been too much for her, given Luke's recent demise. But no, I would have sensed it. I could tell: Patrice was as totally into me as I was her. There had to be another explanation.

I made my way to the bathroom, turned on the light, and splashed water on my face. I stared silently at my reflection, at the droplets of water falling from my chin, until they had all but stopped.

"Where are you?" I shouted to an empty bathroom, then shook my head. I turned around to grab a towel and caught a glimpse into the bedroom that made my heart skip a beat. I did a double-take.

"Oh, no!" I rushed into the room, my eyes darting around and landing back on the chair where I had tossed my clothes the night before.

She'd taken them! I gazed down at my naked body. All of them!

I had two choices: I could wait for Patrice to return, which was unlikely, or look for her, which was also not happening until I had some clothes.

I called JR from the room phone.

"I'm not going to ask."

"It's not what you think," I said, my voice rushed. "The sex was fine —at least, I thought it was. Anyway, Patrice left in a hurry and didn't bother leaving a note. Worse, she absconded with my clothes and cell phone."

"You're kidding."

"At least she was kind enough to leave my handgun and shield. Maybe she thought I'd blow my brains out."

"Ouch. Don't talk like that, Hank. What can I do?"

"I need you to break into my car and bring over my carry-on bag."

"She took your car keys, too?"

"They were in my pants pocket." I gave JR directions to where I'd parked my car.

"I'm on my way," he said, a reliable friend as always. "What room are you in?"

I told him, then sat on the bed, shaking my head in anger. Thirty minutes later, there was a knock on the door.

"Delivery service."

Funny.

I let JR in, a towel wrapped around my waist. At first, he looked like he was going to crack up, but then realized the seriousness of the situation and swallowed his glee. He handed me my carry-on and held out a cup of coffee.

"Thanks." I took a quick sip and placed the cup on the dresser.

"I picked it up after visiting your car. Hope it's still hot. You'll be glad to know I didn't need to break anything." JR grinned then glanced around. "What do you suppose she was up to?"

I slipped on my jeans, pulled the T-shirt on, and shook my head. "No idea."

We stood in silence for a moment until the room phone beckoned me.

I reached for the phone on the first ring.

"Mr. Dubois, this is Cindy from the front desk."

Mr. Dubois, right.

"We spoke before. I failed to mention there's a cell phone here for you. From what I was told, your wife was in a rush when she paid the bill and took your phone by mistake. She asked us to deliver it to you around nine figuring you wanted to sleep in. It's nine o'clock now."

I glanced at JR and shrugged. "Thanks, Cindy, be right down."

Once I'd hung up, I said, "Patrice didn't take my phone after all. She left it at the desk, probably to make sure if anyone called, I wouldn't hear it. She was obviously in a hurry and needed a head start." I picked up my carry-on, Glock, and shield, and opened the door. "Let's find out why."

Downstairs, I collected my cell phone. It was off, so I turned it on. There was nothing unusual—no new voicemails popped up. I scrolled through prior ones, and nothing stood out. However, when I checked my text messages, that was different. The last one had come in at four-forty this morning. Patrice had left the hotel around twenty minutes later.

"Anything?"

"She was definitely in a rush." I turned to JR. "I recognize the number that texted me." I thought a moment, wondering whether the message had anything to do with Patrice's sudden disappearance.

Of course it did.

"She must have read the message and dashed out of here." The early-morning text had come from Sergeant Weech. I read the lengthy message, and when I finished, I tightened my fist and swore under my breath.

"I know why Patrice took off."

"You want to share, amigo?"

"The message came from Sergeant Weech at the Bimini Police Department. He thought I might be helpful regarding a medal one of his investigators found at the crime scene. They dusted for prints and found one set belonging to the victim."

"Luke's."

I nodded. "And another, but it was smudged. Weech believes that from the size, it probably belongs to a woman."

"Okay."

"There's more. Turns out it was a St. Christopher medal. You know, the patron saint of travelers. He's supposed to protect the person wearing it. I guess St. Christopher was off duty that day." I feigned a smile.

JR shrugged. "And?"

I hadn't gotten around to telling JR about the medal Patrice and I had found below the Cliff Walk. "I need to call Weech first."

Weech answered on the second ring. "Thanks for getting back so soon, Detective."

"Not a problem. Can you be more specific about the medal you found?"

"That's why I texted you, mon. I thought you might know some-thing about it. Could help in the investigation."

"Okay," I said quickly. "Can you be specific?" I asked again.

233

"It isn't so much about the medal, but rather the inscription on the back—hold on, let me bring it up to the light to make sure. Right, it says, 'Be safe my love' and is signed 'Patrice.'"

Oh, God.

"Anyway," Weech continued, "if you happen know who this Patrice person might be, I'd like to talk to her."

I bet he would.

"Even if she was unaware of the victim's murder, she'd probably want to know about the medal. It must have been very personal."

Very.

I could hardly breathe, but I mustered the ability to ask Weech to text over a photo, both sides.

"Sure," he said. "Hold on."

I turned to JR and put up a finger, then walked to the hotel exit. Standing on the sidewalk outside, I drew in a lungful of air. Weech was still on the phone with me, but I said nothing as I waited, and neither did he. When the ping sounded, indicating the arrival of his text, I reminded myself before looking that this was a copy of a piece of evidence. Then I peered at the photo, or rather photos. I couldn't take my eyes off the words 'Be safe my love' and 'Patrice.'

There it was: proof that Patrice had been inside Luke DuPont's Bimini hotel room.

"Did you get it?" came Weech's voice at last.

I fought the temptation to tell him to toss the medal into the ocean, to get rid of the evidence and never call me again. I composed myself and said, "Just came through. Thank you, Sergeant. I will certainly get back to you."

"Oh, one more thing, Detective Reed. The suspect we had been looking for, Ricky Ramos—we found him, but let him go after we interrogated him. He had a pretty solid alibi. He was on a Jet Ski at the time of the murder. The owner of the company confirmed that Ramos rented the equipment around the same time. We checked the CCTV around the victim's hotel, and there was no sign of a parked Jet Ski. In fact, one of the owner's employees had to rescue the guy because his engine conked out somewhere in the water." Weech paused. "So, as you can see, it's really important we locate this Patrice."

My brain suddenly shut down and for the first time in a long while, I clearly didn't know what to do. Or where to start.

JR met me outside. "Hank, you okay? You look pale."

I raised my phone. "That call I just made, it was to the Bimini Police Department. I told you about the St. Christopher medal and the prints. There's more."

He raised his eyebrows. "Like?"

I took a breath. "It's the same medal Patrice and I found while searching for Luke at the Cliff Walk. It was below, kind of hidden in the rocks. It was a gift Patrice had given him for safe travels."

"Yeah, but how do you know for sure it's the *same* medal?"

I showed JR the photo from my phone. "See the inscription? Believe me, it's the same."

When JR didn't respond with more than still-raised eyebrows and a crinkled forehead, I said, "My guess is that they got into an argument, and she threw the medal at him."

"I could see that—but it doesn't mean she killed him," JR emphasized.

"I get it, devil's advocate. But everyone else who wanted to harm Luke was either dead or sitting in jail. And Ana was with me at the time of the murder. That leaves only Patrice—and now she's on the run." My eyes leveled at the street as my thoughts continued. I turned back to JR. "The more we looked into Luke's disappearance, the more Patrice seethed over Luke and Elena. Her anger got noticeably worse. At some point, Patrice must have cracked, probably around the time she lied about returning to Paris. She wanted to confront Luke *alone*."

"She shadowed you."

I nodded. "Had to. She must have been hoping I'd find him, and then, at the right time, she'd confront him alone. And she did, while Ana and I were conveniently sitting inside a Bimini restaurant. That's when he was killed."

JR nodded. "It does look bad. And the medal."

"My guess is, after confronting Luke, she threw it at him in a fit of anger, and then killed him."

JR turned his gaze away from me and toward the street. He said, "This sucks."

"No kidding. And the fact that she took off soon after she saw Weech's message only confirms my theory. She could've stayed in the room and explained what had happened. If it had been an accident, I would have tried to help." I shook my head grimly. "Now, she's a suspect."

"What are you planning to do?"

"I told Weech I'd get back to him—only, I'd like to get an explanation from Patrice first, but she's probably gone for good. She's smart, and knows how Interpol works. She could be anywhere."

"We could get out a BOLO, get in touch with Interpol, start there."

I sighed. I'd been a cop for years and usually found solutions. Now, I wasn't sure of anything anymore.

When I didn't answer, JR said, "Don't tell me Hank Reed is giving up."

I met JR's eyes and shrugged. "Maybe I'm just tired of hunting down criminals."

JR held off a moment, then said, "Then maybe you don't want to hear what I have to say."

TWENTY-FIVE

One Month Later

Tempus fugit—time flies. So much had happened in such a short period of time: missing people, murder, fraud, extortion, a few hits to my head, and duplicity. Oh, and a divorce. That last one had finally occurred when I'd returned from New York City.

I vacantly scanned my new first floor garden apartment in Mattituck, Long Island, not far from the house I'd shared with Susan in Eastpoint. At two in the afternoon, I should've been asleep since I'd been working the late shift, but I was too wound up for that. I was still angry about having been played. I couldn't get Patrice out of my head. Was I obsessed with her out of anger, or was I still into her? Maybe I'd put that on the list of things to ask my shrink.

Looking back, I realized she'd used me to track down Luke. The frightened Patrice, who'd feared for her fiancé's life. How could I not have helped? I'd believed her—who wouldn't have? She'd been persuasive and I, vulnerable.

Hell, I'd fallen for it. Sure, she had wanted to find Luke, but not for the reason she'd told me. Had Patrice really thought Luke would change his mind and fall back in love with her when he saw her?

Inside my kitchen, I raided the refrigerator for a bottle of Corona Light—I was trying to lose weight. I popped open the cap and tossed it on the kitchen counter, then drifted into the living room. The apartment was furnished, à la mid-century (in other words, old-fashioned). I'd brought my comfortable easy chair from the house. Susan had never liked the color and had been glad to see it go.

I sat, looked around. Right, old it was. Then again, I felt I was in transition, whatever that meant. JR was disappointed in me for not applying for the NYPD Detective position. And as for my Suffolk County detective job, I wasn't sure how long I'd last there, either. Like I said, I was in transition.

I sighed, took a swig of beer. Our divorce had been amicable; Susan got the house. Quite frankly, I wanted nothing except the chair, and so here I was, in a one-bedroom apartment, alone and away from reality— at least until my next shift. My boss was pleased I'd returned, but I wasn't. Was it the divorce, or Patrice, or both?

It wasn't until JR's revelation last month that I realized just how calculating Patrice had become. While on the phone with Sergeant Weech at Patrice's hotel, JR was talking to a friend from the FBI. The agent had been involved in Hartford's arrest at the airport. What he told JR was that one of Hartford's accounts had been hacked into not long after his arrest. It had been the same account Hartford had been using to wire money to Luke and Ana. Thanks to Ana's ex, Randy, Hartford had reneged on the transfer. Still, he'd been careless about exposing the account.

Looking back, it wasn't difficult to figure out who the hacker was. When Patrice had confronted Luke at his hotel room, she must have threatened him with harm if he didn't provide the account number, and he must have given in—then probably tried sweet-talking his way into her arms again. Too late, buddy.

After killing Luke, the shrewd Patrice would've waited patiently after tipping off the FBI and having Hartford arrested for Medicare fraud before transferring money from his account and moving on to who- knows-where. I assumed it was some enchanted island, maybe the one Luke had dreamed about.

I was obsessing, of course, because I couldn't stop thinking about

Patrice. Like her obsession with Luke, I needed to find her and ask why she'd killed him. Had it been her intention from the start?

Wake up, Reed.

I took another slug and placed the bottle on a coaster that read 'Cheer Up.' It had come with the apartment. I guessed the landlord wanted to preserve the thirtysomething-year-old, worn end table.

The doorbell rang, and I nearly leaped out of my chair. I checked my Fitbit for the time. (I thanked Luke for that idea.) Nobody called on me at this hour—or any hour, to be honest—so I reached for my Glock, which was sitting on the coffee table, and holstered it.

It was the postal guy.

He gave me a slight wave and said hi. I hi'd him back.

With a smile, he said, "Mr. Reed, I have a certified letter I need you to sign for."

Mr. Reed. Must be important. "Sure," I answered. I opened the door wider, looked over the mail carrier's shoulder out of habit, then smiled back.

He handed me a pen and I signed for it.

"By the way," he said, "welcome to the neighborhood. We have a great school system and a terrific police force." Then he noticed my hand gun.

When he looked back up at my face, I told him, "I'm a Suffolk County detective. Thanks for the praise."

He extended his hand, and I shook it. "Brett Harrison. Nice to meet you, Detective. See you around." He turned to leave.

"Hey, Brett, you forgot your pen."

"Oh, right, thanks."

My eyes followed Brett to the white truck, and watched him start the engine and leave. I then gazed at the certified letter in my hands. It was from an attorney in Denver, Colorado. I closed the door, went back to my Corona, and unsealed the letter. My eyes glossed over the official letter until I realized what it contained; then I reread the letter word for word.

Can't be.

I had an aunt, my father's sister. I'd met her years ago when she came for a visit out east. She lived alone—never married, no kids—and had told me more than once that I was her favorite nephew. The truth was I was her only nephew. In this letter, her attorney, a Joseph Enrico, intimated that if I wanted to live like a king, I would have to contact him.

With nothing else to do at the moment, I called Mr. Joseph Enrico. I wasn't sure exactly what I'd been expecting, but I found him to be polite and friendly. He told me that Mary Reed, my aunt, had passed away and had left me quite a hunk of change—seven-hundred and thirty-five thousand dollars in stocks and bonds, to be precise. Plus another four hundred thousand in real estate.

"Say again?"

Enrico laughed, but I honestly thought I had misheard. He repeated the amount slowly and deliberately.

I got it the second time.

I returned to my favorite chair, stunned. I threw down the final swig of my beer as my brain attempted to come to terms with my inheritance.

Finally, I grinned. My favorite aunt! I gave myself a high-five. I had no major debt, and had a clean slate from the divorce. I now had an opportunity to do anything I wanted, within reason. By nature, I wasn't reckless, so I would take my time figuring out what to do with my newfound money.

Closing my eyes, I traveled back in time, all the way to the beginning, when I'd been conned into searching for a supposedly lost fiancé. The time I'd spent searching for Luke had been frustrating, and in the end, deadly. Yet, I had to admit, I'd enjoyed the process. As a homicide detective, I'd be called in to a crime scene and look down at a dead body. In this case, I had been looking for a live one.

Okay, that hadn't really gone well, but they didn't all wind up dead.

I blinked out of my fantasy and walked back to the fridge for another brew. Maybe I'd hang out a shingle. I could call the company Aunt Mary's Private Eye Service. I smiled to myself, snapped off the beer cap, and took a swig. I was getting carried away, giddy at the thought of working for myself. Hell, maybe I'd hire JR.

What if?

But where could my inheritance get me these days? Not a place on some exotic island, like Luke had planned. Or Patrice. I could imagine her on some enchanted island, of her choice, living out her fantasy, now that she had two million dollars to burn. I assumed it was some enchanted island, maybe the one *Luke* had dreamed about.

Back in my chair, I couldn't help figuring out where I fit in. If Patrice's intention had been for us to live together, she had to have known I wouldn't go along with her snatching Hartford's money. It didn't make sense. Would she have tested me first, thinking in her warped mind I'd go along?

I shook my head, sipped some beer and leaned back. That would have been, of course, *before* she listened to Sergeant Weech's voice message. She would have realized if I found out about the medal and made the connection, all bets were off. She'd be taking a chance.

I sighed. What was going through your mind, Patrice?

With that, another fantasy crossed my mind. Maybe I'd start that PI business and make Patrice Dubois my first client. Or rather, I'd be the first client—but you get my drift.

Before I could continue obsessing, my phone pinged with a text message. I hadn't had one since Patrice had gotten my attention over a month ago. I grabbed the phone off the coffee table—also vintage—and checked the message.

UNKNOWN: Miss you!!

Telepathic much?

I instantly replied.

Me: Miss you too. Where are you?

UNKNOWN: Hint, warm and sunny.

I got up and paced the room stopping at the window. I typed again.

Me: You're on an island.

UNKNOWN: Hot.

I shook my head in frustration.

Me: Stop playing games. Let's meet.

Hesitation.

UNKNOWN: I wish. Too much has happened.

Then why bother me?

Me: Why did you kill him? I have a right to know.

More hesitation.

UNKNOWN: Accident.

Me: Then why run? I could have helped.

UNKNOWN: Couldn't chance it.

Guilty!

Me: Why did you drain Hartford's account? That an accident too?

UNKNOWN: You're good, Detective. I had no choice. I needed money to live.

I laughed.

Me: Better than food stamps.

UNKNOWN: You're not helping the situation!!

Touchy.

Me: You put yourself there. We could have found Luke together. This never would have happened. And you wouldn't have left the St. Christopher medal behind.

I stared at my phone wondering if I had pushed too hard.

UNKNOWN: Who has it? The medal?

I held off a moment. Sergeant Weech still had the medal, but I knew I could use it against her at any time. Since we found the medal below the Cliff Walk, Patrice would swear we hadn't. It was my word against hers. I could tell her JR was aware of the medal, but then she'd never show her face again.

And I wanted to see her.

Me: It's safe with me. We can work out a way to resolve this.

UNKNOWN: Be nice to start over, start fresh. I swear he forced me...

I waited for her to expand more.

UNKNOWN: Anyway, would be nice to be with you. Maybe when you retire 😊.

I began to respond but held off. I thought of my inheritance, the sudden freedom. Maybe I should retire. I could search for Patrice until I found her and bring her back to justice before she found me, and...

Me: I am retired. Pension and all.

I felt we were playing a game of chess. Your move Patrice.

UNKNOWN: How fast can you buy a ticket to Costa Rica?

Me: You're there?

UNKNOWN: All alone. Keep me company. For life.

Me: Seriously?

UNKNOWN: I'm staying at the Playa Westfalia in Puerto Limón. Faces the Pacific Ocean.

Me: Sounds romantic.

UNKNOWN: Under the name Patrice Reed. ☻ Call them.

Costa Rica hadn't been on my bucket list, but I wasn't going sightseeing anyway. What the hell.

Me: I'll fly out tomorrow.

UNKNOWN: Can't wait.

The text conversation ended, and I walked over to the living room window, peered out. Autumn was setting in. The leaves were beginning to change colors. I went over to my computer and Googled the Playa Westfalia Hotel, then made a call. Sure enough, I was connected to Patrice's room. She didn't pick up, and I wasn't surprised. She was probably out sunning herself.

I sighed. Two things came to mind. It would be great to see her again. But then reality set in. Patrice would never agree to return for a trial, even with me supporting her. Too chancy. Besides, she didn't have to. She had plenty of money to live out her life.

Except, Patrice might have assumed I was the only person to connect her to the medal and Luke's demise. If I decided to join her in Costa Rica, I would never come back alive. I was crazy, but I bought an airline ticket.

I texted Patrice with the news. I'd be arriving in Costa Rica's capital, San Jose, on American Airlines, at eight fifteen tomorrow night. She said she would meet me at the airport.

I broke the news to JR. He wasn't happy.

"Bad move, Hank. You know what she's capable of. Just let her live her life without your interference. It wouldn't be the first time someone got away with murder. You don't need this. And don't tell me you're in love. With a murderer no less!"

I knew JR was being a big brother and wanted to protect me. He was probably right. But I needed to see this through. I needed to resolve the Patrice/Hank relationship. If there was one.

"I'll be fine, JR."

"Give me the information where you're staying."

Anxious and excited, I finally dozed off. But at three a.m., I got up to pee. Something wasn't right. For one, I felt I wasn't alone. The house was dark and quiet, but my bedroom window was open, and I hadn't opened it.

"A man thing," she said. "Getting up to go to the bathroom in the middle of the night. What will it be like when Hank Reed turns sixty?"

I spoke to where Patrice's voice came from. "I thought we were supposed to meet in Costa Rica. We must have gotten our connections mixed up."

She chortled. "I wanted to see you sooner. I wasn't sure if you'd bring St. Christopher with you."

"He's the travel saint. Of course, I would."

"I need to bring the medal back with me, so where is it?"

We were still in the dark. I had slept in my shorts and T-shirt, an old habit. "I need to turn on the light, Patrice. Otherwise, I might trip and fall and forget where he is."

"Funny." She turned on the light, and I took a deep breath. She looked magnificent, especially with her new Costa Rican tan. But the gun in her hand spoiled the moment.

Patrice sighed. "I missed you, Hank. Really."

"Me too. Can I come over and give you a hug?"

"Sorry. I'd love to, but it would get complicated, me having a gun in my hand."

I shook my head in disappointment. "Seriously, you're here for the medal? Why didn't you tell me before I bought the ticket? It's nonrefundable you know." I smiled.

"You've always had a great sense of humor." She got up from the chair. "You really need to buy a better chair, Hank. This one's worn out."

"My next trip to Ethan Allen. So?"

"I changed my plans. I had a weak moment when we texted, but then I thought you'd probably call the Costa Rican police on me, so I came to you."

"I wasn't going to."

"My mistake. She fingered her hair and sighed.

"But here, I'm local, Patrice. I could have you arrested for the murder of your fiancé. That wasn't my intention. I wanted to join you and start fresh. I was ready, still am. I glanced over at my night table.

"Is this what you're looking for?"

She was holding my Glock.

"Where's yours?"

"Unless you're in law enforcement, you can't take weapons on an aircraft. I'm no longer with Interpol, remember? Besides, this is more convenient." Then she said, "I like your new digs. Hard to see the rest of the place in the dark, but…"

I took a step forward and she moved back one. "Let's stop the bullshit. You're here for the medal. You never wanted me." I scowled.

She waved my gun. "That's not true. If this…problem never happened, I know we'd be together. I still want to be with you, but you don't trust me. How could we live together under lies?" Another sigh. "Please just give me my medal and I'll be out of here. I'll leave your gun in your mailbox. I just don't wanna run forever."

Her pained face appeared real, and I could see that she'd probably had many sleepless nights worrying about me, the medal, and her freedom.

"Fair enough." I pointed to the other room. "It's in a chest drawer. You want to follow me in?"

She waved the gun again. "Go ahead."

I stopped by a wooden chest in the living room and turned to her. "It's in here."

"Move back, Hank. Over to the side where I can see you. And turn on the light."

I complied, and the room lightened up. I watched Patrice stick her hand inside the drawer.

"It's in a small white box on the left side."

Her hand stopped, and she removed it. She then placed the gun on the top of the chest for a moment and opened the box. It was all I needed. I leaped forward and grabbed her leg, sending her to the floor. But she quickly got up screaming and threatening.

I landed a punch to her solar plexus, and she keeled over gasping for air. But then she recovered and held her stomach. "A hell of a punch, Hank."

"It's over, Patrice."

But it wasn't. I was about to grab my gun off the chest when she pulled one out of her leg holster and aimed it high enough so I could see it. "Don't make me kill you, Hank." Her hands shook, but she was in control.

I held my hands high. "I thought you said you didn't have a gun?"

Patrice smirked. "What I said was unless you're in law enforcement, you can't take weapons on an aircraft. There are plenty of ways to obtain a gun in the States."

"Right." I stared at her weapon. "Take the damn medal and get out of my sight."

She coughed then took a deep breath. By the look on her face, Patrice was pissed. She dragged herself to the box and picked it up, one eye staying on me. When she opened it, St. Christopher was lying face up where I'd put him. Only it wasn't the real St. Christopher. Detective Weech had that one. I had one made based on my text copy he'd sent over. For posterity, I guessed. I hoped she couldn't tell the difference.

Patrice turned the medal over and sighed. Looking up at me, she said, "This could have been done without any violence."

I said nothing, let her get up. She put the box in her pants pocket and touched her stomach.

"Sorry about that. So I guess this was our first spat."

"And last." She rubbed her stomach again. "I think I'm gonna be sick."

"Well, use the bathroom."

She growled. "I'm heading out of here. Don't look for me. Live your life in peace."

"I won't follow you, Patrice. But say it, you killed Luke, accident or otherwise."

She was obviously still in pain and in a way, I felt sorry for her. She walked backward toward the front door and scowled. "Damn right I killed him. He cheated on me, said he wasn't in love with me. Said he never was. He laughed in my face, then I threw the medal at him. I would have stopped then, but he kept at it, kept humiliating me. I couldn't take it any longer and lost it. You have to believe that."

Her face turned beet red, and her body quavered. "What would you have done, Hank?"

I didn't answer. I couldn't. I didn't know what I'd have done, but for sure, I wouldn't have killed over it. "Just go."

Patrice reached the door, but before she opened it, she stared at me as though she knew something was about to happen. I turned my back on her and stayed that way until I heard loud voices coming from outside.

"Patrice Dubois, you're under arrest for the murder of Luke Dupont."

TWENTY-SIX

Two days passed since Patrice was arrested. I took no pleasure being a part of her arrest, but I wouldn't have been able to live with myself knowing she was out there enjoying her life without any penalty of law. I could have just sent her the fake medal and wished her luck, though, at some point, she would have analyzed it and realized it wasn't genuine. Oh well. Sorry Patrice.

JR and I were sitting in a local bar near my house in Mattituck. I had downed a few shots of whiskey and was warming up to the idea that I'd done the right thing. JR agreed.

"There was no other way to handle it, Hank. I'm sure if you had gone to Costa Rica, I'd never see you again."

I nodded, thinking he was probably right. She obviously didn't trust I would bring the medal with me, and without the medal, I was the only one who knew the truth.

While I was tempted to stay and see if our relationship would be normal, that little righteous fellow in the back of my head wouldn't allow it.

Patrice got sloppy. Or maybe it was a sign of weakness at the time. By then it was too late. Once she told me where she was staying, I got in touch with JR. He found a Costa Rican private investigator to follow her. He learned she was on a plane heading for New York. From there it was easy. A New York PI was waiting and followed her around. She was heading east to Long Island. That only meant one thing: Patrice was heading my way. After calling me, I called my boss. He understood the situation and had a team in place.

We got you, Patrice.

"What are you thinking, Hank?"

I smiled sadly. "Mixed feelings, I guess. I was stuck on her. Going through a divorce didn't help either. It clouded my judgement. I'll get over it."

JR patted me on the back. "Of course, you will. We need you to find your way to the top of the Sex Academy. I'm tired of being one in the class."

I feigned a smile. "I don't think she would have killed me," I said, trying to stay positive. "She took the medal and headed for the door. Even after I rammed my fist in her gut. She could have shot me, but she didn't."

"True."

I lifted my hand for the bartender. "Another."

"Glad I'm driving," JR said.

I turned to JR. "I'm glad you informed me that Patrice was back in the States."

"We assumed she was heading your way, so it made sense."

"My boss said he was willing to do anything for his favorite homicide detective." I smiled.

"But I have to tell you, Hank, we don't know how she got into your house without us seeing her. If she came by car, she must have parked somewhere out of sight. It was only when your interior lights went on and stayed on, that we became concerned. We headed for the doors and waited. We assumed you were handling the situation okay, if in fact, she was inside."

"Until the crash. I would have called out, but I needed to see how far she would have taken the situation."

"You mean if she shot you?"

"Okay, maybe I was too positive. But now you have her admission of guilt." A weary smile. I was feeling a buzz and needed to sleep. I think JR knew it too and asked the bartender for the bill.

Outside, the air was cool, the night a full moon. JR helped me to my car, took the keys out of my pocket, and opened the passenger door.

"Home sweet home, Hank."

He was right, and through the fog in my head, I knew I would finally have sound sleep.

MENTAL CASE

THE HANK REED MYSTERY SERIES, BOOK 3

Leaving the Suffolk County Police department to become a private investigator was easier than I thought. Especially since I had funds to sustain a smooth transition. Thank you again, Aunt Mary, for the inheritance.

While I was no longer a homicide detective in search of a killer, I was now looking for my first client's son before it became a murder. Ironic, no?

It started an hour ago when I made a hundred-thousand-dollar drop into the Friendly Market Grocery store dumpster. The challenge was to find the kid before he suffocated to death. I prayed the Huntington municipal trash pickup wouldn't show up before the kidnapper grabbed the ransom.

The demand was simple: Don't get the authorities involved or their thirteen-year-old son, Jason, would be killed without hesitation. The family hired me through my ex-wife Susan—we were still on good terms —who begged me to get involved. She worked with Jason's mother, Juliet Godstone, at a local bank, and knew I'd been a Suffolk County Homicide Detective until recently.

Hell, I hadn't even slapped my 'open for business' sign on the storefront window when the call came in.

Perfect timing!

The abductor had called the family around breakfast time. Jason had already left for school, so their other son, Liam, age ten, took the call. After the friendly voice identified himself as Uncle Ernie and asked to speak to Liam's mother or father, things got out of hand. Since there wasn't an Uncle Ernie in the family, Jason's father, Michael, thought it was a crank, until he heard his son crying in the background. Still, it wasn't until they connected with the abductor on Facetime, that they realized it wasn't a ruse.

Jason sat curled up in a metal chair, hands and legs bound with duct tape, his hair tussled, and his eyes red from crying. He sobbed and begged his parents to come get him until the abductor slapped tape across the kid's mouth.

Wearing a black hooded spandex head mask and gloves, the kidnapper stuck his head closer to the cell phone and made his demands.

At noon, it was just me and the kidnapper. After dropping the payoff money, I, pretending to be Michael Godstone, was told to drive to Caumsett Historic State Park in Lloyd's Harbor, the former Marshall Field estate, a twenty-minute drive from the drop. I took Godstone's car and wore his black insulated jacket, and a Crab Meadow golf ballcap. We were close in size, but he was bald. I was hoping the abductor wouldn't find out about the fool me once thing...

With under an hour to the end game, Godstone's black Mercedes S-Class coupe traveled along West Neck Road in Huntington. Now that I was a civilian, my speeding privileges ended. I couldn't afford to be stopped and kept the speed limit.

Ten minutes later, I turned onto a long driveway that ended at a dirt parking lot. Godstone's cell pinged and my heart took a leap. The kidnapper had told him there'd be a texted map showing where his son was buried. I prayed I could decipher it, especially since I had under forty minutes to find the kid.

I turned off the engine and took a breath, then focused on

Godstone's iPhone, and the diagram. I enlarged the text size, which like a treasure map, had sketches of the park minus Captain Kidd's face. A dot near the entrance of the park must be the starting point.

I jumped out of the car, opened the trunk, removed a military survival folding shovel, and jogged toward the Marshall Field House, passing a few barns and onto an asphalt path. Long Island can be brutal in January, but the afternoon sun rays helped keep the freezing temperature under control. I was alone. Who the hell else would be mad enough to be out this time of year?

Thirty minutes. Reaching the house, an early twentieth century brick and mortar edifice with lots of windows, I charged around the side, and when I reached the back, my eyes settled on the magnificent Long Island Sound, which was several hundred acres away.

Christ! My stopwatch told me I had twenty-five minutes to get to the beach and find Jason.

I ran down the hill that ended at a small fresh pond. At that juncture, I wasn't sure which direction was faster. The map wasn't very helpful and heading left would require a swim. Not today. I dashed around the right side and when I reached the beach, I called out, "Jason!"

I wasn't expecting him to answer since he was supposedly buried beneath three feet of soft sand. Or so I assumed. I wiped my forehead, studied the map from my position. It pointed to a small tree sticking out at a bend about ten yards away.

I stepped up my pace through the rocky, sandy beach, wiping my damp forehead and eyeing my stopwatch. Twenty minutes to save Jason. Around the bend the beach was littered with debris probably from a storm. My eyes darted about, but nothing stood out of place. Something wasn't right. My eyes struggled at the map again. He wasn't buried in the sand.

Christ, where the hell was he?

I checked my watch. Fifteen minutes. Bile backed up in my throat and I suddenly felt lightheaded.

Hang in there Reed.

My unsteady hands gripped the phone and I blinked hard at the map. It directed me to climb beyond the beach to a nearby hill. That surprised me; I'd assumed because of the frozen earth the kidnapper would have buried Jason underneath the softer sand.

"Jason," I called out again, but my voice was swept away by the wind. I raced up, grabbing onto stumps and trees and rocks until I reached the top. There were patches of snow and I noticed fresh footprints. I dropped the shovel and got on my knees, my hands brushing away the immediate area. According to the map, I was searching for a rubber tube sticking out of the ground. I didn't see one.

Ten minutes!

"Jason," I screamed when I found it. More echoes, but no Jason. I grabbed the shovel and dug carefully, inches at a time. Normally, the ground would have frozen over, but the dirt was softer, meaning it was fresh. The more I dug, the more I screamed out his name.

"Stay with me, Jason."

My timer went off, but I kept digging deeper and deeper until the tube fell out. It wasn't more than two feet long.

What the hell!

I dropped the shovel, tore off my gloves, and felt around inside until my hand hooked onto what felt like a paper ball. I pulled it out and unraveled it, my hands shaking.

A typed message: 'Nice try,' it read. 'Your not the father.' I stared at the misspelled word and wondered what just happened. The kidnapper must have assumed Michael Godstone would have asked law enforcement to rescue his son. And now he was probably dead.

Bastard! I shook my head in anger and glanced out at the Sound. I was about to stand when I heard a twig snap behind me.

To purchase
MENTAL CASE
Visit Your Favorite Online Retailer or Bookstore

ACKNOWLEDGMENTS

I am grateful to be part of an enormously talented writers group who manage to keep my writing on track. Thank you Sharon Menear, Richard Brumer, and George Bernstein. To my editor Jackie Moon, who knows my writing so well and makes it so much better. To my advance readers, including Joe Enrico and Peg Kelly. To Brian Paules and his staff at ***ePublishing Works!***. Thanks to the Florida chapter of the Mystery Writers of America for their ongoing support. And especially to my wife, Sonia, who calls me out whenever she doesn't like a word, sentence, or paragraph. Thank you dear!

ALSO BY FRED LICHTENBERG

The Hank Reed Mystery Series

The Art of Murder

Murder on the Rocks

Mental Case

ABOUT THE AUTHOR

Fred Lichtenberg is a native New Yorker who lives in Jupiter, Florida. After spending a career as a Field Agent with the IRS, Fred changed gears from crunching numbers to creating fictitious villains and heroes. *The Art of Murder*, the first in the Hank Reed Mystery Series, begins with the murder of an outside celebrity living in a small community on Long Island. Fred has just completed *Murder on the Rocks*, his second book in the Hank Reed Mystery Series. *Murder on the Rocks* takes Hank Reed from Paris to Newport, Rhode Island, Boston, and New York City, in search of a missing person presumably involved in a whistleblower investigation. The book should be available in April 2019.

Fred has also written several stand-alone novels: *Double Trouble* — Mistaken identity grips this thriller when an identical twin separated at birth enters a dangerous game of cat and mouse with the mob. *Deadly Heat at The Cottages: Sex, Murder, and Mayhem* — A humorous South Florida story with a wacky host of characters all living in a retirement community, where people are literally dying to move in. *Murder 1040: The Final Audit*, is an action-packed suspense thriller that plunges readers into the complex realm of one of America's most shrouded government agencies.

Fred also wrote *Retired: Now What?* A humorous bent on finding life into the golden years.

In addition to writing mystery novels, Fred has written short stories and a one-act play titled *The Second Time Around ... Again*, about finding love in a nursing home, performed at the Lake Worth Playhouse.

Fred is an active member of the Mystery Writers of America and International Thriller Writers.

www.fredlichtenberg.com

facebook.com/fredlichtenberg